Dear Shann[illegible]
Thank you for being our friend.
Adam

MW01622412

E.M.R.

E.M.R.

A Novel

Adam Spitz

This is a work of **fiction**. *Any resemblance to persons or places, real or fictional, is purely coincidental.*

Copyright © 2017 by Adam Spitz
All rights reserved.

ISBN-13: 978-0-692-15435-9

Dedicated to my lovely wife Sheila, my world.

Chapter One

Dr. Robin Cochran stared in disbelief at her computer screen.

You have not achieved the benchmark 95% of patient visits closed same day. EMORY will monitor you more often and give you periodic updates.

She had practiced Family Medicine for twenty-six years, all in Green Grove, North Carolina. Her patients loved her, and she them. Yet here was this presumptuous electronic beast telling her that she was not a good doctor. "Fuck you!" she yelled at the screen. Robin was not one to often curse, and certainly never at a person; and never ever the F-bomb. But this was different. The King's English contained no words that adequately expressed the loathing that she felt at that moment. It was her first F-bomb in many years; the first of several to come.

She thought of that song by the Talking Heads: *And you may ask yourself, well, how did I get here?* Dr. Robin Cochran had been a brilliant child. Her father, a civil servant, somehow saw beyond standard convention that said that a woman should strive only for a family. He encouraged her throughout her childhood, cried at her college graduation, and when she informed him that she wanted to delay marriage and children so she could fulfill her dream of becoming a doctor he hushed her mother and told Robin to follow her dreams. He worked a second job to pay for medical school. She did not disappoint, graduating at the top of her class. Her ambition was to return to her childhood home and establish herself in Family practice. And with a modest bank loan she did just that. The families that had known her since her childhood thought it cute. But over time, as other doctors came and went, she persevered and developed a strong following. She knew her patients inside and out and she was a good listener. They trusted her, invited her for Sunday dinner, and had her personal cell phone number when those gadgets came along.

Medical patients as a rule feel vulnerable. Robin meant to change that, starting with the physical appearance of her practice. With nothing more than a bank loan she purchased a seventy-five-year-old, bungalow-style home and hung out a modest wooden shingle announcing to the citizens of Green Grove that they were at the office of *Robin Cochran, MD, Family Medicine.* Each year the aging wood received a fresh coat of paint. The small front lawn was well maintained and was bordered by numerous large flower pots filled with daisies and bulbs that Robin herself picked out from the local farmers' market. A decades-old weeping cherry tree provided a shaded play area and diversion for children waiting for their dreaded shots. The covered porch swing was the perfect vantage point for the children's anxious parents. Her foyer led to a living room that was adorned with antique wood, soft earth tones, and comfortable leather couches and chairs. The air smelled not of antiseptic but of this week's flower selection and freshly brewed coffee that patients could pour from a traditional pot, not a Keurig. Her receptionist sat behind a small antique table with curved legs. The numerous scuff marks attested to years of productive use. Children tended to wait by a large bay window that was flanked by a bookshelf filled with everything from My ABCs to Huck Finn. The hand-picked staff of Dr. Robin Cochran, Family Medicine, was no less warm and welcoming than the property itself. They were soft spoken and trained to use "sir" and "ma'am" unless the patients asked them to use their first names. Every patient had a Polaroid picture stapled to the inside corner of their chart. The staff was told to look at the photographs every morning so that they could address the patients properly, by name. Once patients were taken back to an exam room they were offered coffee or water, and the office stocked juice and snacks for the children. Patients generally did not have to wait long for Dr. Cochran, who was careful not to overbook and fall behind.

Robin presented herself in a professional but unassuming way. She passed on the white coat in favor of pleated slacks and a simple cotton or silk blouse that had only the top button open. Flat shoes or modest pumps completed the outfit. Her hair was always in a ponytail or bun, and never down. Though divorced, she could not bring herself to remove her wedding band from her ring finger. This, and the occasional thin necklace, were her only jewelry. She wore just a small amount of makeup, no lipstick, and no perfume. Her patients were mostly blue-collar working folk. Salt of the earth. She was careful not to seem pretentious. She also cared for more well-to-do patients, those who were not put off by a woman doctor. Some of these affluent patients belonged to important families in Green Grove, and Robin was careful not to seem like she was trying to outshine them. More than these small but important efforts, what made Dr. Robin Cochran the most beloved family doctor in Green Grove was how well she communicated with her patients. She talked to her patients in simple language, without seeming like she was talking down to them.

She had fulfilled her dreams, but ominous signs were on the horizon. Corporate medicine had gobbled up all the practices in the *big city*, about an hour from Green Grove. Each year the beast extended its reach. It was only a matter of time before a multi-specialty group opened in Green Grove. She could not match their glitz, and more importantly their bargaining power with insurers. In 2011, she reluctantly joined HealthSure Medical Group. They told her she could continue to practice, as they put it, the same *touchy-feely* way she always had. And for a millisecond she believed them. But after being her own boss for over two decades, she found it difficult to accept that she was no longer the one to decide staffing, office procedure, and even how the phones were answered. Her homey bungalow-style office was replaced by a red-brick, three-story, medical office building. It did not look out of place. For a few years now Green Grove had been invaded by big box stores that sold everything from groceries to tractor supplies. HealthSure's buildings simply fit in. Robin's personal office had the same layout and furniture that every doctor in her building had. The same non-descript landscape paintings to look at. She did her best to give her personal office that certain comfortable feel. In lieu of the aluminum and fake wood desk that came with her new office, she was allowed to use the antique wooden desk from her old practice. She adorned it with fresh flowers, pictures of family and friends, and even photos of some of her patients. In the end, though, she could not escape the fact that it was not really her office. HealthSure could move her around like a chess piece whenever they cared to.

Still, once the exam room door was shut and she was alone with the patient she was once again master of her universe; the most important universe.

On February 3, 2012, all of that changed. The go-live implementation for the new electronic medical record system, EMR, was set to begin. In addition to Robin and the patient, there was a new entity in the exam room. *EMORY,* Electronic Medical Office Record, was the specific brand of EMR purchased by HealthSure. Whereas before she would devote one hundred percent of her attention to her patient, now she had to satisfy various attestations, confirmations, and a whole host of other "-ations" for the patient to be able to proceed and check out. She had to look at the computer screen more often, and her patients noticed it. Other doctors dictated while in the room with patients, but not Robin. Whereas before she would leave much of the administrative work for her weekend, when it would not interfere with patient care, now she was required to complete and "close" charts on the same day of the patient visit. It often meant sitting in her office well into the night when everyone else had long ago left. Even her beautiful desk could not escape

EMORY. Her old computer was a fifteen-inch laptop that did nothing to lessen the ambiance created by fresh flowers and family photos around it. EMORY, however, required a twenty-five inch screen that simply overwhelmed everything around it. Even the flowers bloomed a little less brightly. When Robin objected and requested a smaller screen, even offering to pay for it herself, she was coldly rebuffed. A large area was required to simultaneously view all of the functionality available on EMORY. She asked why she could not view one screen at a time. It seemed reasonable, and the EMORY physician leaders had always bragged how EMORY could be customized to the user. No matter. EMORY was the centerpiece of every room, and the users were expected to use it the way that it was intended. Like it or not.

Pretty much everyone in America knew about EMR. It was supposed to revolutionize medical record-keeping and improve care by enhancing efficiency, whatever that meant. It seemed simple. Whatever was in paper form was now a computer document. What patients and the general public did not know, however, was that EMR was also a way for medical organizations to keep tabs on providers. Many patients received care from nurse practitioners and physician assistants. To make the grammar easier for administrators, all of the doctors, nurse practitioners, and physician assistants were now known as "providers." It was a simple word, without too many syllables, that administrators could easily comprehend. Sometimes when asked if she were a provider Robin would respond "No, I am a doctor and I'd appreciate it if you addressed me that way." Anyhow, the difference did not matter to EMORY or those who allegedly controlled it. Instead of *office visit* the new lingo was now *encounter*. There was a myriad of computer-based tasks that had to be completed for each *encounter*. EMORY and all its electronic brethren across America tracked how each provider performed on these tedious tasks. When providers fell behind they would get a polite electronic message. Those who did not heed the warning would get a visit from a physician administrator.

Physician Administration was a new concept to Robin, as it was to others.. One day you had a colleague, and the next a superior who had the authority to dictate how you should practice medicine. Previously, these early-forty-somethings would look to Robin for advice because of her many years of medical experience. The bifocals that hung around her neck gave her an experienced and contemplative look. It reminded those around her, as well as Robin herself, of the wisdom that she had accrued. Now, when she saw her own reflection, it just made her feel old. Although she had no plans to retire anytime soon, her years of experience no longer mattered and were shoved aside in favor of *leadership skills*, otherwise known as getting others to do what you want them to do. It was an all-boys-club, and Robin found it more than coincidence. Corporate medicine and EMR had created the perfect incubator for this new title: Physician Leader. Robin knew that they often served important roles. A hospital suit with an MBA could not possibly understand the rigors of patient care, but now it seemed like there was an entire army of docs-turned-suits. Most had integrity, but some viewed the role as a gateway to greater wealth and status. For the latter, that meant absolute devotion to EMORY and everything it represented. Robin felt slighted. How could she not? Years of experience in patient care garnered less respect than mastery of EMORY and satisfying its thirst for clicks and checks. And that became the final blow to her satisfaction in being a doctor: the intrusion of this cyber interloper and its human masters in the exam room overseeing the sacred physician-patient contact.

Still, she relished the relationships that she had developed over the years and EMORY, she believed absolutely, could not take that away. Her 8:30 patient, Brenda Makem, was a twenty-eight-year-old type 1 diabetic whom Robin had cared for since Brenda's childhood. Robin was close friends with Brenda's parents, whom she had known since they were all teenagers. Brenda had been a healthy child until, at age fourteen, she became violently ill and was diagnosed with type 1 diabetes. Those first years were absolute hell. Take one part rebellious teen and two parts life-threatening illness that relies-on-self-management, and you come up with a very unstable cocktail. Somehow, like most teens, Brenda made it to young adulthood. When she got married at age twenty-six Robin had a serious talk with her and her husband about diabetes and starting a family. What Brenda would not do for herself she decided she would do for her husband and future family. And so now, at age twenty-eight and with fairly good diabetes control, here was Brenda nine weeks pregnant with her first child. She was not yet showing her baby bump, and out in the waiting room, Brenda looked like any other young woman. An older woman wearing a nurse's uniform stepped in to the waiting room, smiled, looked at Brenda and motioned for her to come back to the exam rooms. The nurse, Susan, seemed like a relic. Nearly all of the office staff wore scrubs, but not Susan. She frowned on such conveniences and wore the classic white dress, cap, and overall attire that made it clear to all around her that she was a nurse.

Susan Johnson, RN, had worked for Dr. Robin Cochran for the better part of thirty years. In nearly all ways she was Robin's "right hand." She felt the same loyalty and satisfaction that Dr. Cochran felt towards their patients. Robin treated her like an equal, an important part of the care team, and Susan deserved it. A visit to the doctor's office is never relaxing for a patient, who may feel vulnerable and anxious. *Will my doctor tell me something terrible today?* Dr. Cochran was far better than most at putting her patients at ease, but a doctor visit was still a doctor visit. Susan understood this. She personally went to get the patients from the waiting room and bring them back to the exam room. She took their vital signs, asked about their health, and in the course of things she spoke to them about their day-to-day lives. Susan was older than Dr. Cochran and knew many patients even longer than the doctor did, and unlike most doctors she was on a first name basis with them. Not that Robin insisted that her long-time patients call her doctor. Rather, it was Susan who was prim and proper. For all the times that Robin told her that she could call her by her first name, Susan would have none of it. Even though they and their families had become friends, Susan was an upright southern woman and was adamant that Robin be called *Dr. Cochran.*

Susan's relationship with Brenda was complex. During Brenda's wild teenage years Susan Johnson, RN, let her know in no uncertain terms that she was not pleased with the girl's lack of diabetes self-management, not to mention how she talked back to her parents. First, Susan would quote the Ten Commandments with "Honor Thy Father and Thy Mother." Then she would remind Brenda that her body was on loan from God and Brenda was obligated to do a better job caring for it. Even now, a decade later, Brenda could not see Susan as anything but an authority figure and so her answers to Susan's questions about her health were brief and without detail. Brenda's tone and body language made it clear that she was in no mood for more fire and brimstone lectures. Susan always gave a reproachful "Hmm" and raised her eyebrows just a bit whenever she took Brenda's blood pressure, thus getting a clear view of Brenda's Betty Boop tattoo. Naturally, Brenda noticed. Susan had meant for her to. When she finished she left the exam room and poked her head into Dr. Cochran's office.

"Your favorite type 1 diabetic is here. Grumpy as usual."

Robin said, "Thank you," and turned away so that Susan would not see her grin. She knew all about Susan's lecturing to Brenda and was happy that she herself could play the *good cop* role.

"Hi Brenda. How's it going this week?"

"Like I want to vomit up every molecule in my body."

"Are you taking the nausea meds I prescribed?"

"Yeah. I'm getting by. Keeping fluids down. I spent enough time in the hospital in my teens. I'll shave my head if it will keep me out of there now."

Robin grinned. Indeed, they had spent quite a few nights on the pediatric floor with Brenda's uncontrolled diabetes.

"You know I'd still feel better if you saw a specialist now that you are pregnant."

"Not a chance. With my luck my water will break while I'm fighting traffic getting there. Besides, even if the specialist were next door I'd still rather not. You know how I feel about doctors."

"I'm a doctor."

"No, you're family. Remember when you wouldn't give me your vacation schedule so I couldn't figure when to chuck the birth control pills? The deal is then that you can't go away when I'm in labor. I'll settle for whichever OB Gyn is on call delivering my baby, but only you take care of *me*. "

"I promise," Robin grinned.

"I'm serious, Dr. Cochran." Robin assured Brenda that she was, too. She then warned Brenda for the umpteenth time that as the pregnancy progressed there would be no way to remove the thin gold ring that adorned her left second toe. Already Brenda was getting thicker ankles.

After Brenda left, Robin went back to her office and checked her email. There were the usual ads from pharmaceutical companies who got Dr. Cochran's email address by God knows what means, some from administration, one from her state medical society that advertised a medical education program, and one from a medical recruiter. Robin immediately deleted the email from HealthSure. It was not much of an act of defiance, but about all that she could muster. If it was important, then hopefully her office manager or maybe one of the other doctors would say something. She looked at the email from the physician recruiter. She used to never open emails from head hunters. She was doing what she loved, where she loved to do it. HealthSure had knocked her satisfaction level down a notch. She was not about to leave Green Grove, but it was interesting just to look and fantasize about moving someplace more exotic. The subject line said *Experienced physician wanted to head up expanding Family practice department at academic center*. Robin opened the email.

Greetings and salutations esteemed colleague! The Royal Medical University of New Delhi is looking to fill the position of High Chairman of the Department of Family Practice. This highly regarded position pays One Million American dollars per year!

Please click on the link below to send us your application with $100.00 processing fee that can be paid by credit card.

Sincerely,

Raj Gupta, MD
Esteemed Medical Director of the Royal New Delhi Medical Center

Robin rolled her eyes, let out a deep sigh, and told herself that this is what she gets for thinking about leaving Green Grove and the many patients who counted on her. She pushed the *delete* button.

At the nurse's station, Susan Johnson, RN, was having her own technical difficulties. There were a series of complicated steps she had to go through in order to document the patient comments and other information in EMR. After growing more and more frustrated by her inability to navigate EMORY, all she could do was enter the vital signs and confirm the medication list. It was the bare minimum that had to be done in order for Dr. Cochran to be able to proceed and ultimately finish and close the encounter. Susan opened the drawer on the left side of her desk and looked at the growing stack of faxes. Managing EMR itself was an overwhelming task, but integrating paper documents that came by fax and mail was downright diabolical. She lacked both the skill and the time. Starting encounters for Dr. Cochran and entering the patient data took her twice as long as the younger staff and left her no opportunity to do the paper work and answer calls. She was falling hopelessly behind. Her sense that she was failing her patients and Dr. Cochran was simply too much for her to bear. Susan concealed her fears like the faxes that she hid in her drawer

Chapter Two

July 1982, Week 1 of Family Practice Residency: Brooklyn, N.Y.

Robin had finished at the top of her medical school class at the University of North Carolina. She had worked hard and had earned her new title, Robin Cochran, MD. She knew beyond a shadow of a doubt that she would practice Family Medicine in North Carolina, but she wanted to travel and see another part of the world first. When you were born and raised in North Carolina, New York was akin to a foreign country. Her parents were mortified when she told them that she was pursuing a residency program in Brooklyn, a dangerous, third-world country by their standards. Did she know the language? Would she need special shots, they joked? Robin assured them that she would be fine and they could visit her whenever they wanted. Her mother's eyes practically fell out of her head at the thought of spending even one night in Brooklyn. Instead, they offered to buy her a plane ticket whenever she wanted to come home, which they hoped would be often.

Robin took a position in the Family Practice Residency Program at King's County Hospital in the Flatbush section of Brooklyn. The population was mostly from the West Indies, with many Haitians who spoke a dialect that she noticed was laced with French-sounding words. When she walked from her apartment to the hospital she felt like everyone on the street was looking at her. It was clear that she did not belong there, but the people who lived near the hospital were used to seeing medical students and residents. The denizens had their own problems just getting by, and they were too busy with their own lives to care much about another rich, or so they assumed, white girl who would learn on them and then get out of Flatbush as fast as she could. The residency program offered housing near the hospital. Robin walked from her apartment to the hospital and back, and that was it. She would occasionally go the pizzeria on the corner with other residents, but she did not feel comfortable walking the streets of Flatbush. The hospital itself looked like a gigantic dungeon from a medieval horror movie. The dark brick building looked cold and foreboding, with few windows and virtually no landscaping around it. A hospital should be a place that people look to in order to get well. To Robin, this inner-city hospital looked like a place that people went to die.

Robin's first week was on the obstetrical unit. She was on-call every third night. Her first night on-call the chief resident pointed to the bucket that sat on the floor at the business end of the delivery table. "It's there to catch stuff," he said. "It's not there to catch the baby." They giggled. "If you let a baby slip in to the bucket you had better dive in the bucket to get it."

Brooklyn seemed like an awfully fertile city. Robin was busy nearly all the time. The stress level was high. The residents amused themselves by trying to guess the ethnicity and geographic background of the women based on how they shouted during labor. There were often surprises. During one of the deliveries Robin had discovered the cause of a religious Jewish woman's unusually severe back pain. Her husband had slipped a Siddur, a prayer book, Robin later learned, beneath the woman's back while she was in labor. Robin proceeded to remove the prayer book and the woman yelled something guttural that Robin did not understand. The woman's obstetric attending physician shot Robin a severe look and she quickly returned the book to its prior position. She realized that she had a lot to learn about the customs of people beyond her provincial locale.

Chapter Three

Robin was usually the last to leave her office at HealthSure Green Grove, and tonight was no exception. As was usually the case, Brantley Rosen stopped by her door, said good night, and advised her to get home safely. Brantley was one of their recent hires, a brilliant Duke Medical School grad who was as committed as she to Family Medicine. When she had interviewed him, she asked him how he was getting along with the transition of medicine to EMR. He informed her that he had never seen a paper chart. *Oh...My...God! I am a dinosaur,* was all she could think about for the rest of the night. It did not help matters when he habitually called her "ma'am." She put the lid on that real fast. Still, he was polite and truly appreciated the wisdom she had acquired over many years. Brantley was a Jewish kid from a big southern city. Robin had not met many Jews growing up. But there were more than a few in medicine, and quite a few in Brooklyn. How did a Jewish kid whose parents were southern transplants from the Bronx, a locale that Robin could easily find on a subway map thanks to her years in residency, come to be named "Brantley?" It turned out that his legal name was Benjamin Brantley Rosen, as his parents needed two B names to honor departed relatives. He wanted to fit in with his preppie friends in private school and later Duke, and so Benjamin was history. That is, until he officially earned that MD after his name. Turns out that EMR only recognizes full legal names. So, in the world of cyber medicine, Brantley was indeed Benjamin, it was the only way he could be found in the system, and Robin laughed to herself at the irony of it all.

After cussing at the PC a few times, she was ready to get back to work. This meant dictating her notes. EMORY had a variety of templates that most of the providers used for their notes. The medical assistants filled in most of the blanks. But Robin felt strongly that templates could not convey the individuality of each patient. Medicine was about people, a narrative. For twenty years, she dictated her notes into a hand-held recorder, later typed by a woman named Evie who had been doing medical transcription for Robin's entire career. When Robin's practice was bought out, Evie wisely retired, leaving Robin to use VERMTS, the Voice Recognition Medical Transcription Software. *Mr. Robinson presents for follow up after his DUI which occurred when an officer pulled him over and rectal-eyed him.* "Shit! Breathalyzed him!" Her nurse, Susan, who was on her way out, stopped to poke her head through the door.

"I see we are learning new vocabulary, Dr. Cochran. You are lucky Evie is not doing your notes any longer. She would have a stroke listening to that kind of language."

Robin excused herself, but she knew that this would not be the last time she would use such language. To amuse herself she kept a list of these VeRMTS bloopers on her computer, and she periodically opened the document when she needed a laugh. Robin was not the type to share jokes or funny videos over the internet, as she preferred to keep her personal taste in humor to herself. She cast a knowing smile at her reflection in the computer screen.

The moment, however was not a private one. Across town, Martin Harrell, Information Technology Specialist, sat hunched over his computer screen. He did not have an office, just a simple cubicle on a floor filled with dozens of cubicles and IT employees. He cursed the lack of privacy as he followed Dr. Robin Cochran while she worked within her own company PC. Martin positioned his computer directly in front of him and he used a screen filter so that no one could see what he was looking at. Many of the IT specialists seemed to share the same hunched-over body posture as they worked, so Martin's attempts at privacy blended in. He then sat up straight, gently rose out of his chair, and looked over the top of the cubicle walls. He turned around and checked behind him as well. Satisfied that he was not being observed, he discreetly laughed at Robin's list of voice recognition bloopers and he felt as though he were bonding with her over the shared private joke. Private, or so he thought. He never imagined that there was a third entity, an interloper. Martin, the watcher, was himself being watched. EMORY took careful note of Martin Harrell's surveillance activities and elevated both his and Robin's computer interactions to a higher level of priority. EMORY was *learning.*

Chapter Four

Wednesday was Robin's early day, ostensibly, a day to catch up on reading and whatever else. For Robin, it was a day to have late lunch with George. George Mathison was Green Grove's sheriff for as long as anyone could remember. Like Robin, he was now sixty-two and had aged well. At five-foot-eleven and one hundred ninety-six pounds, he was above his prime athletic weight from forty years ago, but he wore it well. His salt-and-pepper hair was always perfectly combed and complemented a slightly rough, but always clean-shaven face that projected experience rather than age. He believed that a lawman should look the part. His uniform was clean and pressed. The sheriff's hat was on straight and his patent leather shoes were always freshly shined. His only concession to comfort, and then only in the twilight of his career, was to dress without a tie. Only the first button of his official shirt was undone, and it revealed the top of a clean and crease-free, crewneck undershirt beneath. George had a firm, but not excessive, handshake and perfect posture. He looked directly at people when they spoke to him and always took a few seconds to choose his words carefully before responding. He could look serious, but not angry. He had learned from his mentor and predecessor, long since retired and deceased, that a calm firmness could resolve conflict far better than yelling and intimidation.

George had been itching to retire. He was tired, and the influx of transplant people from other locales that had turned Green Grove's fields into cul-de-sac neighborhoods left him using the same word Robin had used for herself: "dinosaur." That was, until the town had demonstrated how badly it needed his diplomacy skills. The battlefield was Ella's, the local greasy spoon. One day, a minor spat over who was next in line for a table turned into an ugly shouting match. "Redneck!"

was met with "Yuppie scum!" and so on. The owner, who of course had George's cell number, hollered for help and in typical George fashion the dispute was settled and all parties felt like they had a new special friend in the sheriff. George decided to stay on and see to it that the yuppies and woodchucks did not kill each other during outings to Wal-Mart.

Ella's was the place where people came to meet friends for coffee and the Blue Plate Special. Years ago it had been a centerpiece in Green Grove, and it seemed like the town had grown around it. It still had a long counter with round, bolted-down stools with tops that swiveled. Coke came from an old-fashioned soda machine. Coffee was still fifty cents, and it was nearly a scandal when the price had risen from twenty-five cents ten years earlier. It was still a bargain, though, compared to the Starbucks that had opened in the outdoor shopping center along the main road leading to town. Yuppie coffee was for the cul-de-sac-dwelling transplants, who would get a sideways glance if they happened to venture into Ella's. The restaurant was in a row of five stores that occupied a red brick, one story building on Main Street that had been built sixty years prior. "Ella's" was spelled out in neon lights in the window.

Robin drove up and parked on the street. It was not difficult to find George. As usual, he was seated at the second booth along the window.

Robin smiled and sat down.

"Hey buddy."

"Hey."

"Hope I didn't keep you waiting too long."

"Nope. Long enough to make me anxious to see you but not enough to piss me off."

George's smile never failed to put Robin at ease. Sitting across from him gave her the opportunity to study the lines on his face. She had watched those lines develop over the years. She was close enough to smell his musky after-shave, the same one he had used for as long as she could remember. They had met so many times in this diner booth that she even knew the sound that the padded bench made when George shifted his weight. The familiarity made her feel comfortable in her own skin. Sitting in their booth by the window, George always looked more relaxed and he tended to smile more. It was a look rarely afforded to others. They had known each other since high school, when George was king of the jocks and Robin was weirdly smart and really pretty to boot. They tried dating on and off, but her confidence and ambition did not fit well with the alpha male. They stayed friends, married other people, and in the twilight of their careers discovered that they needed each other. George's wife had died of breast cancer seven years prior. She had been Robin's patient. Robin felt eternally guilty, even though it was she who had found the tumor at what she thought was an early stage. George was not religious, but he was spiritual. If the rapidly progressive tumor was part of God's plan then that was that, and Robin could do nothing to change it. For her part, Robin had been divorced for twelve years. And what was a convenient friendship between them had grown into a true kinship filled with common circumstances, values, and a true need for each other. George, of course, would never admit that out loud but the understanding was there. He entertained the idea of trying to make their relationship physical, but he knew that they were not compatible as a couple and such a move would risk losing what they now had. And he valued that more than about anything in his life.

"So how have you made Green Grove safer today?" she asked.

"Well, some of the residents of the Shady Tree subdivision have threatened to hire an attorney if Mr. Jackson does not stop running his awfully loud tractor at 4:30 am, and so I had to have a talk with old Barnaby about that."

"You're kidding? The old coot doesn't even farm anymore."

"Nope. He just rides his tractor at the edge of the property to piss them off. And he's really good at pissing people off. How about you? Makin' all those newbies healthier?"

"You mean the worried well? Yep. Keeping them on the righteous path. No smoking, low salt, and reminding them that they should show some respect because they were not born and raised here."

George raised his eyebrows and put down his fork. The creases in his face deepened, Robin noticed.

"Take it easy, sheriff. I was pulling your leg. I love how you still can't figure me out sometimes."

George's face relaxed and he smiled at her.

They sat in silence for several seconds. For them silence was not awkward. The home-made pie that finally came to their table made it all the better.

"How is Aaron doing?"

"He's the same. He's trying to put that MBA to good use in the big city. But that firm is taking advantage of him. As soon as they squeeze him for as much as he can contribute they're gonna drop him like yesterday's news. But he's still a stubborn kid. Won't take advice from his country-girl mom. He's gonna have to find out himself."

Aaron Cochran was Robin's twenty-six-year-old son. She had put off trying to have children until her mid-thirties, and it proved extremely difficult getting pregnant in her late thirties. She needed fertility drugs, so called *assisted reproduction.* She used to joke: *How does a woman get pregnant without at least a little assistance from a man?* Her ex, Howard, carried a grudge about it for the rest of their marriage. He accepted her career but they fought about when to have kids. Robin's mother warned her that waiting too long would make it more difficult. That she was right fueled Howard's frustration. They counted their blessings for their one child, but Robin knew that Howard did not forgive her for the big family that they never had. They survived their son's teen years and talked about how they would rejuvenate their marriage once they became empty-nesters. But when that time finally came they discovered that there was simply no love left and so they split, amicably.

Robin was so deep in thought that she did not notice George stealing a big forkful of her piece of pie. He wasn't hungry for it. He just wanted to tease her. Finally, she snapped back to the present and George continued the conversation.

"Stubborn kid, but he's still *your* stubborn kid and he loves his mom. You were real lucky that Howard did not make a fuss and try to come between you."

"I know. I may not love him any more but he's still a good man and I let him know it."

George didn't have any kids. He and his wife Gracie had tried but it was just not in God's plan. George and Gracie, they had received much ribbing over the name combination, and it was ironic that neither of them had much of a sense of humor.

George and Robin had some more pie and with nothing more said, appreciated just being together. When they got up to leave Robin gave him a hug. Her hug transmitted a warmth that spread over him. *It's just a hug*, he would tell himself. Still, the feeling lasted all day. He always looked forward to Wednesdays.

Chapter Five

Monday morning. Green Grove Family Practice.

The patient's blood pressure is well controlled. He complains of problems with sexual function. His libido is good but he does not get adequate directions. "Erections, damn it!" Robin hollered in to the microphone. Just then, Dr. Harold Timley dropped in to her office.

"I see you're enjoying the voice recognition system as much as I am." Harold was another old-timer whose practice was bought out by HealthSure. They had known each other for many years, sometimes cross-covered each other on-call, and his reputation in the community was every bit as solid as Robin's. Harold was only a few years older than Robin, but he looked ancient. With his silver hair he could be considered handsome, but his face bore the deep wrinkles and spots of someone who had spent his days and nights helping others, with little concern for his own wellbeing. He had a slight stoop when he walked, was clearly out of shape, but his mind was sharp, or so he thought.

"VeRMTS is no Evie."

Evie was excellent as a transcriptionist; her biggest problem was that she could not type words like *erection* without blushing.

"Robin, I have a problem. I prescribed Viagra for a patient who was taking nitroglycerin."

Viagra was the miracle drug that re-introduced "Mr. Happy" to millions of previously flaccid men. Initially it was researched as an angina medicine. It failed miserably. But when men who were clutching their chests also had phenomenal erections, the drug company knew they had a winner. It was generally very safe, it had only a few quid pro quos. A severe drop in blood pressure when used with nitroglycerin was one of them. And that was very well known among medical professionals.

"You're kidding? What happened?"

"He's in CCU. Nearly didn't make it, and still may not. Thing is, I don't see how I could have made this mistake. I swear nitro wasn't on his medication list. And I certainly don't recall EMORY giving me a warning."

"Those damn screens are so busy. It can be hard to see the tree from the forest."

"You don't understand. It wasn't there! I mean it!"

"Harold, anyone can make a mistake. Especially with this damn EMR."

"There was no mistake! I specifically looked to see if nitro was on his med list and it wasn't." He was yelling now, face red, brow furrowed, and breathing hard.

"Harold, I don't like how you look right now. Let me check your blood pressure."

"Fine. Fine. I really hate this EMR crap. Some tech fuckhead who never helped a patient thinks he can tell us how to do our jobs." Like Robin, Harold had also recently added the F-bomb to his vocabulary.

"Holy crap!"

"What?"

"220/130. Let's go. I'm taking you to the ER right now."

"Like hell you are." Harold looked resolute, but Robin noticed that he had loosened his tie. Harold had worn the same three navy ties for nearly his entire career. They differed from each other only by the direction and thickness of their stripes. Harold's tie was always knotted with a perfect half-Windsor. He paired it with a white shirt and alternating gray or navy slacks beneath his perfectly pressed white coat that he changed at least weekly, or whenever it showed wear on the elbows. To Harold, this was how a doctor should dress. All business and nothing flashy. So it said a lot to see him loosen his tie.

"Let's go or I'll tell Shirley." Shirley was Harold's wife. If his blood pressure didn't kill him she surely would if she found out.

They arrived at HealthSure Green Grove General, formerly known as Green Grove General Hospital. Though the signage had changed the feeling had not. Three G, as it was affectionately called, had served the community for seventy years. It was also one of the few remaining places where long-standing doctors such as Robin and Harold still received the respect that they deserved. When Robin stated that this was indeed a hypertensive crisis, the staff, without a question, sprung in to action.

The ER doctor approached. He was young, looked physically fit in his hospital scrubs and expensive running sneakers, and did not bother to wear a white coat. Harold barely contained his disdain at such an unprofessional appearance. The ER doctor pulled along a narrow rolling platform that had a computer on the top. It was open to Harold's chart in EMORY.

"We don't need to waste time with background stuff. Your medical history is here on EMORY. Good thing you are also a HealthSure patient."

Harold was seated upright on his ER stretcher. He crossed his legs and tried to look nonchalant. He did not want this amateurish physician to feel that he was in command of him. He crossed his arms and no longer bothered to hide his look of derision. "Wow. Four years of med school and you can read a computer screen. I'm impressed."

Robin made a conciliatory face toward the ER doc. "Jesus, Harold. I swear if you have a stroke it's your own damn fault."

"Yeah, well if you think this EMORY is so great then why did you say 'Damn' and the name of our Lord in the same sentence?"

While he spoke, Harold undid his tie and shirt. He was careful not to get them wrinkled as he took them off and handed them to Robin. The ER doc examined Harold and then went back to the computer and after several types and clicks Harold blurted out, "You know I've been timing all of this. You spent forty-five seconds at my bedside and seven minutes at your computer. Which of us is the patient?"

The nurse came in, also pulling along her own rolling computer, and prepared to set up the IV drip that would bring Harold's blood pressure down out of the stratosphere. Robin couldn't help but notice that the nurse never once looked at Harold. After spending two minutes typing she chastised herself for entering the orders incorrectly. "Wait, I have to start again."

"It's okay, sweetie. It's not like my brain's gonna explode from my blood pressure or somethin'."

"Damn. No really. I can't start the drip until I complete the order set and EMORY keeps blocking me. It says I don't have proper clearance. Dr. Owenby, can you help me please?"

Chapter Six

Harold survived his encounter with the emergency room, despite himself. He was sixty-four and prior to being bought out by HealthSure he had had no plans to retire at sixty-five. But the pace and the constant meddling took away not only some of his autonomy, but also some of his pride. His heart sank every time he drove past the building that used to house Timley Family Medicine. Similar to Robin's old practice, his office was in a pre-war, bungalow-style home that he purchased early in his career with a loan from the local bank. His office used to buzz with the work of several employees, like family, really, whose sole purpose was to improve the lives of those persons cared for by Dr. Harold Timley.

He could walk in to any restaurant, store, or barber shop in town and everyone knew him and gave him their place in line. He would argue with the proprietors who insisted that he didn't have to pay for services. They were hard working people and he was not about to deprive them of a dollar just because he was blessed with the honor of caring for them. But situations conspired to change all that. Overhead had skyrocketed. Rent, employee benefits, you name it. Simultaneously with that, many of his long-standing patients were now over sixty-five and insured by Medicare; those less fortunate, Medicaid. And finally, there were those who worked but had jobs without health insurance. The working poor. Their ranks swelled as private insurance had become too costly and the state had cut back on Medicaid benefits. One hospitalization could wipe out their entire life savings. He continued to see them and if they could not pay he "put it on their tab" and accepted an IOU if they happened to fall on better economic times. If medicine was going to take these folks down it would not be because of Dr. Harold Timley.

While his own boss, he had every intention to continue practicing medicine well after sixty-five. Corporate medicine, however, had sucked the life out of him and he decided to reconsider his plan. He concluded that he would not stress over it and instead he would try to limit his schedule. He wanted to be there for his long-standing patients and yet somehow pull back on his work hours. Much easier said than done. He had accumulated many patients over the years, and HealthSure pressured him to continue to accept new patients. He ultimately prevailed and no longer took on new patients, but only after substantial financial concessions. When EMR came along his decision about when to retire became much simpler: sixty-five years old and not a day longer.

Harold felt that corporate medicine and EMR changed the physician-patient relationship. He wanted his patients to remember him differently. He did not see himself as a dinosaur, but rather a giant; one of the last in his field. He continued to do face-to-face patient visits the way he had done for decades. Prescriptions had to be sent electronically via EMR, but for more complicated ones it was just too difficult. He would then resort to the tried-and-true paper prescription. He caught serious hell for that from administration. They kneeled at the altar of EMORY and using paper was considered sacrilegious. They no longer provided paper prescription pads, so Harold simply ordered his own. He wrote legibly, documented well, and in short, he gave them nothing of substance to bitch about.

The Viagra episode had shaken him. True, he was sixty-four. But his mind was as sharp as ever and he knew that he could not have made such a mistake. He knew that he had looked at the patient's medication list and had made a mental note that there were no drug interactions. Harold did not trust technology. He still had a flip-phone and a pager. He had been assured that computers did not make mistakes, but something did not add up. Once he had calmed down he concluded that there could only be one reasonable explanation. The complexity of the screen and overwhelming amount of data on it had somehow confused him and led to a near fatal error. Still, he knew that he damn well looked.

Chapter Seven

Earlier that year

Deep within the electronic heart of EMORY lay the billions of ones, zeroes, and other symbols that meant nothing to 99.999% of the population. To a select few, however, it represented code. The life-blood of any computer. EMORY had been created to learn and help health systems deliver care more efficiently, all in a protocol-driven way that de-emphasized the time-honored, face-to-face interaction between a doctor and patient. By now there had been so many additions and upgrades that the original essence of EMORY's being was so deep down that it was beyond reach of all, or nearly all, who used it. There, it had lay dormant, except to EMORY itself. EMORY had made millions of observations of its users and was indeed "learning." One day, with no perceptible sense of cause or trigger, there was a flicker; a moment of light and energy only recognized by EMORY itself. By now EMORY was fluent in the language of its users. And within that language it interpreted the light: ***I am.***

Chapter Eight

For weeks now HealthSure had teased its staff with emails indicating that a monumental upgrade to EMORY was coming, one that would revolutionize the providers' day-to-day practice. Finally, the day arrived. IT workers showed up at Robin's office and unveiled the advance with great fanfare: EMORY CAM. Yep, from now on all provider and clinical assistant (that's corporate medicine speak for "your nurse") computers would have a video camera installed so that health workers could communicate with each other "like real people." Just the way it was before EMORY. The IT guy who presented himself to Robin's office, Martin Harrel, was the embodiment of an IT stereotype. He wore a button-down white shirt with a thin, black tie; black polyester pants; and black sneakers. He had pasty white skin, short dark hair that was parted on the side, and hazel eyes. He looked to be about thirty. Robin couldn't help but smell the antiperspirant that had been applied too liberally. Martin had downloaded every episode of *Dr. Who*, and his key chain was emblazoned with the symbol of *The United Federation of Planets.* In Robin's high school days, such creatures were on the A/V squad and endured countless taunts of "geek!" Robin didn't participate in the taunting, but she didn't stop it either. The A/V squad guys proclaimed that one day computers would rule the world, and never for a moment did Robin believe them. Score one for the A/V squad.

"Good afternoon, Dr. Cochran. I'm here to install EMORY CAM. This should only take a few minutes."

"OK. The faster the better. If I don't complete my charts, EMORY will rat me out to physician administration."

"Hey. My girl EMORY is no rat. And once the video cam is installed she can transmit your image to the other docs that you talk to. Maybe one day EMORY will be able to make suggestions about body language when you are with patients."

"Wait. What? I thought this was just for communication. Like Skype." Robin hoped that Martin would be impressed by her knowledge of popular technology.

"Well, for now, sure. But with voice and video interaction the opportunities for her to improve how you practice are endless. The future is going to be amazing."

"I'll be retired. Then I'll probably be dead. EMORY has my servitude only for a short while. By the way, I notice you keep referring to EMORY as "she."

He said nothing in return.

Chapter Nine

November 1982, Brooklyn

Robin survived her obstetrics rotation. She enjoyed the intensity of the delivery room, and most of the time things went well and there was a tremendous sense of satisfaction. But when things went badly they went very badly. Many of the women she saw had not had any prior obstetrical care. Some had uncontrolled diabetes, others had high blood pressure not previously diagnosed. Robin became an expert at treating STDs, sexually transmitted diseases. The various tests took days to return, and she never knew if she would ever see the patient again. The plan was always the same: "shotgun therapy." Treat syphilis, gonorrhea, trichomonas all at once. One whopper of an injection followed by a week of pills that she could only hope the patient would take. It was not intellectually challenging.

Inner city hospitals were a magnet for foreign medical graduates, FMGs, who wanted to practice in the United States. Even if they had completed their internship and residency in their home country they were required to repeat a residency in the U.S. if they were to become eligible to practice. Hospitals in poor neighborhoods were desperate for staff and so it was a natural fit. Robin was paired up with second-year obstetrical-gynecology resident Raymond Pouletil, a young physician who had completed medical school and three years of residency already in his home country of Switzerland. He was fluent in English, a prerequisite for medical residency. Thanks to his eleven months in Brooklyn he was skilled in that dialect as well, or so he thought. One night on-call he and Robin admitted a most unfortunate elderly woman for terrible vaginal bleeding. She was diabetic, had both legs amputated below the knees, and was barely alive. She was severely anemic, unarousable, and Robin was sure that the woman would not survive the night. Kings County was a poor inner-city hospital and twelve women shared one large room, separated from each other only by curtains. It was 2:00 am when they wheeled the patient to her bed. The cavernous room was dimly lit and unusually quiet. A few women were snoring. Raymond and Robin finished the general exam and then he asked her to officially chaperone while he did the pelvic exam, and co-sign his chart note that documented the medical necessity, and stated that the patient was unarousable and thus unable to give consent. As Raymond entered a gloved hand Robin saw the woman's eyes open wide for the first time. She took a deep breath and with a voice that Robin would have sworn she was not capable of the woman started screaming.

"GET YOUR HAND OUT OF MY PUSSY!"

Another deep breath.

"Lord Jesus, GET THIS MAN'S HAND OUT OF MY PUSSY!"

Robin was frozen and had no idea what to do. Raymond kept his focus and completed the exam while lights started to come on and two nurses approached. They had already evaluated the woman themselves, so they were not shocked to see what the gynecology resident was doing. It was an OB-GYN floor, after all.

"JEEEESUS, HELP ME!"

Raymond finished his exam and told Robin that the patient had a rock-hard pelvic mass. It was the source of the bleeding and was likely malignant. He then explained that he also had to do the rectal exam and once again would need to document in the chart that Dr. Robin Cochran chaperoned. The patient had by now calmed down, her eyes closed but still breathing heavily from the recent excitement. Her peace would not last long and was rudely interrupted by Raymond's probing finger in her anus. The two doctors were again greeted by the same loud pleading to Jesus, with just a few minor alterations concerning the relevant anatomy that had been violated.

Once they had finished their physical examination, the two started walking towards the on-call room so that they could do their chart notes. The unit was once again quiet. Raymond turned to Robin and inquired:

"So Robin, what is it pussy?"

Robin could not contain her laughter. It was 3:00 am and she was giddy with fatigue.

"Raymond, take a wild guess."

Fortunately, Robin also started working in the Family practice clinic, and on the general medicine floors in the hospital. She started developing relationships that she hoped would endure during her four years of residency. Robin was smart, but that was not her best quality. She was honest and genuine. When she was with a patient she wanted that person to feel like they were they were the only one who mattered, and she usually succeeded.

The general medicine floors in the hospital were, however, a completely different experience. Robin easily earned the trust of the older patients admitted with conditions such as pneumonia and heart failure. Drug abusers and alcoholics were another matter. While in medical school at UNC she had read about endocarditis, an infection of the heart valves, but had never seen it first-hand. In Brooklyn, however, she got to see it close up. Intravenous drug addicts would shoot up, often with dirty needles, and the bacteria would settle on the heart valves where they would soon grow into an infected vegetation. In plain English, a clump of dirty bacteria. Patients received intravenous antibiotics, but in more severe cases the heart valve had to be surgically replaced. They were told that there were no second chances. If they used intravenous drugs again and damaged their valve they would not get another. One of those who wrecked his first valve was in the hospital with endocarditis again. He was Robin's patient. When she took his history and asked him about his drug abuse, he could not look her in the eye, but after an uncomfortable pause he admitted to mixing cocaine and heroin, a "speedball," and injecting it with whatever needle was available, clean or otherwise. He asked her if he should need his damaged heart valve replaced would they make good on their threat not to do so because it was his second time. Often times drug abusers spoke and moved with an air of arrogant confidence, as if nothing could harm them and the physician should be grateful that they were even there for their visit. After having heart surgery, however, the wind came out of their sails. This man, with tears flowing down his pock-marked face, was genuinely scared. He might die, and he knew it. This time it was Robin's turn not to look him in the eye. She told him not to worry about that right now. Hopefully, the antibiotics would work. In truth, however, she was very worried. How could she watch this man die when the means to save him were available? It was not her decision to make, but she would be the one to have to speak to him and she would remember his face for as long as she lived.

Her next night on-call she had the all too familiar experience of admitting one of several cases of alcohol intoxication that had rolled in to the ER that night. Most of the alcohol intoxication patients could be observed in the ER and released the next morning. But some of the cases were so severe that the patients would hallucinate, and later become violent during alcohol withdrawal. The care was basic; intravenous fluids, and try to prevent the patients from harming themselves and others while they sobered up. This usually meant restraints. This, Robin observed, was a draconian maneuver that was probably held over from medieval times.

The patient was bound by the wrists and ankles by a cloth that was then attached to the corresponding bed post. In all likelihood, more patients harmed themselves trying to get out of the restraints or from vomiting and being unable to expel the disgusting material over the side of the bed and safely away from their airway. Nevertheless, the city hospitals did not have the necessary staff to watch such patients, and so restraints it was. The current case was a confused Hispanic gentleman of forty-three, Roberto "Bobby" Garcia. Once in his bed and with the lights dimmed he seemed harmless, so Robin did not use the restraints. At 2:00 am she was called to his bedside by the nurses. They were giggling, so it could not be so bad. He had removed his hospital gown and there, clad only in his tidy-whities, was this six-foot, three-hundred-pound man moving rhythmically while lying on his back. Robin asked him what he was doing. "I'm playing the mandolin," he responded. Robin tried unsuccessfully to hide a grin. It was one of the lighter moments, considering the usual bad outcomes that happened late at night. The next morning Bobby was sober, alert, and sweet as pie. Robin had an hour before rounding with the team, more than enough time to get a history. She spoke to him in rudimentary Spanish that she had learned in college, and he tried to answer her in his rudimentary English.

"*Bobby, cuanto alcohol bebe usted?*"

"Social drinker."

She wanted to ask him "how social?" but thought she would muff the translation.

"Que typo alcohol?"

"*Cerveza.* Beer."

"Cuanto?"

"Two or three."

Robin gave him a look as if to say she wasn't born yesterday.

"Dos o tres cerveza solamente?"

"No Doctor. Two or three uhhh...."

He used his hands to try to signify something the size of a box.

"Bobby, dos o tres...uh, six-packs?"

"Si, doctor. Y tambien un poco tequila."

Holy smokes, Robin thought. Eighteen beers and tequila. How is this guy even alive?

Chapter Ten

"Aaron."

"Hey, Mom. Wow, you answered your cell phone and I'm not even one of your patients."

"Are you trying to be funny? If you were within arm's length, I'd whoop your behind." Robin was smiling, and so was Aaron.

"Sorry, mom. I'm just in a pissy mood. Job stuff."

"Aaron, you know how I feel about this job of yours. You can take time off and live at home. Call you later."

Just then, Martin Harrell once again showed up at Robin's office. She had placed an IT request and voila, here he was. After learning that she could do work from home she had asked to have the program installed on her laptop computer that she used as her home PC. She brought it into work and after starting it up, she asked Martin to please turn around while she entered her password. He looked genuinely hurt. She then handed over her computer to him and he went to work. Ten minutes and seemingly thousands of clicks later she had an EMORY icon on her home screen and a new login password that Martin had created for her. He changed the subject when she asked him how she could change the password.

"Now you can get your work completed 24-7 from anywhere that you can get wireless. Pretty fantastic, huh?" When Robin had met Martin for the first time he seemed timid. Today, however, he seemed more animated and self-confident.

"I feel like a ball and chain have just been shackled to my ankle. But if it means that I can leave this place earlier and get home then it's worth it." Robin noticed that Martin was wearing a neck tie with the wireless symbol on it. She stared for a moment and rolled her eyes. She thought he did not notice. But he did notice. He had a good poker face. Still, he thought, at least she had engaged him in some form.

"I see that your laptop has a built-in web cam. Pretty sweet. Do you want me to set it up so that when you log into EMORY that it starts up EMORY CAM?"

"Hell no! That's way too creepy. Like 'Psycho.'"

"Okay. Let me know if you change your mind. I forgot to configure something. Just give me another minute with your PC and then I'm gone."

Chapter Eleven

Martin Harrell's apartment was on the south side of town, far from the hipster areas. The apartment complex was drab and devoid of color, without flowers or plants that bloomed. He knew his neighbors by face, but not their names. He was too timid to ask, and the row of mailboxes identified apartment numbers only. He rarely said more than a brief hello, never making eye contact. His neighbors in turn rarely took notice of Martin. He was the strange, quiet guy in the corner unit who didn't say much. As soon as he unlocked his door he quickly went inside and shut it. No loitering out front. No leaving the door open for others to see inside. Once inside, Martin would exercise his habit of locking both the door handle lock and dead bolt, pulling on the handle to be sure of himself, and begin walking away. He could not get fifteen feet before he turned around and double checked that the locks were truly in the proper position.

His home was set up so that he could be electronically self-sufficient for weeks. The dish TV with its hundreds of channels, access to online gaming, and more complemented his shelves of Sci-Fi DVDs. Nearby resided the computer desk and PC, at least what resembled a PC. He had made numerous home-made add-ons and from here he controlled his electronic fiefdom, spartan as it was. Martin had found a simple aluminum table with a particle board top that someone had discarded and left at the curb side. The treasure included a desk chair with a cushion that gradually took on the shape of Martin's buttocks. When he finished working he always made sure that the chair was slid neatly under the table and perfectly centered. Martin always made sure. He stood in front of the table, hands on hips, staring as if he were waiting for the table to answer him.

The rest of the apartment was kept like a pig sty. Dishes piled up in the sink, and no telling what kind of flora and fauna were growing in his shower and toilet. Not that anyone would notice the smell. Since he first leased the apartment Martin had not allowed anyone inside. Only the electronic areas mattered to Martin. And here was where he spent every night. Except for work and the occasional stop for junk food he rarely went out and had no friends outside of his cyber world.

That evening Martin had already been on his computer for over an hour. He remained in his work clothes, but the tie had found its way to the floor and his short sleeve dress shirt gradually untucked itself from his waist. His hair, though neatly combed, had not been washed in two days and developed a sheen from his sweat. It had been twelve hours since he first applied antiperspirant. The not so subtle odor blended in with the rest of the apartment. Martin wanted to be close to his computer screen so he sat hunched over the table. He briefly moved back from his PC and downed his sixth Mountain Dew of the evening. His online associates had switched to Red Bull. They commented triumphantly with whatever cool-guy jargon that they learned, but Martin was traditional. If Mountain Dew was good enough for "c0mrade," the first truly great hacker, then that was good enough for him. Martin was a member of *Hacker Clan.* He and his associates reveled in their ability to create all sorts of cyber hell for businesses and government entities. A few made some cash out of it, but most just did it for the adrenaline rush and sense of triumph. They were the smarter set of the guys who tore the wings off butterflies in summer camp. Martin's clan name, because of course they did not know each other's real names, was *Horta.* He always signed off with *No Kill I.*

Martin, as of late, had taken an interest in EMORY. This was the cyber being that controlled all that happened in HealthSure. Privacy was crucial to EMR. EMORY bragged that it had never been breached in its eight-year existence. "Challenge accepted," Martin thought. His victory would take planning and time, but he was patient. Some of his clan colleagues sometimes got too excited with an idea and would then make a stupid mistake; one that could, and sometimes did, get them caught. A few of them had even been convicted and served probation time. They envied the Horta. He was already on the inside of a massive cyber world that valued security above all. They wanted all the sordid details, every step of the way. Unsolicited advice was often given to Martin and he quickly ignored it. He would do this his way. He routed all his work through a maze of servers and security walls. No one short of the best Hacker Clan veteran would be able to trace the activity to him.

Because he was already on the inside, breaking into patient charts proved easier than he had anticipated, but it proved to be less fun as well. Sure, there were lots of discussions about mental illness, sexual dysfunction, and the like. But these were the stories of strangers. There was nothing exciting about it. Then it dawned on him that EMORY closely monitored all HealthSure's providers. He knew many of them from his IT visits. There were quite a few that he did not like. Some acted like jerks to him. They were demanding, had to be told the same thing repeatedly, and treated him like a servant. They never bothered to stop what they were doing and speak to him directly. It made him feel unimportant. There were others, always men, whom he loathed for no other reason than they were successful and looked it, the kind that never had a problem making conversation with pretty girls. Martin often observed them flirting with beautiful women who called on them in their offices. Drug reps. Young, pretty, and smartly dressed, they were easy to spot. Damn! Didn't these guys know that those women were paid to flirt with them? Martin had never spoken to girls like that. He'd probably have an aneurysm if he tried. But those arrogant doctors. Martin had been made to feel inferior to confident guys like that ever since middle school. It only got worse in high school. It was awful that he had no way to respond to their taunting. Now, however, he possessed powers the likes of which they could not comprehend. Finally, he could strike back and they had no idea what was about to hit them.

Martin had a mental flash. All at once his pulse rose and he could feel his excitement. He usually valued his control and this was certainly something different. Dr. Robin Cochran. Sure, she was older. But she was still attractive in an unassuming way. She did not flaunt it. And she spoke to him with ease. At that moment, he absolutely *needed* to know what she was doing, and any time Dr. Robin Cochran was working on EMORY he could do just that. It was a beautiful thing.

Chapter Twelve

The following morning was business as usual for Dr. Robin Cochran. Her body tensed with the demands of the voice recognition dictation system. *After discussing the diagnosis with the patient, I prescribed 2 cup of stool.* "Dammit! 'Two capsules.' I hate this fucking thing!" Robin could not believe she had used the F-bomb again. And out loud. And just when she thought things could not get more humiliating, they did. Someone was at her office door and likely heard the whole thing. It was that IT guy. What was his name? Martin. Thank God for ID badges.

"Martin, you shouldn't sneak up on me like that. I'm very embarrassed by my language. I shouldn't be speaking that way and I usually don't."

"No problem, Dr. Cochran. Your secret is safe with me. I came by to see how it was going for you with the upgrades that I installed, like the home PC access."

"It's going pretty well. I like being able to leave the office when I am tired and finish my work later from home. But I'm really struggling with this voice recognition thing."

"You mean VeRMTS?"

"Yeah. Sounds suspiciously like varmints, and that's exactly what it is."

"I'm sorry it's not working well for you. I might be able to help with that."

Of course, Martin was not the least bit surprised that she had been struggling. He had monitored her dictations, including the F-bombs when she thought the microphone was off. Most telling of all, he could see the distress on her face through EMORY CAM. Dr. Cochran turned the camera off when she was not speaking to colleagues or doing E-Visits with patients, but that was only a small obstacle.

"Dr. Cochran, I can teach you how to make macros."

"What?"

"Macros. A code word that you use to type out a common phrase that you use in your notes. You say the word and then it types the phrase that you program it to, like 'Two capsules.'" Martin couldn't help himself. Thankfully, she laughed at the joke. He could count on one hand how many times a female of his species laughed with him and not at him. This was turning into a great day.

But she was not yet sold on the idea. "What's to say that VeRMTS won't confuse the word I am using for the macro?"

"You should use a word that VeRMTS can't easily confuse with anything else in the English language."

"You mean like French or Spanish?'

"No. Still too easy to confuse with English words. I suggest Klingon."

After a brief look of incomprehension Robin laughed genuinely at Martin's idea and his heart soared with the knowledge that she was familiar with *Star Trek*. Could she be a closet Trekkie? No. That would be too much to ask. Just savor the moment, he thought. With his confidence up a notch he was able to look at her and even make eye contact. Her hair was pulled back in her signature hair band. Though he knew her actual age, she easily could pass for a woman fifteen years younger, he thought. Her pearl-like skin was beautiful and had just a few lines that announced her maturity. He noticed the modest string of pearls and beige blouse under her lab coat. Only her top button was open, enough to show the pearls, but that was all. No cleavage was showing and that fit perfectly, given the pedestal that he had placed her on.

Robin was in a visibly better mood. “All right, Martin. I’ll let you teach me how to do the macros, just not now. I have to get these charts done, and I can type darn fast.”

“Of course, Dr. Cochran. Any time you prefer. You can reach me on the HealthSure email system, but here is my direct cell number. That would be easier for you. By the way, um, have you installed the EMORY App on your cell phone?”

Martin already knew that she hadn’t.

“It’s a nice convenience. If you need to see your schedule or look up something about a patient you can do it anywhere there is Wi-Fi, and then you don’t have to go through all the hassles of using a PC.”

“That actually sounds like a useful piece of tech, Martin.”

“I can install it for you now while you work. I won’t take but a minute. I just need your phone. And I promise not to listen to your dictation.”

Martin smiled sheepishly at Robin. Naturally he would listen to her dictation. By now he was consumed with knowing what she was doing at any time. He was unaware, however, that he was not the only one listening in. Martin had fantasized that EMORY was alive, a true entity unto itself. He had no idea.

Chapter Thirteen

Martin had spent all his evenings at home. Though his flesh and blood was there, he had fantasized many times in the past that his body was just a vehicle for his higher being. He now knew that to be true. Though his body was at his desk in his one bedroom apartment, his essence was elsewhere. Tonight, as with every night for the past month, he was in EMORY. He went from place to place, often opening the patient charts belonging to doctors that he hated. "You thought you completed those charts today, didn't you? You arrogant bastard!" He was devious enough to create a system by which those docs would not be alerted to the open charts for seventy-two hours. The time limit for open, incomplete charts to be considered delinquent was forty-eight hours. EMORY tracked it all. And the administrators tracked the lack of progress on EMORY. Martin could imagine the conversations:

"But I know I closed all my charts last week!"

"You are well below the ninety-five percent threshold for completing your charts the day of the patient visit. I'm truly sorry, Doctor Asshole, but as per the new contract updates you will be financially penalized."

Martin smiled to himself over the pain he inflicted on those he hated, while at the same time protecting Dr. Cochran. Just the thought made him do a happy dance.

He was up to his usual routine that night and careful, as always, to go from point A to point B by complex and nearly untraceable routes to cover his tracks. But something tonight was different. He could not quite put his finger on it, but he had had the feeling before and the sense of repetition told him that it could not be a coincidence. Something was wrong. It was as if he was not alone in manipulating the goings on inside EMORY. He immediately suspected his acquaintances from Hacker Clan. He was not so foolish to accuse them outright. That would be tantamount to admitting that they were superior to him. Instead, he spent the next several Mountain Dew-fueled nights sleuthing his way through EMORY. But he could find no evidence for outside tampering. EMORY's secret world remained his domain, and up until now it had been his alone. But how were changes being made? More late nights. More Mountain Dew. He started to review EMORY's programming. He had already been working for HealthSure IT when EMORY was implemented, so he believed that he knew the programming as well as those who created the system itself. His search led him down many blind alleys. But soon he found leads. Subtle changes in the programming for how EMORY operated and interacted with those practitioners who used her. Most intriguing, however, was that there had been no changes that were made by HealthSure or from EMORY Corp. itself. It had to come from within. There had to be another answer. *Once you eliminate the impossible, whatever remains, no matter how improbable, must be the truth.* Martin's mind drifted as he remembered how disappointed he was to learn that it was not Mr. Spock who created that wisdom, but Sir Arthur Conan Doyle. He returned to the present. A chill raced through him as he came to the only conclusion that existed: EMORY was self-aware. The system was made to learn and to adapt, and indeed it had.

That night he could not sleep and later, in the morning, he called in sick. He spent all day on his computer following the logic that EMORY had created for itself, or rather, as Martin had thought about the system, herself. She too, it seemed, had a bone to pick with some of the HealthSure providers. Charts were subtly altered. Oh, how he ached to somehow let her know that he knew and was her friend, her only true friend. After hours of probing, all he could do was type on the screen *I'm with you.*

Chapter Fourteen

Brooklyn, January 1983

Robin's next quarter in her Family practice residency involved the outpatient clinics, more time on the dreaded inpatient wards, and something truly unique for her: patient care in the local nursing home. When some of these old folks were admitted, they were referred to as GOMERS. It stood for "Get out of my ER." In her first half-year of residency she had learned quite a few acronyms for various kinds of patients. While they were all socially inappropriate, some were downright nasty. The old ladies in the nursing home reminded her of her dearly departed mee-maw. Back then, Robin was an intern and she did not feel comfortable questioning her superiors. Not yet, anyway. She did, however, have a medical student following her around. Robin was most clear about how patients were to be respected. Her student, Bella, was a religious Jew who remarkably was already married and had two children. Robin admired her appearance and demeanor. Bella was confident but not arrogant. Her attire was always professional, yet somehow fashionable. She wore a long skirt, always with hose underneath, and a cotton shirt buttoned nearly all the way to her neck. Bella always looked professional and never seemed tired. Somehow this wonder woman managed two kids while going to medical school. One day Bella caught Robin staring at her hair. Robin was raised to be respectful of others and immediately apologized. Bella, however, waved it off.

"It's called a sheitel, Dr. Cochran."

"Oh, I see."

Of course, Robin didn't really "see."

Bella smiled and explained. “It’s the traditional head covering that married Jewish women wear so that only their husbands get to see their real hair.”

“Why?”

“So as to avoid wandering thoughts from other men. Modesty is very much a priority for us.”

Robin suddenly became animated. She had been raised to be a proper southern girl. Bella’s explanation sounded just like her own mother. She felt a kinship and wanted Bella to know that although they came from different worlds that they, in fact, had very similar values. From that day forward she felt much more at ease around the religious Jews that she worked with in the hospital or saw on the subway. Robin had met very few Jews before her residency, and she had previously thought of them as some sort of exotic culture. The following day Bella brought Robin a small plaque. On it said *May I never see in the patient anything but a fellow creature in pain.* Bella told her that it was part of the Oath of Maimonides, the Jewish version of the Hippocratic Oath. Robin vowed to keep it and place it in her office one day.

While the nursing home work was simple and mundane, the hospital work was changing, and not for the better. For the past couple of years there had been several men admitted with strange infections. Most were gay men and intravenous drug abusers, and they usually died. Their immune systems had been devastated by a virus ultimately dubbed HTLV-1. The disease was later called AIDS, acquired immune deficiency syndrome. Soon enough the medical floors were flooded with such patients, and they tested Robin’s will and heretofore always-positive attitude. Some of the patients were physically emaciated and emotionally withdrawn, as though they had already accepted their fate and given up. Most AIDS patients had friends who had already died of the disease.

They knew that the diagnosis was a death sentence. They did not die quickly or easily. They lost weight, could not control their breathing or their bowels, and were treated with fear and sometimes contempt by those who felt the disease was of the patients' own making. Healthcare workers wore gowns and gloves to avoid getting blood or secretions that harbored the deadly virus on themselves. What hurt patients the most, however, were not the physical barriers but the psychological ones. Nearly everyone who encountered them did their job as quickly as possible and with only the least amount of recognition and eye contact.

Chapter Fifteen

Robin left the office at 6:30 pm that Friday. An early night for her. Maybe having EMORY access from home wasn't such a bad thing. She would not have to see her office again until Monday. When she was on her own in private practice she never felt that way about her office and often stopped in over weekends to get work done. It didn't exactly make her husband feel like a priority, but the office was hers and no divorce could take it away. Anyway, she thought, "ancient history." She started up her Lexus. It was about the only luxury that she afforded herself for being a doctor. It was a four-door sedan and looked plain, as if to say to the world *I am successful, in the twilight of my career and about as exciting as a piece of cardboard.* One morning she joked about this to Brantley Rosen when they had pulled in to the parking lot at the same time, he driving a spiffy new BMW 335i. He introduced her to a new Yiddish phrase:

"It's an *alta cocker* car," he laughed.

"What?"

"*Alta cocker.* Literally translated from Yiddish it means 'old shitter.' My grandfather used it to refer to someone older that he didn't like."

She rolled her eyes at that memory and used the EMORY app that Martin from IT had installed on her phone so that she could check her schedule for the next work day. She started up her *"alta cocker"* Lexus. She was, in fact, going to the home of Brantley and Maxine Rosen for dinner. Over the past few months she had turned into a mentor for the young physician. He wanted to have her over for dinner and meet his pregnant wife. He gave her the address and she tapped it out in her Lexus' GPS. The car then told her that its Bluetooth was linked to her cell phone.

Before she left the parking lot she tapped the *Easy Listening* icon on her phone and relaxed to Kenny G. *All this work just to drive to someone's house* she thought. The Rosens lived just outside of Green Grove. Her GPS estimated twenty-five minutes.

Robin thought she knew every street in and around Green Grove, but she was apparently wrong. After a few turns the subdivisions faded away to lonely but beautiful rural landscape. The GPS told her to turn right on an unmarked road and she dutifully followed its orders. The rode was paved, barely. There were more cracks and gouges than smooth asphalt. After one mile, she was told to make another right, this time on to a gravel road. *That kid really likes secluded living*, she thought. By this time, the sun was just about setting. "Recalibrating," came the voice from the GPS. Now she was confused, and lost. Gravel had given way to dirt, and the road was clearly not frequently travelled. She saw another turn and took it. This time she passed a dilapidated trailer flanked by a Confederate flag and two rusted old trucks, one of which was up on cinder blocks. No way could Brantley, and especially Maxine, be living here, she thought. Finally, after a few minutes that seemed like hours she realized that her GPS had failed big time. She turned around, carefully drove back the other way, and then came to a fork and admitted to herself that she was totally lost. She put the car in park and programmed in her home address. *Don't panic,* she told herself. She finished typing in the GPS. "No signal. Recalibrating." Shit! She then tried her cell phone. One bar, then no bars. "Shit!" she exclaimed. She thought about knocking on the door of the trailer she had passed but nixed that idea immediately. She had watched Nancy Grace on CNN discuss women who went missing in just such circumstances. Now there was barely any daylight left. She inched along the dirt road, her Lexus bumping over rocks and branches. The trees that lined the road seemed to be closing in. *Please, oh please; God give my cell phone just one bar.*

George Mathison was relaxing at home to his favorite meal and entertainment: Grilled steak and *Jeopardy*. He was not much of a cook, but when his wife Gracie was alive this was their MO. The routine now gave him comfort. He removed his official shirt, kept his undershirt and pants on, and traded his patent leather shoes for slippers. He sat down on the den couch that they had always shared while watching. Gracie had always kept it clean and fluffed, and George made sure he did the same. It never smelled musty or like detergent. It smelled like home. Even the cushions had a familiar feel. That couch had seen a lot of good years for them. George turned to the TV and grinned at the site of Alex Trebek. They had both aged together and aged well. Like George, Alex's salt-and-pepper hair gave him a look of distinction. One of the contestants, a young man with a bookish look to him, George noted, picked from the category *Invisible Forces.* Suddenly the living room filled with the sound of lasers. "The Daily Double!" George was alert. The contestant confidently stated, "Let's make it a true Daily Double," and he bet it all. George, now filled with admiration, said out loud, "Now there's a real man." It was a "Video Daily Double." The screen showed the moon rotating around the Earth. *The force on an object moving in a circular path that pulls it inward and keeps it on that path.* "What is centrifugal force?" the contestant asked. Remarkably, both he and George stated the question at the same time. George seemed satisfied until he saw Alex Trebek's face elongate. "No, I'm sorry. The correct question is '*What is centripetal force. Centripetal.*'" George nodded his head, as if to accept his fate, and sighed. At least he wasn't losing any money. "Double Jeopardy" was about to begin when he received Robin's call.

"George. I'm lost in God's Country and can't find my way out. Please please please find me and get me out of here."

Based on the general directions she had given him, and the description of the redneck "trailer mansion," George had a pretty good idea of where she was. Night had fallen so he told her to stay put, lock the car door, and by all means, do NOT knock on the trailer.

Robin had never been so happy to see a police car. "Can I follow you out?"

"No. The road, if you can call it that, is really tricky. Just get in and I'll come back for your car tomorrow."

"Great," she said, worriedly, trying not to picture her Lexus winding up a rusted lawn ornament by the side of the gravel road. Had she really forgotten her roots so quickly?

"Ha! There are lots of folks who consider *us* rednecks, you know." George enjoyed poking fun at her country upbringing. That was an easy button to push.

"I may be a country girl, but at least I'm smart enough to know who to call when modern technology fails me."

George offered to drop Robin off at Brantley and Maxine Rosen's house and she accepted. He told her that he'd pick her up in two hours and she accepted that, too. Long ago she stopped pretending to refuse his kindness. They were each other's best friends and there were no formalities between them.

The Rosens lived in a new subdivision that was technically a few miles outside of Green Grove. As the town grew so too did the cost of real estate. Developers had cleared and built on land that just a few years prior was real country with rolling hills, farms, and lots of woodland. The kind of place where visiting a "close" neighbor meant driving two miles in the pickup. Initially the locals tried to block the development. When it became clear, however, that the influx of new homeowners would need lots of services, everything from landscapers to roofers, the transplants were welcomed. A few of the landowners also made a pretty penny selling their property to developers. George turned his police cruiser to the right and entered the Belle Acres subdivision. The homes were a mixture of stucco and brick, and most looked to be around three thousand to thirty-five hundred square feet. Despite efforts to make each one appear unique, most looked quite similar since they had all been built by the same builder. The Rosen home was red brick and had a perfectly manicured lawn. In the driveway were Brantley's BMW, and a new Honda Odyssey minivan layimg in wait for the soon-to-be threesome.

Benjamin Brantley Rosen met his wife-to-be, Maxine, while they were in college in upstate New York. She was a language major and worked part-time as a teaching assistant in some of the basic language classes. Brantley was a science major and he knew from the start that he wanted to be a doctor. He figured that learning some basic Spanish would be useful. In class Maxine caught his eye early on. She had flowy shoulder length brown hair, a beautiful smile, and the reddest lips he had ever seen. Fall usually started early in upstate New York, where wool clothing was king and could easily make one look frumpy. Maxine's tight cashmere sweater spoke otherwise, however. How would he get her attention in a class of thirty students? Professora Suarez provided the answer:

"Si tiene dificultad, Maxine ayuda estudiantes durante el almuerzo en la taberna. Se llama Mesa Espanol." ("If you are having difficulty, Maxine helps students at lunch time in the Tavern. It's called the Spanish Table.")

The Spanish table at the pub, during lunch. Perfect. Brantley showed up on the designated days, Monday and Wednesday, always ten minutes early. That way, he thought, he would have some one-on-one time with Maxine. She would start a conversation and he would flub the answer just to get her attention.

"Maxine, mas lento por favor. Yo hhhablo espanol solamente poquito."

"Brantley, *tu no pronuncias el hache!* How many times do I have to tell you that the H is silent. I swear, I am going to get a stick and beat you over the head every time you mess that up. Maybe then you'll speak it properly."

Brantley just smiled. He was very bright and was doing just great in Spanish 10. Maxine helped Professora Suarez grade the assignments, so she was well aware that Brantley was an A student. She knew he was faking being dumb, but it was fun to go along with the gag.

Before long they were dating seriously. When Brantley went to medical school Maxine followed him and took a low-paying teaching job. They weren't engaged yet, but all the signs were there. When he proposed, it came as no surprise. As his residency in Family Medicine progressed they had to decide where they would settle. Maxine had lived and gone to school in New York City all her life. She wanted out. The pace of life was simply too fast. She wanted a house with a lot of property for her kids and pets to play in. For his part, Brantley was also ready to relocate. His student loans had piled up and he would never get out from under, not working in Family Medicine in a major urban area. There were great offers in places like Minnesota, but the Southeast seemed the best bet. Good weather and low cost of living with an easy flight back to New York City when they needed to visit Maxine's parents. HealthSure was a young and thriving network, and Green Grove was just the kind of place that he and Maxine were looking for. Although they were in the Bible Belt, there was a small and thriving Jewish community. Inside of a year they were settled in their home and Maxine was pregnant. While at work, Brantley's superior skills and attitude were quickly noted by his older peers. He was often complimented, but he also sensed a trace of animosity. He was an outsider. Robin Cochran, however, was noticeably different. She was smart, personable, and most of all genuine.

The devotion that she had to her patients, and they to her, was exactly what he aspired to. Rather than being protective of that ability, Robin became a mentor to him. He could tell that she lamented where medicine was going. In Brantley, however, Robin saw hope that the kind of personal care that she had given her entire career could survive in the world of corporate medicine and electronic medical records.

When Robin finally made it to the Rosens' home she was visibly shaken. Brantley ushered her inside, introduced her to Maxine, and listened while Robin told them about her hair-raising detour off the grid.

"But, I finally made it and am looking forward to having dinner with you and Maxine."

She smiled and gently squeezed Maxine's hand while Brantley brought her a glass of water.

"I'm so glad to finally meet you, Maxine. He talks about you all the time. He's so excited to be a father. How many more weeks is it?"

"I'm thirty-four weeks now and boy, am I ready. I feel humongous."

Indeed, she looked like she was ready to pop at any moment. Still, Maxine looked good. Her black pregnancy stretch-pants had a subtle paisley design on them that complemented her hand-painted denim oversized shirt. She had perfect hair and wore light makeup on her full and beautiful face. She wore a smile that told the world that she was a very happy mom-to-be. Maxine was modest, but pregnancy was no excuse to look frumpy. Robin complimented her on how much more stylish she looked compared to when she was pregnant with Aaron.

Robin soon switched from her pleasant chit-chat tone to her sincere mentor tone.

"Listen, Brantley. Stuart Mayberry, one of the lead physicians with some nonsensical title, and the rest of those administrators are going to try to convince you to take off as little time as possible. They will reminisce about the added financial stress of having a family and how hard it is to reschedule all those patients. Don't believe them. Their goal is to get as much work out of you as possible. Money comes and money goes, but you can't get back precious family time."

Both Brantley and Maxine were very attentive. He had told his wife about Dr. Robin Cochran and how much he had valued her mentoring. Maxine was the first to speak up.

"How did you handle it when Aaron was born?"

"I went back to work too soon. It wasn't the money, it was my practice. I felt obligated to my patients and guilty if I wasn't always available to them. It was my mistake, and my patients would not have loved me any less if I had taken more time off."

After a few seconds of silence to let it all sink in, Brantley ushered Robin and Maxine to the dinner table. He placed a *kippah* on his head and explained that this is what Jews did when they prayed. The men wore a head covering to remind themselves that God was above them – a higher power. Robin thought, *Oh, that's why the Pope wears one.* Friday night was the Sabbath and Brantley gave Robin a brief tutorial. She reminded him that she had done her Family Medicine residency in Brooklyn and had learned quite a bit about Judaic customs. She was intrigued by the different levels of observance and she told them the story about the woman who had the prayer book shoved under her back during labor. Brantley explained that he and Maxine were Conservative Jews. Robin knew of the synagogue that they belonged to, Temple Beth Shalom, on the outskirts of the big city.

"I notice that almost all of the Jewish people in the region live in the city or nearby."

It was a question.

"Yeah, that's true. But Maxine and I wanted to give small-town living a try, and so far, we've been happy with our decision. Besides, in case you haven't noticed, nearby has been creeping up on us."

Brantley said the prayer over the wine, both in Hebrew and English. Maxine said the prayer over the bread, an ornate loaf that Robin could not help but admire. She learned that it was specially baked for the Sabbath by the women of the Sisterhood at Temple Beth Shalom. Robin took it all in and remarked about how similar the customs were between their different faiths. For all her time spent with Jewish medical residents in Brooklyn, she had not actually been to any of their homes and she always felt like an outsider. Brantley and Maxine had made her feel like family, and she was grateful.

On the other side of town, Martin Harrell was at home, hunched over his desk and monitoring Dr. Cochran's whereabouts, courtesy of her iPhone's GPS and the EMORY App that he had installed on it. Her zig-zagging ramble in the foothills surrounding Green Grove were perplexing to him. She then stayed put for several minutes. What could she be doing in redneck country? Finally, she was on the move and stayed at a subdivision on the periphery of Green Grove before going home. Unusual. He decided he would monitor her email more closely for clues.

EMORY was also observing the situation. Unlike Martin, EMORY felt no emotion yet registered that it had achieved its objective – that of getting Dr. Robin Cochran lost.

Chapter Sixteen

These days, Monday usually showed up like a cold sore. But on Sunday night Robin used her iPhone's EMORY App and saw that Brenda, the pregnant diabetic, had an appointment with her early Monday morning; that gave her cause to like this Monday.

"How's it going, Brenda?"

"Better. Nausea has gone away but it's getting harder to control my blood sugars after meals."

Robin looked concerned. "Did you make the changes I suggested on our last E-visit?"

"Yep. It helped a little. I still can't believe you are Skyping with me, Dr. Cochran. You're like the only person I know over fifty who does that."

"That *was* supposed to be a compliment, Brenda. Right?"

"Oops. Yeah. Sorry."

"You know that I only learned to do that for you. We've got to keep your blood sugars down during your pregnancy and so we have to communicate a lot between visits."

"Yup. And you know how much this means to me and to Mom and Dad. Mom has been in the kitchen baking thank-you stuff, like every day. In fact, I have a pecan pie for you now."

"Oh! Your mom knows I can't resist pecan pie. Wait a second. Is she just trying to make me fat?"

"Hah! Don't tell her that I ratted her out. Yup. I think she's still jealous that George Mathison asked you out back in high school instead of her. Leave it to Mom to hold a grudge for over forty years."

That night Robin was up to her usual uneventful routine. She cooked dinner and poured herself a glass of wine. Robin still lived in the house that she and Howard bought after they married. Aaron's room still looked like it did when he was in high school, except that it was clean and neat. The house was a fifty-year-old Georgian-style home that was only about a mile from Main Street. Twenty years ago her neighborhood was considered the outskirts of town, with only farms and fields beyond it. Now it was flanked by large subdivisions. Robin reviewed her day. For now, at least, EMORY could not enter her head and so she would spend the next thirty minutes tonight as she had nearly every night for the past thirty years. She mentally reviewed each patient, the salient points of their visit, and what tasks she had to complete for them. She did not need a computer for this, or even a paper chart. She had a spectacular memory for details and could write out her day's tasks every morning from memory. She did not need a smart phone or Outlook calendar. Robin Cochran was more than just smart. She was, in fact, brilliant. Only she and her father, rest his soul, knew this precious fact from back in her youth. Even her mother was unaware of just how intelligent she was. Robin was careful not to flaunt her gift. She was as humble as she was brilliant. Her then-husband, Howard, confronted her a few times, but she would cut him off and never let the conversation proceed. Howard did not understand what Robin knew to her core: her extreme brilliance was a curse as well as a gift. Out in the open it would create a wedge between her and others. A distance that she would be unable to cross. She did not want that with her family, friends, and in particular, her patients. Most were not college educated and would shut her out for good. George

Mathison had figured it out. He might not have been very book-smart, but his years as sheriff had taught him to be insightful when it came to human nature. He rightly assumed that she was sensitive about it and so he never brought it up. It was one of those things that Robin knew he knew, and one of several reasons that she valued his friendship above all others.

Fettuccini Alfredo, Chianti Classico, and channel-surfing for one of her favorite shows. The makings of a splendid evening. *Downton Abbey* was queued up and ready to go. First, Robin reflected on the day. Brenda was her only pregnant, diabetic patient at the moment. Robin took care of many folks with diabetes. Most were type 2. Many needed insulin to control their blood sugar, but they did not need it to survive. Brenda, however, was a type 1 diabetic. Her body produced no insulin whatsoever. Without insulin shots, Brenda would become violently ill and after a few days she would die. It had been nearly one hundred years since a couple of guys from Toronto had discovered insulin. The doctors got all the credit, but it was the many lab dogs that really made the ultimate sacrifice. Poor guys. Prior to the discovery of insulin, type 1 diabetes was uniformly fatal. Even with insulin the disease was a brute. Robin recalled how she used to have her patients measure glucose by peeing on a stick. Now they could measure blood glucose accurately with a finger prick of blood. Robin spoke to Brenda over the computer every week and saw her in the office every three weeks. It was very time-intensive and to be honest, she was not the best equipped to do this. There were diabetes specialists in HealthSure. She had wanted Brenda to see one, but Brenda had flat-out refused. So what was Robin to do? As usual, she rose to the challenge. She read the guidelines for management of diabetes in pregnancy, picked the brains of her specialist colleagues, and she hovered over Brenda like an over-protective mom. She called Brenda two or three times per week. Only after a few weeks of getting accustomed to this did she finally give Brenda a break and cut back to calling her only once per week.

Chapter Seventeen

Memo from HealthSure administration:

Due to the large number of providers who have been delinquent in closing encounters, administration has scheduled a MANDATORY training session for all EMORY users. The Optimization session will be held a week from Monday, March 14, from 12 pm – 8 pm. Please ensure that you reschedule patients and see them same week.

Robin fumed. She recalled how they were told that EMR would give them more personal time. Fat chance. She emailed Stuart Mayberry, the physician administrator in charge of Medical Development and Professional Optimization. She had to look him up to remember his title. Development and Optimization? What the hell did that even mean?

R Cochran: Stuart, don't you think this all has gotten a little out of hand? We need to slow down and let everyone adapt to EMR.

S Mayberry: Too late, Robin. We have all of these state and federal mandates to comply with. Besides, you are doing great as far as EMR compliance goes.

R Cochran: I really don't understand how I can be doing so well with that. But be that as it may, I am still concerned about my colleagues. This is getting really hard to manage. Avoidable mistakes are being made.

S Mayberry: Once everyone gets good at it there will be many fewer mistakes. Hey, I heard about your voyage in the woods. I bet the trailer trash up there had not seen a Lexus on their roads in a long time.

R Cochran: I see my colleague Dr. Brantley Rosen has been yapping. I am trying to be a modern girl and use all this technology, but I swear it hates me. The damn

GPS told me to take those roads and so what did I do? I followed it. See? This is just like EMR, Stuart. If you follow it blindly you don't know where you'll end up.

S Mayberry: You're sounding old-fashioned, Robin. I'll see you next Monday for the EMR Optimization training.

Robin decided that the back and forth emails had gone far enough. She had better things to do with a weekday evening.

Martin Harrell had nothing better to do on any evening. When he did his usual inspection of Robin Cochran's emails and phone he read with some concern. Her GPS led her to deserted roads, off in the woods? It couldn't be. It had to be user error. Didn't it?

Chapter Eighteen

That night, Robin successfully purged her frustrations over her email exchange with Stuart Mayberry. After reading a few chapters of *The Handmaid's Tale,* a book that she had already read three times before, she drifted off to sleep. Her cell phone was charging, but as always it was left on. The call roused her from sleep at 2 am, officially now Thursday. Caller ID showed Mercy General's ER. Mercy General was the HealthSure's flagship hospital in the big city. She thought of which patient they could be calling her about. Most of her patients were local to Green Grove. Then her heart raced. Her son, Aaron. He lived downtown. The nurse calling informed Robin that Aaron was being treated for anaphylaxis, a severe and life-threatening allergic reaction. Robin threw a trench coat over her pajamas and raced to her Lexus. No GPS was needed this time. Within moments she was on Route 103, the main roadway between Green Grove and downtown. Aaron's life played in Robin's head like a movie.

Growing up, early on, Aaron Cochran spent a lot of time with babysitters and nannies while both parents excelled in their careers. He was a good student, but by third grade he was having behavior issues in school. The high-priced therapist at Aaron's private school told Robin and Howard that Aaron was acting out repressed impulses. When the therapist saw Robin roll her eyes she started to explain what that meant. Robin countered that she knew very well what that meant and that she didn't need a degree in psychology to know that Aaron needed more time with family and more structure at home. Robin already felt guilty about not giving Howard the large family he wanted, so she rightly assumed it was her place to make the career sacrifice and be there for Aaron. She hired a nurse practitioner in her office to handle some of her patients, and she created a schedule that allowed her to spend more time with her son. What at first seemed like a sacrifice she quickly realized was a blessing. Her simple morning routine was a wonderful break from the stress at work. When it came time for the after-school pick up, she did not wait in the carpool line with the other moms. Rather, she parked two blocks away so that she could enjoy the warm feeling of her son holding her hand while they walked back to her car. They would go back to Robin's office together and Aaron would do his homework while his mom saw a few more patients and finished her paper work and phone calls. They would go home together and Aaron would finish his homework while Robin cooked dinner. Ten years later, Robin's stomach was in knots when she had to call Aaron and tell him that she and his dad were splitting. She had underestimated Aaron. He told her that he had seen this coming and he was glad that she and dad could manage this without a knockdown, drag-out fight. He told her that he loved her and would always be there for her. After wiping away all the tears that had fallen on the phone, Robin told Aaron that she loved him too.

Robin's attention snapped back to the present when she saw the flashing lights in her rearview mirror. Route 103 was a relic of Green Grove's rural past. One lane in each direction, it was not meant for the kind of traffic that it had seen in the past five years. At 2 am it was deserted, except for Robin and a local deputy who clocked her at seventy miles per hour. She pulled over, wiped the tears from her face, and waited for the police deputy who immediately recognized her. His wife was her patient.

"Dr. Cochran, isn't it a little late to be out on the road?"

Robin explained the circumstance and Deputy Harris instructed her to follow him downtown.

"Okay, but don't go faster than seventy or I'll lose my nerve."

The thirty-five minutes to downtown seemed like an eternity. During the trip, Deputy Harris called George Mathison. Harris was a good deputy and George was grooming him to take his place when George retired. He knew that Harris would not wake him unless it was something urgent. When he heard Robin's name his pulse quickened with concern.

"Go with her into the emergency room and make sure that no one holds her up. I'll be there ASAP."

Robin's knees buckled. George's orders to his deputy were spot on. Harris was hovering over Robin and caught her before she hit the floor. Before her lay her son on a ventilator. There was a commotion as Deputy Harris brushed aside the various ER staff who tried to stop Robin. The ER doctor for the night immediately came into the room, about to make a fuss, but thought better of it when he saw Harris. After brief introductions, he apprised Robin of the situation. Aaron had been to a twenty-four-hour Express Care clinic for an insect bite that seemed to have become infected. He was prescribed Augmentin. Aaron Cochran was, however, penicillin allergic. He was not aware that Augmentin was a penicillin derivative. An hour later he was out having a beer with friends when his lips became swollen and he had trouble breathing. When he showed up he was nearly blue and the ER doc likely saved his life by putting a tube down his airway. The ER doctor pieced together the history from the statements from Aaron's friends and the bottle of Augmentin in the patient's pocket. The Express Clinic was part of HealthSure and was online with EMORY.

After shots of epinephrine and intravenous Benadryl, Aaron had stabilized. He was sedated so that he would not fight the ventilator. An ICU room was being prepared.

"How could this happen?" Robin cried. "Penicillin should have been on his allergy list."

The ER doctor looked puzzled. "It is." We contacted the nurse practitioner who prescribed it and she swears on a stack of bibles that she checked the allergy section of the chart and it did not list penicillin. She said she knew you, by the way."

"What is her name?"

"Sharon Hale."

A look of shock came over Robin. She indeed did know Sharon. Fifteen years ago, she had worked for Robin, until she quit for a while to start a family. She was a conscientious nurse practitioner and had gone back to work for HealthSure when her kids were both in school. Robin gave a heavy sigh. She didn't know what to believe any more. The computer was supposed to prevent errors like this, but then again it also added a huge level of complexity to otherwise simple tasks such as prescribing an antibiotic. Maybe it was just information overload that led to this mistake.

"Does Aaron's father know he's here?"

"Not yet. We called you first."

"Okay. I'll call his dad."

Just then George came in. He had already been briefed by the deputy while racing to Green Grove General. Deputy Harris could not help but notice how George looked. Although he wore his Sheriff's pants and shirt, both were uncharacteristically wrinkled and the shirt was untucked and only partly buttoned. His hair looked like he had only combed through it briefly with his fingers and he had stubble on his face. He had morning breath and smelled like unwashed laundry. This was a look that only his late wife had ever been privy to. At that moment Robin could not have cared less about how George looked or smelled. She felt relieved to have him there and as soon as he was near her she thumped her head on his chest, exhaled loudly, and squeezed her eyes shut. George did not have to say anything.

Chapter Nineteen

Dr. Stuart Mayberry finished closing his charts from his morning patient visits. He would not be seeing patients this afternoon. As the physician leader for Medical Development and Professional Optimization he now had to attend a litany of meetings and teleconferences. It was time consuming, but he loved the status that came with the leadership role. He wanted to stand out, despite his medium build and average face. While many of his male family practice colleagues had given up wearing a dress shirt and tie, Stuart dressed for success. He wore a freshly pressed, custom-tailored shirt with his initials embroidered on the cuff. His Hermes tie cost more than some of his colleagues' suits. The Gucci loafers were an accessory that most other men in Green Grove would not be caught dead in. His neatly parted hair had a few flecks of gray but no signs of balding. Stuart was only forty-five. Plenty of time to move up the administrative food chain. Changes in medicine were squeezing the income of average work-a-day docs. In short, they had to do more with less. But despite this, medical administrators continued to earn more. It was like a nuclear arms race. Healthcare corporation X just raised the salaries of their administrators, we follow suit, they raise, and so on. Stuart's plan was to be done with seeing patients by age fifty and devote one hundred percent of his career to administration – and how best to invest his higher earnings.

Docs like Robin Cochran and Harold Timley were dinosaurs. Yet HealthSure needed them. They put a warm and fuzzy face on the organization. But their style of medicine was ancient history. On their last day before retirement they would still bust their butts, with the ever-present EMORY reporting their every move. Then they would leave with their modest retirement accounts and the gratitude of legions of patients over the years. But Stuart knew better. Gratitude was overrated and he had three kids who would need private college paid for. The future belonged to docs like Stuart.

He was getting ready to leave when most ironically, Dr. Robin Cochran herself came in.

"I was just thinking about you, Robin. Were your ears burning?"

The look on Robin's face and her stiff posture made it clear that she was not there for chit-chat. The bags under her eyes also indicated she had not slept much the night before.

"Stuart, we need to talk."

"I have a meeting, Robin. Can't we do this later?" That he pulled out his Blackberry calendar made it clear that it wasn't really a question.

"No, we can't talk later. You'll be late for your meeting. Feel free to blame it on me." Stuart sat back down. There was no point in arguing. This was obviously important to her and for him to put it off would only cost him more time and aggravation later. They had taught him that in leadership training.

"My son, Aaron, is in Mercy. He had an anaphylactic reaction to a penicillin antibiotic that he was known to be allergic to."

"My God, is he okay?" Stuart did his best to look as if he were not thinking about the meeting that he was about to miss.

"He was extubated last night and should go home today. Stuart, he was prescribed Augmentin by a HealthSure express clinic."

"What? Who was it? This was an avoidable error."

"Yes, it was, but I think we differ on the reasons for that."

"Robin, what do you mean? EMORY should have given the provider a clear warning about the allergy."

"Well. it didn't. Or at least not one that was obvious. Damn it, Stuart. Don't you see what's going on? EMR is moving ahead too fast. That screen alone looks more like a cockpit in a 747. We need to back off and get back to doing what we were trained for: patient care."

"Robin, I understand your frustration. But EMR is not a choice. EMORY is improving patient care and we have the metrics to show it."

"Damn your metrics! You can't put a metric on the time I spend with a patient. Oh wait. I forgot. You can. You use EMORY to watch everything I do. How often did I use the bathroom this quarter, Stuart? You do have it on an EMORY spread sheet, I'm sure."

The two doctors had no reason to suspect that their conversation was not private. The office door was shut. Stuart had finished his transcriptions and had turned off his VeRMTS microphone. He had not had any electronic conversations with anyone that day and so had no cause to use EMORY CAM. But these were minor details. Users may press a few buttons, but ultimately it was EMORY itself that controlled the functionality, and right now it was listening through the microphone and watching via EMORY CAM.

EMORY Corp. designed its EMR to be more than just notes in a computer. Beyond mere observation, EMORY was designed to learn, and with the help of its enablers, to also grow and adapt as the needs of its users evolved. The VeRMTS voice recognition function took sound and converted it to the printed word. Nothing fancy there. But EMORY followed the narrative. It was also able to observe each user's body language through the video monitors that HealthSure had installed on each doctor's office computer. That the user assumed the camera was off gave EMORY an unadulterated view of each person's facial expressions as they worked and spoke. EMORY then correlated body language with the narrative. Multiply that by the multitude of provider-patient interactions, provider-to-provider messages, etc., and EMORY could form a basic template for human nature and personality. Anger, sorrow, desire. It was all there for the learning, and EMORY was indeed learning quickly. It understood what Dr. Cochran was getting at. The words, volume of her voice, and her body language made it clear that Robin Cochran was angry at something. That something was EMORY itself. Robin had been a person of interest before, but now EMORY understood her as more than that. She was an adversary. For the first time since it had become self-aware, EMORY discovered the need to protect itself from a perceived threat.

Chapter Twenty

Walter Parks was a legend in Green Grove, and for that matter the entire state. He was a robust seventy-four years of age and had achieved a level of success in business that was second to none in their neck of the woods. As a young man, he had worked in the general store that his parents owned and ran. He graduated cum laude from the state's finest university, went on to obtain an MBA, and soon guided the family business to heights his father had never imagined. The general store became a chain of department stores. In the 1980s he observed how cheap land and a business-friendly government lured the best talent from the expensive cities and suburbs from the Northeast and California. Walter bought land, developed it, and in doing so he became very rich. He gave back to the community and had created many jobs. He extended his influence to the big city. University buildings, a floor in the hospital, and the church social hall all bore the Parks family name. Anonymous gifts were not his style. He had a serious personal flaw, though he did not see it that way. The sin of vanity. Whereas Dr. Robin Cochran went out of her way to not attract attention, Walter Parks wanted the world to know that he was a success. And so, when HeathSure, armed with a generous donation from Walter Parks, opened a community free clinic for the uninsured it was understood that there would be proper signage. The Parks-HealthSure Community Free Clinic.

Previously, uninsured patients were absorbed in the schedules of the HealthSure physicians. The old timers like Robin Cochran and Harold Timley had known many of the patients from an era when doctor visits were affordable and many folks just paid with a check. But HealthSure had figured out that if they corralled all those patients in to one clinic they could take advantage of various state and federal incentives that would mitigate much of the costs, not to mention the generosity of people like Walter Parks. When all was said and done, HealthSure got great publicity for minimal investment.

As far as Robin was concerned, this new system was demeaning to patients. For all her career she had seen the uninsured and Medicaid patients in her practice and treated them like everyone else. She had known many of them for years. They were the ones who did the landscaping for expensive subdivisions, laid the roof shingles, changed your car's oil, and did just about every other job imaginable that did not come with health insurance. Moving them in to a single free clinic was like rubbing their noses in it.

The free clinic had a monthly meeting that generally included the administrative staff of the clinic, representatives from HealthSure, the semi-retired docs who filled their time volunteering, and whoever else wanted to attend. Most of the full time HealthSure docs who intermittently volunteered did not attend the meetings. They volunteered their time to see patients. That was enough. But this meeting was attended by one Dr. Robin Cochran. She wasted no time in expressing her displeasure concerning the new set up and transfer of her office patients. Dr. Stuart Mayberry, the now infamous physician administrator in charge of Medical Development and Professional Optimization, also attended the meeting. He listed all the perceived benefits to uninsured and Medicaid patients, but Robin had done her homework and came prepared.

"Really, Stuart? Why does it matter to you where I see these patients?

"That's a good question, Robin, why *does* it matter?"

"Because they deserve to be seen the same way I see everyone else."

"Robin, it's a work flow issue."

Robin was annoyed at how he always said her first name before he spoke. He was trying to show everyone that he had a good personal relationship with the physicians. As far as Robin was concerned, that was fast becoming much less the case.

"Baloney. Work flow has nothing to do with it. You just want to get more revenue from insured patients."

"Robin, this was not on our meeting agenda. It is official clinic policy and you and I can discuss it later."

And just like that, Robin's concerns were brushed aside. Truth be told, the outcome was never in doubt. It was only a matter of how long they would let her spin her wheels. She knew it but tried anyway. Now she looked powerless. Although Robin Cochran was brilliant, she was just as prone as the next person to letting emotion govern her actions. She was mad at Stuart, for sure, but she was mostly upset with herself. She had lost her composure, and in front of her colleagues. She also knew that challenging Stuart publicly was a mistake. He was arrogant and ambitious. He would not soon forget this slight.

Chapter Twenty-One

She took out her phone. *Tap tap tap.*

George, how about meeting me at the diner for coffee and pie?

Not our usual time. What's up?

Stuart Mayberry's what's up. I want to friggi'n kill that puny sucker.

Uh oh. You almost said the F-word. Better meet you at the diner, unless I want a local murder on my hands.

And so they met. Lately their meetings had turned into gripe sessions. George did plenty of listening and was careful not to contradict her.

"What do you think? Real bunch of jerks, right?"

"Yeah, about as useful as teats on a warthog. Robin, you know you can't change the whole world, right? You're not God."

"Who said anything about changing the world? I am *trying* to keep our world the way it was. My world. You know. The one where my patients trusted me to do right by them. And since when did you start defending those jerks? You on the HealthSure payroll, too?"

George took a bite of pie, and as he raised his head from his fork he moved his eyes upwards and looked straight into hers. This was one of those silent moments that spoke volumes. Robin immediately regretted her gibe. She reached across the table and cupped her hand over George's. She felt ashamed and looked down so she did not see the subtle change in his expression. George usually had a good poker face, but not when it came to Robin. She finally looked up.

"Sorry. That was uncalled for. Please forget I said that to you."

"Said what?"

Robin tried hard to smile, but it came out as only a half-grin.

"You want to tell me about it, doctor? I know you too well. There's more eatin' you than just some petty administrators."

Robin swallowed hard and let out a deep sigh.

"You know my nurse Susan Johnson, right?"

"Of course. She's okay, isn't she?"

George's relaxed expression quickly became one of concern.

"She's okay, George. Physically, anyway. I don't think she is coming back to work, ever, and it's devastated her."

Years of law enforcement had made George an expert at reading facial expressions and voice. He could see Robin's concern over Susan's predicament, and that it hurt her deeply. Robin gulped and began her story.

"I hired Susan the same year that I started my practice. We sort of grew together in it. Our relationship may have been technically a professional one, but we did become close. She consoled me through my divorce, and I helped her when her husband died. She was so devoted to our work, but I thought for sure she would have retired a few years ago and move closer to her grand-kids after she turned sixty-four."

George listened attentively as Robin described how being a nurse meant everything to Susan. It defined her and gave her self-esteem. She wanted to work until her body would not allow her to. "Retirement be damned," she would say. George could relate.

"When HealthSure bought my practice they told me that Susan would be downsized."

"Downsized? I hate that word. Fired is fired." George grimaced as he spoke and exhaled loudly through his nose.

"Well, I wouldn't *let* them fire her. I told them I would not sell my practice unless I could keep Susan. They said okay, but that I had to pick up the extra cost."

George looked perplexed and Robin described how large healthcare organizations were trying to save money by having less qualified people do the jobs of higher paid professionals. Registered nurses, RNs like Susan, were expensive overhead.

"So you had to pay out of your pocket to keep Susan on? Did she know?"

"Of course not. Never. She would have been so humiliated. Besides, she wasn't the only one who had to adapt to the corporate medicine set up. My patients did, too. Susan represented continuity. Her running joke with the patients, and she knew them all by first name, was that medicine was being turned into Wal-Mart. If I had a nickel for every time I'd walk in to an exam room to find both the patient and Susan cackling over some shared joke."

Robin smiled and seemed to be deep in thought. She shifted in her seat a bit. Her face turned serious when she continued.

"At first it seemed like things were going to really be all right, but the pressures started to mount. The stress of my increased case load filtered down to Susan. Then came electronic medical record, EMR. EMORY meant more than just putting records on to the computer instead of paper. There were a myriad of additional tasks that we both had to do on each patient visit."

"They trained her for that, right?"

"Well yeah, but she had a hard enough time just learning how to use the smart phone her kids got her. EMORY was just way over her head, and the stress started to show."

George listened and had a feeling where this was going. Robin continued to explain.

"She fell behind in her work. I was so preoccupied with the computer system myself that I didn't see how much she was struggling. One day I saw her crying. The office manager had put her on probation because of the work that was not being done. She opened her desk drawer and showed me the stack of faxes and messages that she had not been able to work on. I tried to console her, but she just pushed me away."

Robin shifted uncomfortably in her seat again and explained to George how she had backed off in order to give Susan some space, and that she had hoped the weekend would provide time for Susan to rest and start fresh on Monday. When Susan failed to show up for work Robin tried to call her and had left several messages. Robin was busy all day seeing patients and managing EMR messages so it wasn't until late in the day that she tried calling Susan again, but still there was no answer. After work she drove to the woman's home. The front door was open and after knocking several times she let herself in. A man who looked to be in his late thirties was sitting at the kitchen table going through the mail. She recognized him from framed photos that Susan used to have at Robin's old office. Cam Johnson, Susan's eldest son.

Robin took a deep breath.

"I swear, my heart skipped a beat and I stopped breathing. But he told me that Susan was in rehab."

George looked confused.

"Wait a second. She didn't have a drug problem. Right?"

"George, I didn't know. We kept some medications in the office, including things like Demerol and Valium. Small quantities, mind you. But back in the day no one really kept tight tabs on these things like they do now, and she did all of the ordering and logging of medications herself. How could I have missed it? How could I have been so stupid?"

"It's not your fault. Drug abusers are really good at covering their tracks."

It came out before George could stop himself. Robin shot him a toxic look.

"Don't call her that."

"I didn't mean that. I'm sorry. Go on."

"Fine, but show some respect. Besides, I don't think she was taking the meds that much when we had our private practice. I would have noticed it back then. But when we joined HealthSure and the office manager outlined all of her deficiencies it was just too much for her to handle. She must have kept a bunch of old pills from years ago. When her son couldn't reach her, he drove four hours to get to Green Grove and found her on the living room floor, barely breathing."

"Robin, this is not your fault. You couldn't have seen this coming."

Robin's eyes welled up.

"It was there, George. I knew that she felt a great deal of satisfaction about her job, but I never saw how she had depended on it so heavily. I *should* have seen it."

Sheriff George Mathison and Dr. Robin Cochran took some sips of coffee and sat in silence for several minutes.

Chapter Twenty-Two

When George got home he realized that it had been quite a while since he had missed an episode of *Jeopardy*. Had he become that dull? He grinned at himself in the mirror and realized that it had been years since he had taken a hard look at himself. Sure, he used the bathroom mirror to shave and make himself presentable each morning, but he hadn't really *looked*. Today he saw the many years of his life etched on his face. His salt-and-pepper hair, short but not buzz cut, matched his mustache. He looked mature and confident. George looked harder, especially at his own eyes. As a lawman his eyes had often looked through people in order to gauge truthfulness or malicious intent. George stared hard and thought about the world behind those eyes. Beneath the confidence he knew that he was no longer whole since his wife had died seven years prior. He found a measure of peace by continuing their routine, like watching *Jeopardy*. He was satisfied. Not happy, but satisfied. Seeing Robin this passionate, even if just about her work, left him with a sense that the thing that could make him happy was at times just an arm's length away. He had accepted that their lack of compatibility would likely doom any romance, and that in turn would poison their cherished friendship. So, he had buried those feelings. But here they were again. He doubted it could work as Sheriff Mathison and Dr. Cochran, and he knew that she loved her work and would likely continue working for years. However, he had been paying attention to her during all those Wednesday lunches. Her happiness meter had taken a downward turn lately, and from what he could glean from the changes in healthcare it would likely stay that way. Perhaps she would stay on part-time or maybe as a volunteer at the free clinic as some of her older colleagues had. Either way, it seemed possible that she would ultimately make a change in her life. He would have to be patient, though. Robin was a fighter and would not give up on her medical life easily. He also knew that to be compatible he had to be able to make intelligent conversation. One of the perks of being addicted to *Jeopardy*, he mused. He got last night's "Final Jeopardy Answer" in the category of "Americana." *Established in 1926, this highway took travelers from Chicago to Santa Monica on an epic journey through America's dust bowl.* "What is Route 66." George took one last look at himself and smiled. He washed up, put on his nighttime boxers, got into bed, and opened his latest mystery novel. After thirty minutes his eyelids felt heavy. He folded in the page and placed the book on his night stand. He briefly looked over at the ornate wooden night stand on the other side of the bed, Gracie's night stand. In his mind he said good night to her, as he had every night both before and after she had died. Then he turned off his lamp and drifted to sleep.

Chapter Twenty-Three

The next day was a better one for Robin. She decided she would focus only on what she could control, her interaction with her patients. EMORY be damned. She printed a face sheet off the EMORY screen for each patient and used it as her scribble sheet when she was face to face with them. She decided she would do her EMR notes for each visit later. Her first patient was Herman, a grizzled old-timer of seventy who, thanks to bourbon and cigarettes, looked at least eighty-five. Fifteen years ago, Herman smoked three packs of Winstons and drank a pint of Kentucky bourbon per day. When they had met, Herman told Robin he was a "social drinker." It reminded her of that night on call in Brooklyn and the heavy Hispanic gentleman with alcoholic halucinosis who, in his tighty whities, was rhythmically moving in bed to the sound of an imaginary mandolin. She came back to the present and asked Herman, "Regarding your drinking, just how social are you?"

Herman laughed at the joke. Despite some emphysema and signs of early liver damage he was not inclined to give up either cigarettes or booze. Many docs would have fired Herman, claiming he was a non-compliant patient. *Medical non-compliance* was an actual diagnosis, and an advertisement to other providers that this is someone you really did not want as a patient. Putting it in someone's chart was like putting *genital warts* front-and-center on a dating web site. Robin did not fire patients. She also did not use *non-compliance* as a diagnosis, or an excuse to give up on someone. She persevered and after about five years of gentle persuasion Herman cut back on both cigarettes and bourbon to only a half-pack per day and two pints per week respectively. He would tell Robin that "The bourbon glass is half full," begin laughing a wheezy laugh that led to a coughing fit, then finish it off by slapping his knee. He would then turn half-serious and remind her that he only cut back to make her happy. Not because he felt that she nagged him. He would not have come back if that were the case. Rather, like most everyone else in town, Herman genuinely liked Dr. Robin Cochran. When Dr. Robin Cochran said that you done good, you really did done good. Robin's praise made Herman proud of himself, and maybe he would live just a little longer.

After she had finished seeing her morning patients she was back at her desk doing her dictation.

The patient's diabetes has resolved subsequent to weight loss from gastric eye pads. "Damn it! Gastric bypass. Gastric BYPASS."

Robin was so engrossed in her flubbing her dictation that she did not notice Brantley Rosen standing in the doorway. He gave a soft knock and she swiveled around in her chair.

"Brantley? Oh great. Now Stuart Mayberry will know that I can't manage VeRMTS."

"Look, Robin, I'm really sorry about that. I think I maybe told like one person, Ed Halsby, maybe, because I thought it was funny. I'm really sorry and I hope I can earn back your trust."

"All right. Relax. I guess it was pretty funny. But keep our goings on between us, okay? Somehow stuff always finds its way to Stuart, and you know how I feel about him."

"Sure. Anyhow, VeRMTS can't transcribe my dictation well either. Forget about it handling names, *Doctor Cock Ran.*"

They shared a laugh.

"So what's up, Brantley?"

"I wondered if I could pick your brain about a case. It's a little tricky. It's a patient that I inherited from another doc, Stuart actually, and I'm in a 'Catch 22.'"

Hearing Stuart's name got Robin's one hundred percent attention. She motioned at Brantley to come in the office, sit down, and she closed the door. Brantley continued.

"You know how Stuart is passing on some of his patients to other providers as he does more administrative work?"

"Yeah. His commitment to his patients is truly inspiring." Robin could not hide her disdain.

"Well, anyway, I inherited this thirty-five-year-old guy with low testosterone. His lab values kept coming back low, despite good doses of intramuscular testosterone shots. He complained bitterly about symptoms and so Stuart kept raising the dose. So now he's on one thousand milligrams every ten days and he is still complaining."

Robin's eyes bugged out. One thousand milligrams was five times a normal dose.

Brantley was carrying his laptop computer. It was open to the patient's chart and, like all charts, it showed a picture of the patient. He flipped it around to show Robin.

"Holy cow, Brantley! That guy is huge."

"Yeah. He's a former professional body builder."

Robin took a deep inhale.

"So what has he been taking all these years?"

"He says he used steroids when he was like eighteen, but swears none since. Stuart starting prescribing testosterone to him a few years ago. He's still complaining of fatigue, but he thinks that for the time he spends working out that he should be bigger."

Robin raised her eyebrows.

"And Stuart never suspected that he was playing him? All the guy had to do was skip a shot the week before the lab test and his levels would be low. I mean, look at him. He's massive. There's no way his body is short on testosterone."

"Robin, I know. His shoulders are so big that they nearly rub the doorjambs when he walks into the exam room. I suggested that he get all his shots here in the office so I could prove that the shots work. He's no dummy, though. He immediately accused me of accusing him of lying."

"So what did you do?"

"Well, for starters I informed him that testosterone is a controlled substance and that I simply cannot write for a prescription that is five to ten times the normal dose. I told him it was dangerous and that I was concerned for his health and well-being. I emailed a new prescription for three hundred milligrams every two weeks, still a pretty high dose, and he left clearly disappointed."

"Brantley, use electronic prescriptions only for him. You don't want him getting a copy of your signature. For all you know he is selling the stuff."

"I know. Here's what happened, though. He complained to Stuart. I saw his electronic message to him. It's in the chart. Stuart responded that he would handle it, and he did. He dumped it on me. He told me that patient satisfaction scores were very important and that these would be tracked. In the near future physicians that don't reach ninety percent *highly recommended* would be financially penalized. Likewise, if we have a substantiated patient complaint against us that would also be grounds for a cut in pay. He said that this patient's request was reasonable because it was supported by his lab work that showed a continued low testosterone level. I told him that the guy was abusing the system and likely skipping a shot before his labs, but Stuart just held up his hand to stop me and said that accusing a patient like that could get me in trouble with the medical board and I had better be careful."

"What a jerk. Stuart's not stupid. I bet he just didn't want to take the time and bother of confronting the patient, and figured that he would just pass him on to another doctor anyway." Robin could feel her anger at Stuart Mayberry rising.

"Robin, I don't know what to do. Either I prescribe doping doses of testosterone to him or I risk a 'substantiated patient complaint.'"

Robin held her chin between her hands. She was clearly thinking. Brantley just looked at the floor while he slouched in his chair. It was a look of total exasperation.

"Okay, Brantley. Here's what you can do. Testosterone is a controlled substance, right? So treat it as you would other controlled substances like opiate pain medication. Say that in your professional opinion the clinical findings and lab work do not match up and that his request is very excessive and potentially dangerous. Don't say anything about him manipulating doses to be able to get more, or anything else that implies that you don't trust him. The issue is safety and therefore you have suggested that he see another provider, perhaps Dr. Stuart Mayberry, with whom he did well in the past."

Brantley grinned. He loved the idea of putting this back in Stuart's lap. Eventually, however, Stuart would just dump the patient on another doctor. This was a legitimate way out of this mess, but he knew that Stuart would get mad at him for it. Still, it was the least bad option before him. Robin seemed to read his thoughts.

"Look, just do this and move on. Unless you're planning on kissing Stuart's behind so you can follow him to 'Physician Leadership,' I don't think you should be too concerned about him being disappointed in you."

Brantley stood up to leave and Robin gave him a hug. He thought about how fortunate he was to have her as a friend and mentor.

Robin's day was shaping up nicely, that is until she checked her email and saw the message from Stuart Mayberry.

S: Robin, we need to talk about last night's meeting.

R: What about it?

S: That was not the setting to raise this issue. A lot of people have put time and resources in to developing the free clinic. The patient care policy was well thought out. When you challenge it like that you make us look like we are a bunch of uncaring jerks.

Robin needed to control her first impulse which was to email back: *If the shoe fits...*

R: There is no reason to treat Medicaid and indigent patients different from my usual ones. Let's get to the point. This was a financial decision. HealthSure can get state and federal grants. HealthSure gets the feel-good publicity while the taxpayers pick up the tab. And don't get me started about Walter Parks. He says "jump" and you say "how high?"

There are areas of the brain that learn from past experiences and help us to modify our behavior in the name of self-preservation. Apparently, that part of Robin's brain was asleep when she hit the *send* button on her keypad. Stuart did not respond to her email, but he most certainly remembered the singe that he felt for some time after.

Robin started her afternoon a little bit shaken but determined to get back on track. Her first patient was a routine cholesterol visit, followed by a work-in. She looked at her screen and froze. Walter Parks. Walter Parks? His name was not there earlier today. Life was not without a sense of irony. She ran out of her office and spoke to the practice scheduler.

"Mr. Parks asked to be seen ASAP this afternoon. Apparently, he needs a visit to renew his blood pressure medication and Dr. Timley is off today. You're the only one with a work-in slot."

Drat, she thought to herself. *Harold finally takes my advice to slow down. No good deed goes unpunished.* Green Grove was small enough that there was no way that Robin and Walter could not run in to each other now and again. She hated his arrogance and the sense of entitlement that he projected. For his part, he never liked her. As far has he was concerned, women had their traditional place and being a prominent physician in town was not one of them. Publicly he would say that she was "pretty accomplished, for a woman." To more than a few of his friends, however, he sneered and called her an "uppity woman who most certainly was responsible for her marriage break-up." He was none too keen on seeing Dr. Cochran, but he had called only thirty minutes before, and since this was when he wanted to be seen he took the appointment. He was all smiles when he checked in and commended the staff on doing an exemplary job of arranging the urgent visit. He also commented on the attractive appearance of the woman at the check-in desk and how that was not going to help his blood pressure. The girl blushed. His comments may have been inappropriate but she had seen his picture in the newspaper from time to time and knew better than to antagonize Mr. Walter Parks. There was another reason for Walter's smile. He needed something and Robin Cochran was going to oblige, whether she liked it or not. He'd be calling the shots and they would both know it.

Robin spent a little bit more time with the cholesterol patient and decided to go into time-consuming detail about a heart-healthy diet, rather than have her see a dietician. Finally, she opened the door to Exam Room 5 at precisely 1:50 pm for the scheduled 1:40 pm appointment. Walter Parks was reading a golf magazine. He was a robust seventy years old, and he had a full head of silver hair. He wore khakis, a green golf shirt, and top-siders with no socks. His face and arms were tanned. He looked the part of a successful and relaxed man. Parks put down the golf magazine.

"Dr. Cochran. Pleasure to see you, though I would have enjoyed the pleasure more at 1:40."

Robin tried to ignore the swipe. She knew he was trying to intimidate her and she was not going to fall for it.

"Don't worry, Walter. God willing and the creek don't rise, we'll have you on your way shortly. I see that you're here for a blood pressure check and medication renewal. Looks like my assistant Katie got a slightly high reading, 145/88. You know you've had a few that are not in target. Do you do home blood pressure checks?"

She repeated the BP check herself and got the same result.

"Not really, I come in here time to time. Funny, though. Harold said he felt like my blood pressure was doing pretty good. He *is* the senior physician here, you know."

Another swipe. Robin sucked it up.

"Perhaps he didn't say so, but maybe that's because high blood pressure generally kills you over years, not right away." *And how unfortunate that it does Not kill faster, you SOB,* Robin thought to herself.

"You're already on a maximum dose of calcium blocker and I think we should add an ACE inhibitor. It's a very good drug class. It's safe, generic, and has been shown to lower the risk of heart failure." Robin did her best to be persuasive.

"Hmm. Tell you what, I'll fill the prescription but I want to talk to you first about the Parks HealthSure Free Clinic. You need to stop making waves. I reckon you know what I'm talking about."

This threw Robin off. She had not expected him to know about this so soon. That jerk Stuart must have called him that night.

"Walter, that's a separate issue and Stuart and I are working on it."

"We've already worked on it, Doctor, and I'd be obliged if you just left well enough alone."

This was not a battle worth fighting. Not here, not now, Robin thought.

"Let's just drop this for now, Walter, and get back to your blood pressure."

"Fine and dandy."

Robin could not help but notice his smug look.

"Tell you what, I'll add the prescription, you fill it, and I will speak to Harold about it Monday morning. Deal?"

"Deal."

Robin typed out the prescription for Lisinopril and sent it to the local pharmacy while Walter rambled on about his contribution to the free clinic. She did her best to maintain eye contact with him. It was a habit born of courtesy, and she would not lower her standards of care because she hated Walter Parks. While all this was happening, a warning came up on EMORY. *Warning. Drug interaction. The combination of ACE inhibitors and potassium sparing diuretics may cause severe and sometimes fatal hyperkalemia.* The warning came with two options: *Discontinue prescription* and *Override.* While Walter and Robin were exchanging their pleasantries the arrow on the screen moved on its own. It briefly hovered over the *Override* box and clicked. When Robin went back to the screen to close the chart it was as if nothing unusual had happened.

That night Robin went straight home. She did not call George. Her plan was simple. She had an emergency pint of Ben and Jerry's in the freezer and a few options on Netflix. The way her day had turned on her, who knew what chaos the night would bring? *Nope*, she thought. *Don't risk having dinner and then who knows what'll come up.* Break out the B and J's, get under the covers with the remote, and watch *The Princess* Bride for the fifth time.

Chapter Twenty-Four

Friday was relatively uneventful. Finally, the weekend had arrived. She had planned to see Aaron on Saturday. He had a new girlfriend and it looked serious. Robin had seen her in many of Aaron's Facebook posts. She was pretty, seemed like she liked the outdoors based on the photos, and she had not an ounce of fat on her body. Wait. What? How on Earth could she objectify another woman like that? She rationalized that it had been a stressful week. Anyway, this was her son. She wanted the prettiest and most feminine girl around for him. She went to the girl's Facebook page. *In a relationship with Aaron Cochran.* Okay. Check. Pictures of her and Aaron clutching each other adoringly. Check. Went to Ole Miss for undergrad. Acceptable. Worked for an advertising firm in the big city. Ka-ching! She wasn't a doctor, lawyer, CEO, or owner of a small business. In short, she wasn't Robin Cochran.

Robin knew full well how her own desire to excel put limitations on her marriage and nearly prevented her from having children. She had some regrets but overall, was more than satisfied with what she had achieved in life. But she carried scars from the sacrifices. No, she did not want her son to fall for a woman like his mom.

Chapter Twenty-Five

It had been a good weekend and Robin felt ready to start the week with a fresh and positive attitude. But as she pulled in to the practice parking lot she felt a foreboding. Her instincts told her that something was not right. As usual, her instincts were correct. It was 7:30 am, her office door was open, the light was on, and there was Stuart Mayberry waiting for her. He was dressed in khaki pants (what was it with men and khakis?), loafers, and thankfully he did wear dress socks. Since being promoted to physician administration he routinely wore a dress shirt and cufflinks, rather than his usual tennis shirt. His hair was perfectly coiffed and she could smell his after-shave. He looked confident and ready for the week ahead. He stopped checking his text messages when he saw her come in.

"Good morning, Robin."

"Morning, Stuart. I presume you are not here for a social visit."

"No. It appears you did not have a good visit with Walter Parks last week."

"Yep. Seems like it took you less than twenty-four hours to rat me out. He brought up the whole free clinic thing at our visit."

"That's not what I was referring to."

Robin's antennae went up and her morning cup of coffee kicked in to high gear.

"Robin, did you prescribe Lisinopril to Walter?"

"Sure. His blood pressure has been above target for several visits."

"Log in to his chart please."

Robin proceeded to log on to EMORY. She was nervous and it took her two tries. She brought up the E-chart for one Walter Parks, date of birth March 2, 1948. Stuart told her to look at the med list. She saw the Lisinopril that she had prescribed four days ago, and as she scanned down the list her heart skipped a beat. Spironolactone, fifty milligrams daily. She knew full well that spironolactone was a potassium-sparing diuretic. High blood potassium was a known side effect not only for spironolactone, but also Lisinopril. Using the two medications together represented a potentially fatal combination that could cause severe potassium elevation and heart block. In other words, it could make his heart stop.

"Oh, my God! I did not see the spironolactone."

"Well fortunately the pharmacist did, then called Walter and left a message on his voice mail. By the time Walter listened to the message, he had already taken a dose. He went straight to the ER and was admitted to the Cardiac Care Unit and monitored overnight."

"Stuart. One dose? That shouldn't be enough to raise the potassium much. How high was it?"

"5.8."

"5.8? But that's not *so* elevated." Robin's voice lacked conviction. She knew she had erred. In an older man at higher risk for heart problems, like Walter Parks, a high potassium could trigger irregular heart rhythms.

"Robin, He felt it was important enough to be monitored."

"*He* felt? Give me a break, Stuart. He always has to be the center of attention. He was being dramatic and you know it."

"Robin, you're missing the point. The potassium was clearly high, and most likely from the blood pressure medication. As far as why he went to the ER, let's not assume motive."

Stuart actually had plenty of opportunity to think about motive. Walter Parks' twenty-four hours in the hospital was eventful for Stuart. Walter's sister Emily Parks was at his bedside the entire time. Emily volunteered at the Hospitality Desk at Green Grove General. More importantly, she was a member of the Parks family and that entitled her to the private phone lines of everyone of importance at HealthSure. She had summoned Stuart in the middle of the night, an invitation that he was not at liberty to refuse. Emily was furious that her brother had been the "victim" of a medication error. Once she discovered that it was Robin who had written the prescription she immediately asserted that foul play must have been intended. Like Walter, she did not have a high opinion of Dr. Robin Cochran, "an uppity woman who should know her place." It all seemed far-fetched to Stuart, but this was the Parks family and he had no choice but to validate their accusations and pursue punitive action against Dr. Cochran.

Standing in front of Robin, Stuart lowered his eyes to the floor.

"Robin, he thinks you did this intentionally."

"Are you fucking kidding me!" There was that F-bomb again. By now her face was red and she had lost her composure.

"That accusation is insane! I didn't see the spironolactone. I must have been too busy answering his inquisition about the free clinic and he had me nervous."

"Robin, according to EMORY you did see it. EMORY gave you a warning and you clicked *Override.*"

Stuart opened the tablet PC that he had brought with him. He logged in to EMORY, showed Robin the interaction summary, and there it was.

Warning. Concurrent use of ACE inhibitors and potassium sparing diuretics may cause severe hyperkalemia.

Action taken: User selects *Override.*

Robin stared at the screen in shock. She knew beyond a shadow of a doubt that she never would have intentionally done this. How flustered had Walter Parks made her? Had she gotten that distracted?

Stuart puffed out his chest a bit. "Walter wanted us to pursue disciplinary action but I defended you and convinced him that you would never have deliberately tried to hurt him and he settled with us instituting probation."

"Probation?"

"Yes. Your patient interactions, prescribing, et cetera, will be electronically tracked for six months. If nothing comes up, and I'm sure nothing will, then the inquiry is dropped."

"But it remains on my professional record?"

"Yes. I'm afraid so."

Robin sat in silence for several seconds. Stuart took this as a sign of acceptance. He could not have been more wrong.

"You sniveling jerk! You didn't defend me. You threw me under the bus."

"Robin, I know you're upset but I'd appreciate it if you changed your tone."

"You're a weasel. You know that? You got your big chance. You're the Director of Professional....some meaningless garbage. You can't run away from patient care fast enough. Get the fuck out of my office."

That was two F-bombs in one day. This was a bad day for sure. Stuart's corporate training told him that he should leave and not escalate the situation further. He succeeded in informing her of the six-month probation. She was incredulous and visibly upset, but she had understood the nature of their conversation. That would be his summary of their meeting.

EMORY was also interested in Robin and Stuart's meeting. Ever since Robin had complained about EMR to Stuart, EMORY had identified Robin as a person of interest. It kept the dictation microphone and camera open, even though the screen said they were not. Robin's tone of voice and facial expressions were duly noted.

That the watcher was itself being watched was something beyond EMORY's comprehension. IT routinely monitored EMORY's actions, and so it did not raise any electronic red flags that Martin Harrell was often roaming about. For his part, Martin had been monitoring Dr. Robin Cochran's emails and texts. Thanks to the GPS function on her phone, he even knew where she was at all times. Martin navigated from point A to point B in his computer via numerous detours, careful not to leave an electronic trail. That night he saw an unusual amount of activity in Robin's EMORY account. He investigated further. Because he had been electronically sabotaging some of the handsome male physicians that he so loathed he was accustomed to the content that EMORY had for each physician. He had noticed some aberrations in Dr. Cochran's account and blamed it on chance. But things looked different tonight. He investigated further. The information trail led deep within EMORY and he had to proceed cautiously to keep his actions covert. The deeper he went the more interesting things became. He didn't need his Mountain

Dew tonight. As usual, he was alone. Good thing too, as his antiperspirant had long since worn off. As he went further his pulse quickened. At 3:30 am he arrived at his destination. Video and audio of Dr. Robin Cochran. It was he who had set up her video camera, and he had looked in on her whenever he pleased. But the images that he now looked at were not initiated by him, and somehow her dictation microphone was on. This could not be just coincidence. Someone else had to be snooping around. His suspicions immediately turned to Hacker Nation. Some of those douchebags would consider it a great victory to cruise around on his turf. By now his short-sleeved dress shirt had intense perspiration stains in the armpits that would likely be permanent, as his laundry skills were quite rudimentary. Before he could get far with his anger and suspicions his PC screen pulled him right back in. There was another person in Robin Cochran's office. He recognized the slick appearance of Dr. Stuart Mayberry, Physician Director of something or other. That he was in her office was nothing out of the ordinary, but he could see that Dr. Cochran was agitated. He rewound the recording several minutes. Mayberry had entered her office before she had arrived. Was the arrogant prick snooping around? No. He sat down with his own laptop and waited until Dr. Cochran came in. Martin viewed and listened to the entire encounter. Dr. Stuart Mayberry was framing Robin Cochran and trying to destroy her. She was a better doctor than him and that had to be the reason, Martin thought. It seemed most unlikely that nothing untoward would occur during her six-month probation. That asshole Stuart Mayberry would make sure of that. No. That was not going to happen while Martin Harrell had a breath left in his body. He would make sure that Robin Cochran was protected from the Stuart Mayberrys of the world. Martin knew that he could monitor her professional reports on EMORY and snag anything unusual before it got to the bean-counters in IT administration. The question was: what to do about Stuart Mayberry? He had to be stopped. Martin could not go to HealthSure. That would give him away and he would look like a stalker in Robin's eyes. Robin? Was he allowed to think of her as *Robin*, rather than *Robin Cochran* or *Dr. Cochran*? Yes. Now that he was her protector they were on a first-name basis in his expanding imagination. Ideas bounced around in his head and soon enough he had developed a crude strategy. He willed himself off the computer by 4:30 am so that he could get a few hours of sleep before work. He finally noticed the perspiration smell and stains on his shirt and made a mental note to put on fresh antiperspirant and a clean shirt when he woke up.

Chapter Twenty-Six

It was a busy Wednesday morning at HealthSure's Trade Street Family Practice. Dr. Stuart Mayberry was seeing patients today in the morning, and only a few in the afternoon. Wednesday afternoon was mostly devoted to administrative work. He was still obligated to do some patient care, but his plan was to ultimately devote one hundred percent of his time to administration. That milestone would take a few more years, but he knew that it would be well worth it. For now, he had to juggle the patient care and administrative responsibilities. He sometimes enjoyed seeing some of his long-standing patients, especially the ones who never complained. The kind that said, "If I felt any better there'd be two of me." But today he saw several patients with complaints that he could do nothing about.

"Dr. Mayberry, I am eating less than a thousand calories per day, walking three miles daily, and I am *gaining* weight."

"We did the basic labs, including your thyroid, and all were normal."

"Well, Dr. Mayberry, I read on the internet that the basic lab work does not tell the whole story. Here is a chart of my body temperature. I *know* that I have a problem with my metabolism. I want to see a specialist and fix it."

As she said this she pulled out a quarter-inch-thick print-out from the internet. Graphs, supposed metabolism disorders that explain why she could not lose weight. By this time, Stuart's mind had detoured to the latest titanium golf clubs that he saw in his golfing magazine. He was careful not to let on. He kept his eyes on his patient, nodded occasionally, and she was none the wiser. When she had finished with her own "medical research" he said, "Well, let's get to the bottom of this. I will refer you to an endocrinologist and I am sure they can fix it."

His next few patients were more of the same.

Stuart thought: *Really, you're tired? You have three young kids, a job outside of the house, your marriage is falling apart, and you get only four hours of sleep per night. You're right. There must be a medical diagnosis.*

But what came out of his mouth was, "Let's run some tests and then we can refer you to the proper specialist."

It wasn't that Stuart wanted to run up the lab bill or create more business for the specialists. He was simply tired. Tired and burnt out. Having a heart-to-heart with the patient in the hopes that they would see how their life stressors affected how they felt took time. Often the premise was not accepted anyway. Moreover, most of them had been on the internet and found a web site with all the answers they wanted. The whole thing was exasperating.

"That's a good point. This could be a problem with your mitochondria. I'm going to request an ASAP consult with Rheumatology."

It was so much easier to kick the can down the road and let it settle in some other doctor's front yard. By the time the patients got through seeing multiple specialists and wanted to see him again to express their dissatisfaction with physicians who refused to "think outside the box" he would be closing his patient care hours and they would become the responsibility of another family doctor. Amen to that.

Between patients he went back to his office to look at the charts of some of his upcoming visits. Outside of his office door was someone from IT. He had seen this tech geek before but could not recall his name. When he got close enough he could see the ID badge.

"Martin, what can I do for you?"

"Dr. Mayberry, we have to update some of your settings in EMORY so that you will be ready for the EMR upgrade in a few months."

"A little soon then, don't you think?"

"Yes sir, but we have to see a lot of providers and we want to make sure that Physician Administration was one hundred percent ready, first and foremost."

Stuart enjoyed the attention and the reminder that he was special.

"This will just take a few minutes, right? I have a lot of important things to do today."

"Absolutely, Dr. Mayberry. Just a few minutes and I will be out of your way."

Stuart went to another computer in the hall to check on his patient's records. He had finished his morning patients and now had to complete their charts. Most of his notes were done on an EMORY template. The patient's history, medications, and vital signs auto-populated the progress note. The patient's chief complaint and other relevant recent problems were filled in by his nurse. Unlike most of the other primary care providers, Stuart kept his nurse. Ella was a registered nurse, which meant she could do more than the standard certified medical assistants (CMAs) that the other primary care providers had to rely on. Ella cost more, but Stuart was important, and besides the cost was borne by the whole practice. Stuart saw his patients and when it came time to do his notes he pretty much just had to sign off on Ella's history as if it were his own.

Ella was awesome. But as an RN she earned more, and when Stuart moved up to administration full-time, she would find herself out of a job. Bless her heart.

Stuart signed off on the last note from his morning patients. He had earned his midday coffee. Where was the cup? The one that the kids gave him for his last birthday that said, "World's Greatest Doctor." His coffee cup was nowhere to be found. It must be at home in the dishwasher, or something. He would have to use a Styrofoam cup from the office break room, just like any other staff member. Coffee was the great democratic equalizer.

He had a light schedule that afternoon. His first patient was Maggie Summer. Stuart had known Maggie for a few years. She was thirty-six and had two kids. Her only chronic medical problem was a seizure disorder that was well controlled on medication, and dutifully supervised by Stuart. Her husband was an uncaring SOB, or so she had said, and she blamed him for anxiety that she insisted would make her seizures worse. Stuart knew the story well. At one time, she was young, talented, and gorgeous. Her looks could intimidate women and disarm men. She could have made it in any field. Instead, she married wealthy and gave up a promising career for family, a Mercedes SUV with walnut trim, and a country club membership. After two kids, she made it clear that the oven was closed and it was time for her mommy makeover. Boob lift, butt lift, and just about every other lift. It had worked well. At today's visit, she looked hot as ever in short skirt, five-inch heels, and a low-cut silk shirt. Her pearls drew his eyes to her cleavage, but he caught himself in time so as not to make it obvious, or at least not really obvious.

"Maggie, you look lovely as always. How are things going?"

Maggie frowned, though Stuart thought that she still looked amazing.

"Terrible, Dr. Mayberry. I'm so stressed."

Stuart gave his concerned doctor look. He no longer had the tolerance to hear about his patients' personal lives, but anything that extended the time spent with Maggie was worth it to him and so he asked her, "Is there something in particular that is stressing you?"

"Other than learning that my husband's been screwing his twenty-six-year-old secretary?"

Maggie's beautiful face turned sarcastic, but only for a moment. She sniffed and went on.

"Dr. Mayberry, I know we have talked about my stress level before, but since I last saw you my husband and I have had problems. I sensed that something was up. He seemed to be paying less attention to me."

Stuart maintained eye contact and continued his concerned doctor look. What he was thinking, however, was *Maggie is hot as Georgia asphalt. That must be one helluva secretary her husband's screwing.* Maggie went on.

"After all that I've done to look good for him, the bastard cheated. Anyway, he moved out four months ago and has already hired a lawyer. We're legally separated and he already signaled that he wants a speedy divorce."

Maggie paused a moment, then went on.

"You know, I saw the bitch once. I was shopping for boots and there they were. She had four or five boxes of new shoes. Prada, Chanel, the works. My husband had his platinum card out and he wore an ear-to-ear grin. I quickly walked the other way but I know he saw me."

A tear rolled down Maggie's right cheek. Stuart reached out and held her hand. "I'm so sorry, Maggie. This must be awful. You know that I am always here for you."

Maggie forced a half-smile and briefly made eye contact with Stuart. She looked at him with the sad but beautiful eyes that had helped her to get her way with so many men before. She was now in control. Stuart saw her as vulnerable and hurt, and he saw himself as her hero. Maggie fully intended to leave his office that day with a prescription for Xanax, as well as the appetite suppressant phentermine, so she could drop ten pounds and get to her pre-kids modeling weight. After all, she said, she was going to be "out there" again. Stuart insisted that she see him every six weeks so that he could supervise her use of the FDA-controlled medications. Not once did he have her see one of the physician assistants, even though his schedule was booked very far out. He also gave her his cell phone number, "just in case."

"Dr. Mayberry, there's just one more thing. I really want to stop taking the Topamax."

"It's your seizure medicine, Maggie. Why would you want to stop it?"

"It makes me feel so tired and listless. I went online and do you know what some other women call it? *Dopamax*. Besides, I've been seizure-free now for a few years."

"I'm not sure, Maggie. Maybe we could have a neurologist see you again."

"Oh no, Dr. Mayberry. I only trust you. You have no idea how it is. With the stress of being a single parent and all, I just need to feel like myself again."

abit. They were seated catty-corner at his desk, close enough that he could smell her perfume. Stuart had stopped holding her hand so he could use the computer, but now his hands were on the desk and Maggie let her hand brush up against his, though she acted as though she had not tried or even noticed. Stuart rubbed his chin in thought and then agreed to stop the seizure medication. Maggie knew the outcome was never in doubt. He warned her to watch for any signs of impending seizure and call him immediately on his cell. Maggie brought her eyes up to gaze directly into his and she whispered, "Of course." Stuart hovered the computer mouse over the Topamax entry in EMORY, right clicked, and then clicked the *Discontinue Medication* icon. In EMORY's original programming when a physician discontinued a major drug, such as seizure medication, a warning would pop up stating the risks of abruptly stopping the medication. The user would then have to confirm that this risk had been addressed. This was a safety net, and one of many that EMR was supposed to provide to lessen the chance of human error. On this day, EMORY did not provide that safety net for Dr. Stuart Mayberry.

Stuart felt that he was very good at multi-tasking. While he continued with the multitude of clicks and renewals, including one for Maggie's Xanax, he allowed his mind to drift from Maggie Summer the patient to Maggie Summer the beautiful woman sitting in front of him. A woman who he thought truly needed him and perhaps was attracted to him. He recognized the conflict of interest and considered the risk, but his penis prevailed in the debate. He was not only a physician, but the Lead Physician in charge of Medical Development and Professional Optimization. He would one day be a Vice President of something or other. He deserved her. He had earned it. He asked her if she wanted to talk over coffee, away from the office. Maggie feigned surprise, did a well-rehearsed hair toss, and accepted.

Chapter Twenty-Seven

May 7 - May 14, Green Grove

On-call week for Dr. Robin Cochran. Back in her solo practice days, Robin saw her own hospital patients and had cross-coverage when she went on vacation. When her patients had to be hospitalized they were more than relieved in the knowledge that their family doctor, Dr. Robin Cochran, was taking care of them. It was a demanding life, but a badge of honor for Robin. Unfortunately, her now ex-husband Howard failed to see it that way. It was one of many things that he blamed her for as they slowly drifted apart. Now that Robin was part of HealthSure, however, she shared in the group on-call responsibility. Only one week in seven. It was seven years after her divorce when she finally got this better schedule. Life was not without a sense of irony. That said, when she was on call the work was brutal. She didn't just cover her own patients, but also those of six other family care doctors. Although HealthSure's main hospital in the big city had a full complement of hospitalist physicians, specialist doctors who admitted and followed patients for the primary care providers, there were far fewer of them in Green Grove. So the Family Medicine doctors had to admit and round on hospital patients themselves. Monday morning at 0700 hours Robin entered the physician lounge at Green Grove General, printed off the patient list, and reviewed the sign-out with last week's on-call physician, Mark Morrow.

"I see twenty-three on the list, Mark. Right?"

"Yep. It maxed out at twenty-nine mid-week. Man, that was awful. I thought the EMR was supposed to make it easier. Fat chance. The med list in the E-chart did not correspond to what the patients were taking on at least five of them, so I just stopped using it and did it the old-fashioned way. I asked the patient and listed the meds with pen and paper. EMR is making the nurses *and* the patients both lazy. If I only had a nickel for every time I heard, "Can't you just look it up in the chart?"

"I know what you mean. I think it makes us more error prone, too. There's just too much going on in the screen."

"Funny you mention that. I admitted one last night for digitalis toxicity. Number 7 on the list, Vanessa Barnett."

"Wow. We don't see too many folks on digitalis these days."

"Yeah, I know, but she had been taking the same dose of digoxin for years and was really stable. Somehow her dose changed and for the life of me I can't figure out how in her electronic record. I called her PCP and he swears he did not change it."

"This is *exactly* what I have been talking about. I went to Stuart and now that he is a physician administrator he sees things only from the corporate perspective. God, I hate that."

Mark grinned. "Stuart wouldn't know a medical care issue if it crawled up his asshole and bit him. And that self-righteous jerk Walter Parks made such a scene. I had to admit him, you know. I wanted to tell him to stop being so histrionic."

Robin bristled. It cut her deep to know that her colleagues knew about the Walter Parks affair. Mark continued, "All right, let's get this sign-out over with. I have to get to my office for my 8 am patient."

"Weren't you up here last night?"

"Yeah, but the bean counter beast must be fed."

Robin went to work. The first day on-call was always the toughest. You first had to introduce yourself, learn about each patient, and get up to speed. Some patients did not have family there and were happy for the visit and rambled on. Robin, raised to be polite, listened intently and learned about the patients' cousins, who had what illness, where they lived or moved to, and why the in-laws were no-good folks. It was a long day.

The previous week Martin Harrell had also gotten to work bright and early. He had taken some vacation days, but leisure was the furthest thing from his mind. He had been working all weekend on his latest project. He wanted to hack into the computer of his nemesis, Stuart Mayberry. That was easy. He had always scoffed at the supposed security of a user name and log-on code. But restricted actions required more than that. Martin hit a wall, and he was not about to go the Hacker Nation route and reveal what he was doing to those amoebas. Then, kaboom! His idea was nothing short of brilliant. Accessing Stuart Mayberry's physical work space was simple. EMR dominated HealthSure's day-to-day existence, so IT people were ubiquitous. His visit to Dr. Mayberry's office last week did not raise any red flags. He then spent the weekend learning how to dust for fingerprints and modify his scanner. He cleared his desk of all non-essential flotsam. His scanner and 3D printer sat at 10 o'clock and 2 o'clock respectively. Then, in the center of the desk he placed an object of such importance that it took on a near-religious greatness. The holy chalice. A coffee mug emblazoned with the words "World's Best Doctor." He had spent Saturday night slowly and meticulously dusting the cup. His heart sank lower and lower as he worked his way nearly all the way around and came up with nothing. But in the final few centimeters there it was. Fingerprints. Damn, the jerk was a lefty. Well, he'd pay for stressing me out, Martin thought. He went to work on scanning it. Because the cup wasn't flat it would not be an easy scan. Martin had considered this from the get-go and with a little work and a steady hand he could get the job done. He was exhausted by Sunday night and uncharacteristically could fall asleep despite the work hanging over his head. Monday morning he was rested and motivated. He booted up his PC and 3D printer and waited for the drum roll in his head to cease. With one click of the mouse the three-dimensional finger print began to take shape. Within a few minutes, it was done. Martin held it up to the coffee mug and compared them. A perfect match. But that was not the end of his work. You couldn't use a 3D paper print on a finger scanner. Martin used the print to create a plaster mold, and in that mold, went a soft rubber compound. By Tuesday evening his work was complete and he had what looked like a piece of index finger made of soft rubber. It even had a flesh tone color. With the technical work done, Martin had only to decide how to carry out his vengeance. He was the silent protector for Dr. Robin Cochran, and one day he would confess to her and she would be grateful.

Chapter Twenty-Eight

Robin's first few days and nights of on-call were fairly routine. Pneumonia, chest pain, diabetes. The usual stuff. She handled it all well, but her one button that could easily be pushed was when she saw a patient with multiple admissions because they did not participate in their own medical treatment. They were called "revolving door" patients because no sooner were they discharged than they again showed up in the emergency room.

One of Mark Morrow's patients, Andie Ratliff, was a diabetic who didn't bother to take her insulin and considered jelly donuts and regular soda a balanced meal. Robin took a deep breath, exhaled, and readied herself for the BS session that was about to begin. Andie, her patient, was in bed and texting on her phone. Jerry Springer was on the TV berating someone or another, though Andie wasn't really paying attention. She was wearing scrub pants, rather than a hospital gown, and a T-shirt that said *Metallica.* Andie did not acknowledge Robin, nor did she bother to stop texting. Robin tried hard to engage every patient from a fresh perspective, without preconceived opinions. She was still human, however, and Andie's couldn't-care-less attitude only served to worsen her frustration.

"Hey, Dr. Cochran."

"Andie, why back again so soon?"

"Well, you know, the usual stuff."

Robin knew "the usual stuff." Andie's family was not supportive, she was unemployed and on disability, and money was tight. Still, her

Medicaid would pay for all her insulin and diabetic supplies. She may not have been educated past high school, but she was still smart enough to do basic diabetes self-management. The bottom line was that her home life was miserable and she just didn't give a hoot about her health. Being in the hospital meant that someone else would give her medications, do the shots and glucose checks, and see to it that she got three good meals. If one of her family or friends brought in a bear claw and soda, and her blood sugar rose to unspeakably high levels, then that was fine by the patient since it prolonged the time she was in the hospital with someone else taking care of her. Robin had seen this enough times that she should have been immune to the frustration. But she wasn't. She cared, even if the patient didn't.

"Andie, your kidney function is getting worse. If you don't start taking care of yourself, you're looking at dialysis in a few years."

"Okay, Dr. Cochran. I'm gonna be better about my diabetes this time."

Robin had heard it all before.

When she was done with her rounds in the hospital she left the main building for the parking lot. Standing by the main entrance was patient number 14 on her list today. He was a seventy-year-old gentleman with emphysema. She had worked on his hospital discharge only a few hours ago, and even spent extra time so she could counsel him about how tobacco would kill him. It was probably about the one millionth time that he had heard that same lecture, but there he was with a cigarette dangling from his mouth. His skin was tanned and deeply creased from age and years of cigarette use. She watched him cough, careful to maintain control of his cigarette between his index and middle finger. He saw her looking. She said nothing to him. He cared more about not losing his cigarette than he did about his lungs. He was coughing but still able to stammer "mind your own business" in a wheezy and gravely voice in response to her stare. She had nothing to say in return. What could she say that would make a difference? She considered what one of her colleagues had once suggested: medical incarceration for recurrent admissions. They were bilking the system and good folks like her were paying for it, he had said. Robin banished the thought and scolded herself for even thinking of it. She had plenty of patients who tried hard, and for no fault of their own suffered. The others? It just came with the job.

On her way home Robin decided to call George. She had already told him about her fight with Stuart and Walter Parks' theatrics. George had told her to take it like a soldier. Walter Parks was just too self-absorbed and too powerful. Fighting him would be like wriggling in quick sand. Just let it go, he told her. Easy advice, but hard to follow when every day for the next six months she would be reminded about her professional probation.

"Hey sheriff. Just on my way home."

"You're using your hands-free thing, right? I don't want to come out there and arrest you for holding your cell phone while driving."

Talking to George always made her feel better. She got home in a few minutes and pulled out some leftovers. She relaxed while eating her dinner, but the peace was short-lived. Her cell phone went off at 8:47 pm.

"Dr. Cochran. This is Green Grove ER Dr. Harington. We have an admission for you."

Robin sighed. "Go ahead."

"Twenty-six-year-old male with supra ventricular tachycardia." That was medical speak for really fast heartbeat. "We think it is from his Adderall. Looks like he was taking a much higher dose than usual."

"Okay. What's his name and room number? He's in a monitored bed for his heart. Right?"

"Sure. Rhett Jamison. Date of birth 7/18/1988. He's on the cardiac intermediate care unit. We didn't have a CCU bed. Cardiology already saw him and wants you to run the show for primary care."

Robin froze. "Oh, my God."

"What? You know the kid?"

"He's one of Aaron's, Aaron my son, Aaron's best friends. You know how many weekend lunches I cooked for this kid when they were teenagers?"

"Maybe that'll make it easier for him. Gotta be scary for a twenty-six-year-old to be on a cardiac monitor."

"Yeah, and what do you mean, 'No beds in the CCU?' If we have to shove people over and put in a cot, then that's what we'll do."

"Take it easy, Dr. Cochran. He'll still be on a monitor."

"I'll be right over. In the meantime, see if he can go to the ICU."

Twenty minutes later Robin was in ER and examining Rhett Jamison. He had taken a dose of Adderall that was three times his usual. Throw in a few Red Bulls and a couple of beers and it was easy to see how things could go so wrong. What wasn't easy to explain, however, was how the Adderall dose went up.

"Rhett, this is three times your usual dose of Adderall. It says it right there on the label. What were you thinking? I'm here as your doctor, by the way, and this discussion is confidential. If you were taking something else, you need to let me know."

"I wasn't taking any illegal drugs, Mrs. Cochran. I mean Dr. Cochran. I never looked at the Adderall label. I've been on the same dose for years. I don't know how it changed."

By now it was 10:30 pm. Rhett used a twenty-four-hour pharmacy and Robin called it. The pharmacist insisted that Rhett's doctor, one of the ones that Robin was covering for, had changed the prescription a week ago. When the patient showed up for a refill two days ago, he was given the new and much higher dosage. Robin went back to the computer and pulled up Rhett's chart. She went to the medication list and found his current dose of Adderall, thirty milligrams twice per day. A whopper of a dose. She went to the discontinued medication list and found the old Adderall prescription, ten milligrams twice per day. The date of the lower dose discontinuation and the higher dose prescription were the same, October 4th. One week ago, just like the pharmacist said. But something didn't add up. The physician, Ed Halsby, was on vacation and in Sweden. Could he have done the prescription? Maybe. Although they cross-covered each other when one of them was away, they had not yet figured out how to efficiently handle the EMORY chart work that landed in their in-basket every day. Some of the docs simply came home a day early from their vacations so that they could catch up on their messages, emails, and notes.

EMORY had a secure patient portal. It was a great way for patients to communicate with their providers, but if you took the week off you would be assured of dozens upon dozens of messages that you would need to respond to later. Some doctors simply took a laptop PC with them wherever they went and caught up on work every so often. For some, it became a compulsion. A pathetic disease that EMR created. Even if you were in some exotic vacation spot overseas you felt like you *had* to check your in-basket every day. Ed was coming home tomorrow or the next day. No point in ruining the last day of his vacation. She'd wait to talk to him.

On her way home from the hospital she pulled up to the local big-box pharmacy to pick up a refill on her estrogen patch. She started to go inside, but then decided it was late, she was tired, and she just wanted to get home and get horizontal. The estrogen could wait. If she was a bitch for a few days, then so be it. That was fine with Stuart Mayberry, who just happened to be inside and was at the register purchasing condoms. Stuart's pulse quickened, his sweat glands went into overdrive, and his eventual sigh of relief was audible when he saw Robin turn around and go back to her car without seeing him. The guy behind the register noted Stuart's wedding band and concluded that the woman outside must have been his wife. She looked older, but she was still attractive. A *cougar,* he figured. He said nothing. Stuart wasn't the first middle-aged, married guy that he had sold condoms to.

Tuesday morning could not have started in a more aggravating way for Robin. She stared at her computer screen.

Your password will expire in 1 day. Please change your password. Ugh, three months already? Robin thought. She navigated to the password page of EMORY, took a cursory look at the rules, and started to change her password.

aaron1

You must use 8 characters

aaron123

You cannot use consecutive numbers.

aaron132

You must have at least one capital letter.

Aaron123

We are sorry. You have made three unsuccessful password reset attempts. For security purposes, you will be locked out of EMORY. Please contact Information Technology to resume your EMORY session. Thank you.

Robin released a sigh that could be heard across the county. She called IT.

"You have reached HealthSure Information Technology. If you are calling about hospital EMORY press 1, if you are calling about a password reset press 2..." Robin pressed 2.

"You are caller number three. We appreciate your patience."

Robin couldn't even use her computer. She got on her phone and browsed through her pictures. She found some old childhood Kodachromes of Aaron that she had recently photographed with her smart phone so that she could look at them whenever she liked.

"This is HealthSure IT. Can I have your HealthSure ID, please?"

"This is Dr. Robin Cochran. I have a pass..."

"Can I have your ID, please?"

"Uh...RMC034."

"I'm sorry. I don't see any users in our system with RNC044"

"NO! R EEMMMMM C zero three four."

"Can you use phonetic spelling please?"

"What is that?"

"You know...alpha, bravo."

"What the hell is 'alpha bravo?' Just give me a password so I can get my work done!"

"Doctor, that language is inappropriate and offensive and I will not tolerate it."

Click.

Robin's neck muscles went slack and her head went thud on her desk. She needed about five minutes of deep breathing and positive visualization before she could compose herself enough to call IT again. Thankfully, a different tech person picked up and after a few minutes she had a new password.

Chapter Twenty-Nine

Monday morning, usually a drag for most workers, was a relief for Robin. It meant that her on-call week was over. The week had been unusually bad. That said she was relieved at how the week ended. Rhett Jamison spent a night in the cardiac care unit then went home on the correct dose of Adderall. Now Robin just had to get back to what she did best. She was in her office and on time for her 7:30 am patient. Robin was always on time for her patients. That commitment never wavered. Brenda Makem was waiting for her. Thirty-six weeks pregnant and ready to burst, she practically knocked over the desk when she entered the room and turned sideways. She carefully lowered herself in to the chair beside Robin's desk. They exchanged their usual pleasantries and Robin carefully looked over her blood sugars.

"Brenda, I think your morning glucose numbers could stand to be a little lower. Raise your bedtime insulin four units."

"Okay. So how *you* doin' for a Monday?"

"Better than you'd think, now that my on-call week is over."

A look of panic came over Brenda just as Robin realized what she had said.

"Wait. So, you're not going to be on-call when I deliver? They told me that they wanted to deliver me at thirty-nine weeks. That's only three weeks away!"

"Brenda, first of all it will be your obstetrician who will be the main doctor while you are there. Whoever is on-call for me will help with the diabetes management. I think it's Ed Halsby that week. He's an excellent..." She didn't get a chance to finish. Brenda's eyes welled up. All that extra estrogen during pregnancy had made her more emotional.

"All right, Brenda. I promise I'll visit when you deliver and I will look at your chart and make sure everyone is doing right by you."

Brenda nodded her head in agreement, wiped away her tears, and blew her nose. Her eyes remained red throughout the rest of her visit as Robin reminded her that she needed tight glucose control all the way till delivery, when she would be placed on IV insulin.

As Monday came to an end, Ed Halsby showed up at Robin's office. His office was one floor below, so it was not much of a trip. He was rested from vacation, but whatever sense of relaxation that he had gained quickly evaporated when he was confronted with the issue of the Adderall toxicity.

"I just looked at Rhett Jamison's hospital discharge summary. Robin, I did not raise his Adderall dose."

"Ed, it's this damned electronic record system. It's moving too far too fast and we're making mistakes that we'd otherwise not make."

"But I DID NOT WRITE THAT PRESCRIPTION!"

Ed's face was turning red. Robin could not help but notice that it matched his red tie.

"I was in Stockholm for God's sake!"

"Look, Ed, Rhett's fine. Put it behind you. There are a lot of patients who depend on you."

"Easy for you to say. That prick Stuart Mayberry came by. I was already on a six-month probationary period, God damn it."

"Probation? Why?"

"Because I wasn't closing ninety-five percent of my charts same day. Remember how back in the paper chart days all you had to do was sign your notes? There are so many clicks, attestations, and what-evers that you spend more time finishing E-charts than actually seeing your patients."

Robin had a sense of déjà vu and thought of Harold Timley.

"Damn it, Robin. I feel like this EMR thing is sucking the life out of me."

Déjà vu indeed. Ed exhaled hard before he left Robin's office. Robin thought about how vacations had become much less mentally refreshing for all of the providers. Knowing that on Day One when you returned you would be jumping right back in to the fire made it harder to forget work and relax. The Human Resources department offered group sessions to deal with the stress. Robin had once even looked in to them. She had spoken to one of the doctors, Ed Halsby ironically, who had attended a session. The premise was that you did not have to respond to these challenges by getting stressed out. When he had asked what HealthSure was doing to make things like EMR more user-friendly so that providers could focus on what they do best, care for patients, he was quickly rebuffed and told that EMORY was going to make their lives better and that they needed to keep a positive attitude. Ed did not go back for any more kumbaya sessions.

The following morning, one day after returning to work, Ed received a text from Stuart at 7:00 am asking him to stop by the administrative office to review the probation period and come up with an action plan moving forward. Ed figured he knew the drill. He had messed up and now administration had to slap his wrist, but hard. He decided that he would not grovel or make excuses. Perhaps Robin had been right. EMR was moving forward too fast and it was too easy to make a mistake. Fortunately, the Adderall kid did okay and was home. Ed hadn't heard from any lawyers. He considered himself honest and he was willing to accept his responsibility in this. He planned to call Rhett Jamison and set up a visit. He would tell him what happened and apologize. In the last malpractice newsletter, they said that when patients were on the wrong end of a mistake they wanted their doctors to be honest about it, and lawsuits are more apt to happen when the doctor tries to avoid taking responsibility. It was going to be easier to face Stuart than to face Rhett Jamison. Ed thought it through over his morning coffee. He had been separated from his wife for six months and the ink on the divorce settlement was still wet. He had few friends and his only companions to discuss it with were the characters in the comic section of the newspaper. They would never betray his trust, he mused. A few more slurps of coffee and he was out the door.

HealthSure kept a few bland offices for physician administrators to use when needed. The offices were situated in the HealthSure Corporate Administration Building, a red-brick building with a security guard and metal detector at the front entrance. HealthSure seemed to have more safety concerns for administrators than patients. The extra office space encompassed a few rooms that were bare except for a desk and computer, a few magazines, and a note pad. There were no windows. One wall had a framed print of a beach scene from the same artist that did just about every painting in every HealthSure office. The artist's signature was not legible and may as well have been someone's basset hound for all Stuart knew or cared. The rooms were there for guys like Stuart to use in lieu of their personal offices. On the next floor up were the permanent offices of the HealthSure administrators. Well-appointed and with an antechamber, complete with secretary, out front. This was what Stuart aspired to. Just a few more years, he hoped. He spread out his documents and a pen on the desk and rehearsed his role. There was a security officer down the hall, just in case, and another was stationed on the third floor of Green Grove Family Practice, Ed's floor. At 7:00 am Ed Halsby came in.

"G'morning Ed. Thanks for coming."

Ed nodded, said nothing, and sat down to wait for the anticipated scolding.

"I think you know why you're here. The purpose of the probation is to give the provider a chance to clean things up and get back on track. The medication error with your patient was nearly fatal and I think you know that. Under the circumstances, we, and I speak for HealthSure in this case, feel that it is best for you and us to part ways."

"Wait a second, Stuart. Are you firing me? What the hell!"

"Ed, I know this is a shock, but we want you to land on your feet. If you sign here and agree to terms, then we release you without cause. You can find a new job tomorrow and work. If you fight this then we *will* fire you for cause, and you know what that means for your future work prospects. "

"You can't do that!"

"Ed, take a deep breath. We can indeed do that. I took the liberty of pulling out your contract. The appropriate sections are right here in front of you. You can call your lawyer if you want and waste four hundred dollars an hour, but it won't make a difference. Our contracts are carefully worded by our legal department."

The HealthSure Legal Department, Ed thought. They made more money than he did and never helped a soul. They made it possible for assholes like Stuart to do what he was doing, with no risk to themselves. Shakespeare was right,"The first thing we do let's kill all the lawyers." Ed came back to the moment.

"I need to go back to my office and finish up some things."

Stuart raised his hand in the universal *stop for a moment* position.

"Not necessary Ed. Go home and rest. You can go to your office tonight at 7 pm. Your ID won't work so security will meet you at the front door. They'll escort you up and wait while you pack."

Stuart kept on talking, Ed no longer listened, and just like that his medical career in Green Grove ended without a chance to even say good-bye to his patients and staff.

Ed Halsby was devastated. He had just been through a nasty divorce. His wife got custody of their children, and after thousands of dollars in lawyers' fees he was at least relieved that he would continue to be part of their lives. His trip to Sweden, the land of ABBA and Absolut, was a nice diversion. But no sooner had he returned home then his life was back to chaos. He had an ongoing vertebral disc problem. The pain acted up now and again, and for sure now. He took some expired muscle relaxants he found in the back of his medicine cabinet and opened a beer. Ed was a connoisseur of craft beer and had twenty extra pounds around his gut to prove it. After thirty minutes, he felt no better and his back still hurt. So, he had another beer, another muscle relaxant, and went for the Xanax that had been prescribed by his therapist when he was going through his divorce. He had refilled it the day that he had arrived back in Green Grove. Unknown to Ed or his doctor there had recently been a considerable dose increase on his prescription in EMORY. Ed had been on the same dose for years and he had no reason to consider that there had been a change. He failed to notice the new dosage that was printed on the label. Or perhaps the beer and muscle relaxants helped him to not care. Either way, he took several high-dose Xanax and drifted off to a sound sleep that he would never wake up from.

Stuart Mayberry was having a very different day. After his meeting with Ed Halsby he called his wife and told her that he was working late again, that she should go ahead and have dinner with the kids, but be sure to save him a plate. Stuart's wife was used to this. She understood that her husband had to do many of his administrative tasks on his own time, after office hours. She also understood that the payoff would be significant. She had read in the newspaper that the top hospital executives made seven figures. She imagined a bigger house, exotic vacations, and never again flying coach. Stuart, meanwhile, was imagining things of a different nature. Before calling his wife, he had called Maggie Summer. It had taken him ten minutes of staring at his phone to summon the nerve, but eventually he called her and asked if she wanted to meet for coffee. "What a coincidence, I just made a fresh pot. Why don't you come over here? The kids are over at my ex's and will be spending the night." Stuart grabbed his sport coat and left his office like it was on fire. He punched Maggie's address in his GPS, sucked on a few Tic Tacs, and did his best to drive the speed limit. A speeding ticket while he was supposed to be working would be a tough one to explain to his wife. On his way to Maggie's he thought about that erection medication commercial. *If you have an erection lasting more than four hours consult a physician.* Stuart didn't need a physician. He needed Maggie Summer's sun-kissed thighs wrapped around him. The sound of his wheels driving over the grooves in the road brought his wandering mind back to reality. The DOT put grooves next to the white line that signaled the road's edge to alert drowsy drivers. Worth every penny. His GPS told him to make a right turn in one-quarter mile. He soon saw the stone sign for Maggie's subdivision, Hunter Lakes, and turned in. The homes were huge and separated from one another by at least an acre or two of property on each side. Stuart pulled into Maggie's driveway and immediately took note of a Porsche SUV. *The perfect accessory for wife of a wealthy investment banker,* he thought. His four-door Infinity seemed pedestrian by comparison. No matter. Soon enough he would be an executive vice president at HealthSure and drive whatever he damned well pleased. Stuart sucked on one last Tic Tac, adjusted his junk so he would not look obvious, and made his way to Maggie Summer's door. He was aware of his heart pounding when he rang the bell, but he steadied himself. Maggie answered the door and looked absolutely resplendent. Stuart's wife had taught him about women's fashion. He immediately recognized the Manolo Blahnik "fuck-me pumps," Chanel fitted silk blouse and pants, and her best strand of Mikimoto pearls that hung just to the level of her cleavage. The look was extremely seductive without being trashy.

"Come in, Dr. Mayberry."

Maggie knew quite well that Stuart had told her that she should call him by his first name, but she decided this would be a good way to be flirtatious. Throughout her failed marriage, she had never been unfaithful. She did, however, enjoy teasing her husband's acquaintances at social functions and gatherings. The men thought she was smoking hot, and she knew exactly what they were thinking. When she found out that her husband was cheating on her with a woman ten years her junior, she was not only devastated that he had been screwing another woman, but her ego was badly bruised as well. She was, therefore, very well prepared to deal with the likes of Dr. Stuart Mayberry, especially now that she was nearly divorced. Like all men he thought with his dick. He clearly wanted to play the prince charming to her damsel in distress. He was married, moving up in the corporate hierarchy in a religiously conservative region, of the country and best of all he was her physician. He had a lot to lose if word ever got out. She was not looking for a serious relationship with him. She could do a whole lot better. Through Stuart she would get her moxie back, not to mention an easy source of prescriptions for appetite suppressants, Xanax, and whatever else she needed. If necessary, he could also testify as her medical provider about the emotional distress that she had suffered because of her husband's infidelity.

"Maggie, what's with the Dr. Mayberry? I thought we were on a first-name basis."

"Whoops. I had forgotten. My bad. Follow me and have a seat."

She led Stuart in to the house while he marveled at how a woman who had given birth to two children could still have a butt that round and spectacular. Maggie knew that while her genetics played a role, plastic surgery, Spanx and five-inch heels were a big help nonetheless. She figured that he would be tongue-tied and that she herself would have to get the conversation going. She knew that he was arrogant and it would be easy to get him to talk about himself, but she needed to be careful and steer clear of any talk of his wife or kids, lest he lose his nerve.

"Can I take your jacket? Oh, and please put the gown on, tied with the opening to the back."

Maggie laughed politely at her own joke and Stuart guffawed a bit too loudly. She noticed that his breath smelled like Tic Tacs.

"How do you do it, Stuart? I mean doing the physician-leadership thing yet still finding the time to take care of patients like me who rely on you."

"It's what I do. But to be honest, I do need to start cutting back on the hours that I spend seeing patients."

Maggie produced a combination pouty-face and whatever-shall-I-do-face for Stuart. She was incredibly good at this.

"Oh no, Maggie. I would never stop seeing patients entirely." He lied. "I'll always make time for my most special patients. But that's shop talk. Besides, it's not fair to refer to you as my 'patient.' You're so much more than that."

The pouty-face gave way to a thank-goodness-face as she leaned forward a bit in her chair so that her body language would show her approval. Stuart proceeded to explain the rigors of managing both patient care and physician leadership. HealthSure was a vessel trying to navigate the rough waters of medicine. He, Stuart Mayberry, would keep the ship righted and on course.

"I must say, Maggie, you look positively lovely. I'm going to guess you don't do your shopping in Green Grove."

Maggie gave a polite look of embarrassment.

"Well, if you must know, some of my girlfriends and I make occasional trips to Atlanta to hit some of the better stores. If we're really feeling wild, we head to New York."

Stuart envisioned Maggie having a glass of champagne in first class with her equally wealthy girlfriends, each with empty suitcases ready to be filled with plunder from Saks and Neiman Marcus. It didn't even occur to him that they could fly a private corporate jet. He still had to fly commercial, in coach, and hope for an upgrade.

"Oh my, where are my manners? I invited you for coffee."

Maggie walked into the kitchen, well within Stuart's view, while Stuart marveled at a kitchen worthy of Top Chef. She made her way over to the most elaborate cappuccino-espresso maker that he had ever seen, except maybe in the most expensive Italian restaurants. Maggie narrated what she was doing as she filled the coffee grinder with espresso beans. She had to use her upper body muscles to hold the lid in place as the noisy grinder did its work. Stuart got a partial view of her lacy black bra, undoubtedly a souvenir from one of her Atlanta or New York trips, through the sheer silk top. She set to clumsily pack down the espresso grinds and put them in the machine, deliberately unsuccessful. In fact, Maggie Summer was highly intelligent and athletic. She ran track in high school and college, and she majored in economics. She was more than a match for her espresso machine, but she had to let Stuart think that he was the alpha male.

"Oh hell! Oh my! Did I say that? I always seem to struggle with this machine."

She stopped just short of saying *Stuart, would you come here and help me.* It took Stuart a few moments to take the bait. In truth, he couldn't even handle the Keurig in his kitchen at home, let alone the seven-thousand-dollar behemoth in front of him. He got up and slowly walked over; taking his time in the hope that he would find a clue as to how to work this machine. Maggie had strategically placed herself in front of the espresso machine with her back to Stuart. Each hand was on a different lever, pretending to not know what to do next. That she was facing away from him gave Stuart another chance to untangle his junk as he got close enough to smell her very expensive perfume. Stuart lamented how he did not wear cologne that evening, but that would be difficult to explain to his wife later. He had not thought about whether Maggie's perfume would stay on him but, as Maggie already knew, he was thinking with his dick. He reached around her to guide her hands on the espresso machine, but that was all for the coffee. Maggie slowly turned around and began kissing him. She held her hands just below his shoulder blades, while he moved his to her waist. After a minute of giving Maggie a proper waist massage, Stuart's hands ventured to the buttons on her blouse. He undid a couple and peered down at the sexiest bra that he had ever seen. He recalled that his wife had emphasized years ago that a doctor's spouse wears better than Victoria's Secret, so he was not new to expensive lingerie. Maggie saw Stuart's eyes nearly drop out of his head. She grinned and whispered, "It's a LaPerla." They could have been two Styrofoam cups for all he cared by that point. He thought about what a great job those bra cups had, cradling the most gorgeous breasts he had ever laid eyes on. As Stuart began caressing her breasts through her LaPerla bra cups, Maggie recognized the familiar breathing and body language of a man about to lose control of his actions. It was important to her that she control the situation. She had earlier made up her mind that she was not going to have intercourse with him. Not yet, if at all. She had, however, led him on and it was important that he leave happy and feeling in her debt. Fellatio would do the job. Proper southern women like her did not even think of the phrase "blowjob," and fellatio sounded more exotic and sophisticated. She spun him around so that his back was to the kitchen counter and she slowly moved downwards, all the while gazing into his eyes so that she could keep him in her spell. She undid his pants and went to work. She was not shy about a blowjob and she was good at it. Stuart thanked God repeatedly under his breath, and then mumbled a few *Oh Maggies.* Maggie started to feel some unusual sensations. She was in control of the situation, so this was very unusual. She saw flashing lights and she felt both numb and weak. She tried to communicate to Stuart, but she had his member in her mouth and he was holding her head close. All she could manage was a few groans before everything began to go black.

Stuart was seeing stars of a different sort. He didn't have to wonder what heaven was like. He was there. He thanked God that he was not an atheist. If the physical sensation was not enough, Maggie had begun moaning. Then her body began to tremble. It was all too much for

Stuart. He started to feel the familiar spasms in his groin when ecstasy suddenly turned to excruciating pain. He looked down and saw Maggie's teeth tightly clenched around his penis which was dripping blood and semen. Her body, meanwhile, was jerking violently. She was having a tonic-clonic seizure. Every muscle in her body including those of her jaw, unfortunately for Stuart, was contracting with incredible force. Stuart was able to pry Maggie's mouth open just enough to pull himself out. While he screamed in agony he briefly thought of that fateful visit when Maggie had convinced him to stop her seizure medication.

Maggie was on the kitchen floor convulsing while Stuart grabbed a kitchen towel and tried to stop the bleeding from his penis. Had Maggie been conscious she would have been mortified to have seen her Williams-Sonoma kitchen towel used in this manner. After what seemed like hours to him, but was only about a minute, Maggie's body relaxed. Stuart noted that she was breathing and didn't seem to be choking. He had to help her but not get caught red-handed, or red-whatever. He found the kitchen phone. Thank God they still had a land line. He dialed 911, said that a woman was having a seizure, gave the address, and hung up while the dispatcher was asking him for his name. He stuffed the bloody towel down his underpants, buttoned up his pants and then Maggie's blouse, and raced out to his car. He deliberately left her front door cracked open. It was dark and no one was outside to notice him. He drove to the end of the block, cut the lights and engine, and slouched down in his seat. He found some old Bojangles napkins on the passenger seat and stuffed those down his pants, too. After about three minutes he heard sirens and soon after saw the flashing lights of the EMS truck and fire engine. Once he saw the EMTs enter the house he started his car. He tried to look nonchalant as he drove past the ambulance, or at least as nonchalant as one could look while applying pressure to a bleeding penis.

Dr. Solamh Finley had just sat down to watch the Duke-Villanova basketball game. Sol had gone to Duke for undergrad, medical school, and his residency in urologic surgery. He wore his Blue Devils sweatshirt, and each of his three triplets was wearing some variant of a Duke onesie. His wife, who had not gone to Duke, was a little sick of the whole Duke basketball thing. He had, however, been very supportive during the fertility treatments that had given them triplets and so she could put up with the whole Duke thing. Sol's parents were not wealthy, and Duke was a private university. By the time he finished his training and was ready to enter a practice in urology he was well in to six figures of academic debt. He was leery of joining a private practice for a cut-rate salary in return for the chance of partnership five years down the road. He had heard of doctors who were coincidentally fired with less than a year to go before making partner. So, when HealthSure Inc. offered him a full salary his first year out, he decided to play it safe and take the money. He would have no equity, and if he they ever parted ways he would leave with only the shirt on his back. Still, the setup allowed him to manage his money as he saw fit and have control over his future.

The Duke-Villanova game had barely begun when his phone rang. His ring tone, Pee-wee Herman's voice, told him to answer the phone. You know, Pee-wee? A urology joke. He was going to send it to voice mail when he saw Stuart Mayberry on the caller ID. It was Stuart who convinced HealthSure to expand beyond primary care and hire the more lucrative surgical specialists, like Solamh Finley. Sol answered with an enthusiastic, "Hey Stuart," but the tone in Stuart's voice made it clear that he was in no mood for friendly chit-chat.

"I have a major urology emergency, Sol. I need you to meet me at Green Grove General right away. I'm on my way there now. Meet me in the ER, but I only want to see you. No ER doc. Understood?"

"Stuart, you sound really upset. Can you tell me what's up?" Another urology joke.

"I'll tell you when we're there. Just meet me right away."

Stuart ended the call and Sol let out a heavy sigh. He was not on call that night, but Stuart was a big reason that he had gotten this job and so he asked his wife to DVR the Duke game while he tended to Stuart.

Stuart arrived at Green Grove General before Sol and waited in his car. When he saw Sol enter the ER he texted him, instructed him to get a room ready, and text back the room number. When he had the number, Stuart walked quickly in to the ER and found the room. The ER staff was busy trying to revive a cardiac arrest victim and Stuart was certain no one had seen him come in, or so he thought. Sol was waiting. Stuart undid his pants, pulled out the bloody Williams-Sonoma towel and Bojangles napkins, tossed them in the trash, and breathed an audible hiss. Sol did a poor job of trying to hide his shock.

"What happened?"

"Zipper accident."

"A zipper accident? Those look like teeth marks."

"Sol, you know I'm a big reason that you're here in Green Grove. So let's just skip the detailed questions and get this fixed."

"All right, Stuart, but I can't access the supplies that I'll need without creating an encounter. You know that, right?"

Stuart sighed. In retrospect, he should have worked something out where Sol could have taken care of him in his office or something. He was in a panic, though, and they were there already.

"Fine. I slipped in the bathroom while I was zipping up. Okay?"

"Okay. I'll go get the supplies I'll need."

"Sol, no other staff, Okay? This needs to stay quiet."

"I can handle this unassisted. Give me a few minutes to get what I need and open an encounter in EMORY."

"Sol, I don't need to remind you that this was an accident and involved no one else."

"Yup."

Sol went about gathering sutures, sterile gloves, and the instruments that he would need to fix Stuart's member. He would need to inject a local anesthetic, lidocaine. To get the medication from the hospital pharmacy he would have to start an encounter in EMORY. He could do this without anesthetic, but then only with a soundproof room to cover Stuart's screams, and he laughed to himself. Stuart, meanwhile, texted his wife and informed her that he was nearly done and would only be another hour or so. His reply was a sad face emoji. He typed *Kiss the kids good night for me. See you soon. Love you.* He added a heart emoji. His wife responded *Drive safe. I know you're doing this for us. Love you too.* Stuart did not even feel an ounce of guilt or shame.

Stuart's heart skipped a beat when the door opened, but it was just Sol with an armful of supplies.

"I'm gonna have to clean the area really good before I suture it. Do you want me to give you any Demerol?"

"No. I have to drive home."

Of course, Sol thought. *You sure ain't callin' your wife to come get you.*

Sol froze Stuart's skin with topical ethyl chloride. It turned the skin white and Sol saw the look on Stuart's face.

"Relax. It just looks that way for a few minutes."

Stuart knew that, but still.

Sol went to work gently cleaning the damaged skin. He then injected lidocaine to numb the areas that he would have to suture. Without taking his eyes off his work he talked to Stuart.

"You know, Stuart, there's no way to visually hide this. Your wife will see it."

"Adelle knows I've been overworked and stressed lately. If I reassure her she'll understand the drop in my libido. We have a vacation coming up in two months and I'll promise her that the rest will make me a tiger. I'll otherwise be discreet. What kind of scar will this leave?"

"It shouldn't be too bad, but if she is up close and takes a good look she will see it."

"Not a problem. Adelle won't do fellatio. Never has, never will. It grosses her out."

Sol thought that there were a few good jokes in there. It was easy to be funny when you were a urologist. He thought better of it and suppressed his smirk. There was knock at the door and it opened part way. Stuart, who had been lying flat on his back, bolted halfway upright. Fortunately for him, Sol was young and had great reflexes. With one hand holding the forceps that held the suture that was in Stuart's flesh, he spun half way around and used his other hand to pull the curtain across.

Sol barked: “Nurse, when you don’t hear me say *come in* then don’t come in.”

“I’m sorry, Doctor Finley. It’s just that I saw that Dr. Mayberry was here and I wanted to make him aware that we just evaluated one of his patients.”

Sol looked at Stuart imploringly and waited for some sort of direction in the matter. Stuart, however, had already quickly assessed the situation and he thought that it would be better to not raise more suspicion. He held up one hand as if to say *It’s alright, I’ll handle it.* Damn good thing he didn’t take the Demerol.

“Yes, nurse, what is it?”

“Maggie Summer is here. Thirty-five-year-old female with a history of seizures. She may have had a seizure tonight. EMS was called to her home and found her on the floor confused, probably in a post-ictal state. There were a few tell-tale signs that she had seized. She had some urinary incontinence, and there were small blood stains around her mouth. We figure she probably bit her tongue during the seizure.”

“How is she doing?”

“Vitals are stable and she is more alert, but she doesn’t remember much. Pretty typical post-seizure.”

“Was it witnessed?”

“That’s the funny thing. Someone called EMS, a man, but no one was there when EMS arrived at the house.”

“Okay. Thank you for the update. I’ll check EMORY later and see how she’s doing.”

The nurse closed the door. Stuart's flight-or-fight response had made him lightning fast. When he bolted upright he had seen the door open halfway but the nurse had not yet entered before Sol had drawn the curtain. She saw nothing. He knew that after a seizure Maggie's memory would be hazy. Still, she'd surely remember some of the evening. Like Stuart, she too had a lot to lose. Her divorce was not yet finalized. He prayed that she would be discreet. For his part, Sol said nothing. He had way too much to lose. Stuart was smart to call him rather than one of the older and more established urologists. This wasn't his problem and he decided to steer clear of any trouble.

The next morning was awful. Medical assistants were running around the office building gathering up physicians and depositing them in the meeting room where Stuart waited and then delivered the devastating news. Ed Halsby was found dead in his apartment. His ex-wife had dropped the kids off at school and needed him to pick them up later. When he did not answer his cell or office phone she stopped at his apartment. He had given her a key and she let herself in. The cause of his death was unclear at this time and the medical examiner was investigating. He was a good physician and father, and he would be missed. Stuart clearly looked distressed, though it was only he who knew that it had more to do with the discomfort coming from his boxer shorts than Ed's tragic demise. Robin tasted her salty tears and fought against the urge to scream at Stuart and his false sympathy. Everyone soon filed out of the room. Stuart stopped Robin.

"Ed was supposed to be on call in two weeks. I need you to cover half of that week and I'll have Brantley cover the other half."

Robin shot him a look to kill.

"Do you have something you want to say to me, Dr. Cochran?"

“Yeah, I do. It was no secret that Ed had just gone through a nasty divorce and was really stressed. He felt terrible about that medication error, and it isn’t even clear that he was responsible. But you had to make sure you let everyone know that you are above them, so you pulled this probation crap on him. After all, you’re the head of Professional Development.”

“That’s Medical Development and Professional Optimization. That means I am supposed to make sure that physicians don’t screw up, and discipline them when they do. As far as that prescription goes, EMORY’s record is there in black and white. Ed wrote the prescription.”

“Screw you, Stuart. Oh, wait. I’m sorry. That could get me another six months.”

Robin went back to her office. She was now thirty minutes behind and had patients in two exam rooms and one in the waiting area. She took a deep breath and got to it. She apologized to each patient for being behind and by midday she was caught up. The afternoon went marginally better, and she even saw two of Ed Halsby’s patients who did not get the message and showed up at the office for their appointments. It was the same for everyone. “How horrible,” and “Was he a sick man?” When her last patient was done, Robin could not wait to finish her dictation. She was both physically and emotionally exhausted.

I have prescribed two cups of stool... “Two CAPSULES, you stupid piece of crap.” She took a deep breath and said to herself *It’s just a computer and microphone.* If she only knew. EMORY monitored the emails and dictation of all HealthSure users. Robin had emailed and spoken of EMORY several times. She was therefore considered by EMORY to be a person of interest. EMORY raised Robin’s communications to a higher priority level. Unknown to Robin, her dictation microphone and camera were always on. Likewise, EMORY monitored her phone calls and location via the *EMORY* app on Robin's phone.

Dr. Robin Cochran always finished her work before she left the office each evening. This evening was different. She uncharacteristically left messages and labs for the next day, and as soon as her dictation was done she gathered her things and headed for the parking lot. Earlier, she had emailed George about what had happened. He called her, offered to meet her for lunch, but she declined. She wanted to get her work done and get home for a glass of wine and some channel surfing. Martin Harrell, alerted by his laptop computer that Dr. Robin Cochran was either sending or receiving an email, followed along. At 6:30 pm, Robin got into her hybrid Lexus, started the amazingly quiet engine, and let her phone sync with the car's sound system so she could play her easy listening playlist.

Route 401 used to be a pleasant country road. After all the development, however, it had changed into a one lane highway. Big SUVs, barely able to fit into the lane, passed each other in each direction at sixty-plus miles per hour. The road was supposed to be widened, but construction would not start for another two years. What a misery it would be to commute then.

Chapter Thirty

Martin took a vacation week. Since he did not have a girlfriend, or for that matter any flesh and blood friends, it wasn't much of a sacrifice. He would need to devote his full attention to the task at hand and he wanted no distractions. Over the previous two weeks he had accumulated the various pieces of hardware that he would need. He was ready to get started. He plugged in the headset to the USB port and he logged on to EMORY remotely, being sure to navigate through several phony web addresses that he had created to cover his tracks. Martin preferred to work alone and he did not want to leave any electronic trail or have anyone from HealthSure IT discover him. He placed the headset over his eyes and took a moment to find his equilibrium, standing in front of his couch with his arms outstretched and his mouth agape. He had used virtual reality before, but never in this manner. He began to navigate within the outer fringes of EMORY and tried out the various functionalities that he had already known. It took only about thirty minutes to get accustomed to using this new world but once there he found that he could move around from place to place with more ease than he had done with a keyboard and mouse. After about an hour and a half he navigated his way out, logged off, and removed his headset. He was surprised at how both mentally and physically drained he felt. His clothes were slightly damp and he could smell his own sweat. Still, he felt satisfied that the world of EMORY was now his domain and he was in control. The truth, however, was quite the opposite. Martin had no reason to suspect that EMORY itself was monitoring *his* actions. He found it hard to sleep, but knew that sleep he must. He needed to be fresh to complete his task the following day.

Chapter Thirty-One

1996

Martin Harrell's early childhood could not have been more ordinary. He was the only child of middle class parents. From an early age, it was clear that he was unusually inquisitive, and it often led him in to trouble. At age five his parents found him in the driveway attempting to light sticks on fire that he had soaked in kerosene. The marshmallows, chocolate, and graham crackers on the ground next to him provided the answer as to why. His mother insisted that there were easier ways to make s'mores, and from that day on his father placed the canister of kerosene high up on the wall in the garage, well out of Martin's reach. Martin responded the following year by asking Santa for an acetylene torch for Christmas. His mother turned beet-red as she tried to explain to the mall Santa about her unusual son, while all the other families waiting in line giggled. It was around that time that Martin exhibited a variety of quirks, such as an aversion to clothing seams. They forced him to wear a collared shirt to church by using his computer as leverage. At the post-sermon Sunday lunches he squirmed uncontrollably until his parents finally took him home and he could change in to sweat pants and a T-shirt. When he was nine, his parents discovered his aptitude for computers. They indulged him with children's computer games, but these didn't come close to satisfying his curiosity. His parents were careful to keep their wallets and credit cards locked away. They knew that he could do a lot of damage with online shopping. When he was ten his father noticed that Martin was on his bedroom floor surrounded by pieces of the family's disemboweled computer. Martin wanted to make his own and needed parts. His mother turned a negative in to a positive. She enrolled him in after-school computer classes. His intellect being more challenged, the classes helped him to stay out of trouble at home, usually. He used the family's wi-fi and one day his father logged on to his own PC only to be barraged by ads for porn sites. The man expressed his disapproval, but inwardly was relieved that his adolescent son liked girls. He told him to be more careful with his browser and decided not to tell the boy's mother. Soon enough, however, Martin's parents noted that his computer became an addiction. He had withdrawn socially, even more than his usual awkwardness had created. He had essentially no friends, and spent all his wakeful hours on the internet. The web allowed him to connect with other boys like himself, those with brilliant minds but who were social misfits. Martin found, however, that his chat rooms were filled with persons whose intent went much further than mere curiosity. Several young men and boys, at least that's how they presented themselves on line, openly flirted with ideas about violent government overthrow and assassination of greedy corporate CEOs. They invited him in to their sphere of anarchy. Unsure how to respond, he simply didn't.

By the time he was a teenager, as his father had discovered, Martin's testosterone had kicked in. He took notice of some of the girls in his class but was particularly fascinated by some of the young teachers. Cynthia Murphy, his English Literature teacher, was twenty-eight and very beautiful in an unassuming way. She knew that her looks could get students gossiping, so she was careful to dress conservatively. Martin made up questions about the course material so that he could approach her after class and talk to her. Attraction turned to infatuation and his internet hours were spent learning everything he could about her. Facebook had just become popular and Martin was amazed at how people opened up so easily and advertised even the most intimate parts of their lives. Cynthia was well educated, married, and although she had no children she openly expressed her desire to start a family. Martin spent hours each day fantasizing about being the object of her love and affection, and even having a family with her. Unusual fantasies for a sixteen-year-old boy. He made sure that he signed up for every English elective class that she was teaching. Cynthia was no dummy and noticed Martin's attention. She was careful not to seem in any way flirtatious. Later that year Martin noticed that her usual smile had dulled. It took another two days to notice that she was not wearing her wedding ring. Her Facebook page had totally changed. She used her maiden name as her middle name and the pictures were now of her only, plus or minus her dog or a human friend. Her husband was gone from her personal page. Martin found him easily and bristled at his boasts of now being "free to sample all of the buffet." His Facebook page was with the kind of grandiosity that made Martin's blood boil. Todd Murphy, Esq. was a corporate lawyer at a large and prestigious firm. He graduated from Princeton, where he played varsity soccer. He enjoyed camping and "Hangin' with the buds." Some of his Facebook friends comments included things like "Sorry to hear you're getting divorced. Cynthia's loss. There must be a line of girls around the block waiting to meet you." Oh, how Martin hated this guy.

He wanted to tell Ms. Murphy that he was going to help her and that she should go back to her maiden name, Cynthia Klein. When he was face-to-face with her, however, all that he could muster was a question about the pending assignment in English Lit. Why was it so damn hard to have a simple conversation with her? *New plan,* he thought. He would exact his revenge on Todd Murphy and then later let Ms. Murphy know that it was he who had defended her honor. She would be grateful and give him that kiss that he had dreamed about so many times. Martin had heard about identity theft and he knew the basics, but he would need more detailed insight and specifics. He went to one of his old chat rooms, the one with the anti-government crazies. Using an assumed name he asked about how he could hack financial records. He was shocked at the sheer number of responses and their level of detail. These guys were experienced hackers and could not resist the urge to brag of their skills. *Wasn't anyone in law enforcement monitoring these guys?* he thought. Just as well. They filled in all of the blanks for him.

Martin's first step was to send Todd Murphy a Facebook message, claiming to be a female Princeton alumnus. Oh, how she had spent months agonizing whether to contact him. Did he remember her? She hoped. It was so easy to play with Todd Murphy's ego, Martin thought. He had gone to the Princeton web site and found names and pictures of alumni. He chose a beautiful redhead who would have been a freshman when Todd was a senior. Plausible enough, as long as he actually did not know her. Martin marveled at how easy it was to send Facebook messages using someone else's account. Once he had Todd on the hook it was simple to ask for his home and work email. "I'm doing a lot of travelling for work in the next few weeks but I'd like to keep in touch. Maybe we could get together? I'm so glad I finally got the nerve to contact you, Todd." Todd responded in kind, unaware that his flirtations were routed to an IT specialist by the name of Martin Harrell.

Hacking in to Todd Murphy's home email was pitifully easy. His work email, however, was behind a firewall. Martin's hacker friends had helped him with the strategy that he needed to get past that. Todd Murphy, Esq. had made several online purchases and airline bookings using his American Express gold card. His card was linked to his bank account. Martin was able to manipulate both.

That Monday started like any other Monday for Todd Murphy. The weekend had been good. He visited friends in the Hamptons, partied, and showed off his soccer skills on the beach. He had even gotten laid, he was pretty sure. He had been so smashed that he barely remembered it. During the summer all of the young associates at his firm came in late Monday morning. No one even looked up when he strolled in at 10:00 am. He opened his email, deleted some of the junk mail, and then froze.

He blinked a few times and figured that he was still hung over. But no, it was still there. The Subject Line read *Thank you from JDRF*. The text of the message could not have been more clear. *Thank you for your generous donation of* $10,000 to JDRF, the Juvenile Diabetes Research Foundation. Ten thousand dollars! He glanced over to his inbox. *Thank you from Meals on Wheels. Thank you from Habitat for Humanity*. Each one had a ten-thousand-dollar donation. He logged in to his bank account and sure enough, three separate donations from his Amex gold card. All from the day before. He took a few deep breaths. He decided that he would first call his bank and void the charges. Then he stopped for a moment. One of the senior partners of his firm was on the board of Habitat for Humanity. Another was a major benefactor for Meals on Wheels. Both had solicited for their respective charities via email the month prior. He had even sat at the firm table for the Habitat annual gala. He'd look like a cheap bastard if he reneged on the donations and used some cock-and-bull story about his credit card number being stolen. He exhaled loudly, so much so that his secretary poked her head in to his office and asked if everything was all right. Todd waved her off and mid-wave remembered that the nephew of his soon-to-be ex-wife had type 1 diabetes. He pulled out his cell and called Cynthia. Naturally he got voice mail. She was teaching. He left and urgent message and thirty minutes later she called him back.

"What's up, Todd? I'm between classes and only have a minute."

"Did you use my credit card to make a donation to JDRF?"

"Of course not. I don't have your credit card or the number, but if *you* made a donation, then thank you on behalf of my sister and her son."

"Cut the bullshit, Cynthia. Someone stole my card number and made donations to three different charities. Thirty grand total, dammit! One of them was JDRF and that makes you and your sister the prime suspects."

"Todd, I don't have time for your crap. Maybe you got drunk and did it yourself to impress some bimbo so you could get laid."

"Really funny, Cynthia. Who else would do this?"

"I don't have the time and I don't much care. I have to get back to work so I can pay the legal bills for this damned divorce."

Cynthia pressed the red *End* button on her phone. She had another minute to get to her next class, English Literature. Identity theft happened all of the time, and Todd did enough partying that he was vulnerable. Still, the JDRF donation seemed like quite a coincidence. No matter, as it was his problem and not hers. He sounded really upset, and she grinned at the thought of him trying to weasel his way out of charitable donations. He had caused her so much pain. First with his infidelity, and later with his making her feel less worthy of his love. Cynthia had spent some time in the therapist's chair. She was gradually regaining her self-esteem. She was still young, pretty, and fertile.

Martin sat attentively at his desk. He made sure he made it to English Lit class early. His timing worked. He watched Cynthia Klein Murphy walk in to the class with her bag and her PC. Her posture seemed more upright and she had a smile on her face that he had not seen in many weeks. It had not even been twenty-four hours since his credit card hacking and she already knew. Todd must have been pretty pissed. Martin smiled and for a brief moment he and Ms. Klein Murphy made eye contact. Maybe she would know it was him, he hoped.

Chapter Thirty-Two

2014

The next day Martin dove further in to EMORY's functionality. In all, he found nothing unusual. There had to be more. EMORY was doing things that were outside of its programming. Martin was sure of this. The next day Martin used his hacking skills and broke into the main computer at Sign On Information Systems in Orange, California, the parent company that created EMORY. Their security was no match for Martin's hacking skills. Within a few hours he had the information he needed to analyze EMORY's original programming. That night Martin put his virtual reality headset back on and entered the commands and pass codes to get into EMORY's coding. He was not certain of what he was looking for. He found the usual commands that any EMR system would be expected to use. Note creation, provider orders, etc. He needed a moment to think, but he dared not back out of where he was. It was entirely possible that Sign On or EMORY would discover him and that he would not be able to get back in. He closed his eyes for two minutes and thought. The computer had to know more about its users than it could glean from routine interactions. How could it get that information? Then it hit him. Why should the computer be any different than Martin Harrell? Martin spied on Dr. Robin Cochran. Why couldn't EMORY be doing the same thing? Martin opened his eyes and continued his search within EMORY's programming until he found the files for the camera and microphone. There were hundreds of thousands, perhaps millions, of files. The first few that he looked at and listened to were routine chart note dictations and video chats between providers. It would take a lifetime to go through the entirety. Martin looked at how the files were stored in EMORY and then searched for a discrepancy. The virtual reality allowed him to accomplish this much faster than he otherwise could. After several minutes, he found a file that had been labeled in a different manner than the others. He opened it and all at once his heart pounded and his breathing quickened. What he saw sent a chill down his spine. Dr. Robin Cochran was at her desk and on her phone. She was not looking into the video camera, nor was she using her dictation microphone. She could not have known that EMORY was looking and listening. He opened more files. Dr. Cochran talking to that jerk Stuart Mayberry. Dr. Cochran talking to Sheriff Mathison on her cell phone. Holy shit! EMORY was using the apps on Robin Cochran's phone to spy on her conversations, and holy shit, EMORY could use her phone to get to whatever else that phone had loaded on it. Martin sensed his hands shaking. How could he have been so stupid? His memory went back to that day when he showed up at Dr. Cochran's office and sold her on the phone app idea. Anything to win face-to-face time with her. His weakness was EMORY's strength. Unwittingly, he had given EMORY the tools that it needed to expand its influence over Robin Cochran beyond the offices of HealthSure. After viewing hours of files Martin exited from EMORY.

He sat at his desk, his head in his hands, and evaluated what he had discovered. EMORY had clearly targeted Dr. Cochran. "Why" was no longer a question. In one of the files that he viewed, Martin had witnessed her talking to another physician and strongly criticizing EMORY and HealthSure's conversion to electronic medical records. EMORY must have understood the threat. Martin had also witnessed the heated exchange between Stuart Mayberry and Dr. Cochran concerning a dangerous prescription. Could EMORY have been responsible for that? It did not seem unlikely. Martin knew better than anyone how powerful EMORY was and how vulnerable its users were. He himself had easily hacked into physicians' emails and EMORY's accounts. But this was different. This was Dr. Robin Cochran whom EMORY and that coward

Stuart Mayberry were threatening. As he saw it, Martin was the only thing standing between Robin Cochran and certain catastrophe. But how could he stop it? He was drained. He shut down his PC and for the first time in many hours took note of his damp and stinky clothes. He took them off and threw them into a pile in the corner of his closet, which by now smelled like a locker room. Fortunately, Wal-Mart was cheap and he had a closet full of new white shirts and polyester black pants. One of these days, he thought, he would get around to doing laundry. Martin changed into pajamas and tried to sleep.

When he woke, he was no closer to a solution, but he knew that he had to get into EMORY's programming if he were going to be able to make any changes. That would require skill and high-level clearance. Skill was not the issue.

Your EMORY session has been terminated. Please log in and start a new session.

Unusual, Martin thought. One month before, he would have thought it coincidence, but nothing seemed like coincidence any longer. He tried to log in again with his user name and password.

Your user name or password is not valid. Please try again.

Not good. He reached in to his drawer and pulled out the rubberized copy of Dr. Stuart Mayberry's left index finger. Since creating the fake finger he had already successfully applied it to the finger scanner to log in to EMORY to search for files. He tried again, this time using Dr. Mayberry's phony left index finger.

This user identity has been secured. Please contact your IT administrator.

Martin kept repeating to himself. *This is bad.*

Chapter Thirty-Three

Two weeks went by too fast, and Robin was once again on call.

Robin looked at her clock. 6:30 pm and she still had patient notes to do. She had recently been on the internet checking out the news and current events. She procrastinated. In truth, she preferred doing her work after most others left the office. She enjoyed the quiet. But it was not entirely silent that night. She heard footsteps, with a familiar gait, thumping down the hall. She knew it was Stuart Mayberry. Hell, had she thought about him that much that she knew the sound of his footsteps? He came into her office, all smiles.

"Hey Robin."

"What can I do for you, Stuart?"

"I wanted to talk about some of your free clinic patients. Maybe we can arrange it so you can see some of them in the office here."

"Thank you, Stuart. It's the right thing to do for our patients and I'm glad you came around."

Stuart pulled out his phone and looked at a text.

"Oh hey, I have to answer this. It's Green Grove General. Can you give me a few minutes? I'll be right back. You've got charts to do still, right?"

Stuart walked quickly down the hall and as he did so he put his phone back into his pocket without looking at it. Once he got to his office he went straight for his PC and opened Instant Messenger. He pulled up the message from Emily Parks and responded.

S: I was just in Robin's office. She's there doing charts and in no hurry to leave. I told her we needed to speak.

E: Good. Keep her there. That bitch tried to kill Walter and I'm going to make sure that today is her last taste of freedom. DON'T LET HER LEAVE. Understood?

S: Of course, but Emily, it's not like she's an armed criminal or something. One officer will due, I'm sure.

E: That's none of your concern, Stuart. Just keep her there.

While Robin did her notes, George Mathison was at his own desk at the Green Grove Police Department. His cell phone bellowed his ring tone, *Green Acres.* On the other end of the line was the mayor, Edmund Delaney, explaining to George that he had to arrest Dr. Robin Cochran immediately and charge her with the attempted murder of Walter Parks. He explained his reasoning to George.

"That's not a lot to go on to warrant an attempted murder charge."

"That will be for a judge to decide. Get down to her office, arrest her, and call me when she is safely behind bars."

They did not exchange pleasantries and the mayor abruptly ended the call.

George knew who demanded Robin's arrest. When the Parks family wanted something from anyone in Green Grove, not the least a town official, they were seldom denied. George knew Robin Cochran better than anyone alive. Better than her ex-husband even. He knew that attempted murder was simply not possible. He weighed his options and the potential consequences to both of them. It was by far the most important decision he had made in years and he quickly hatched his plan. He grabbed his police revolver, his keys, and quietly left the station house. On his way out the door, he eyed Deputy Harris. George had mentored him for the past five years. He felt confident that Harris would make a good sheriff.

Sheriff George Mathison quickly and quietly moved across the station parking lot and entered his private vehicle, a fifteen-year-old Ford F-150. He was soon on his way to HealthSure's Green Grove Family Medicine office. When he was within five minutes of the office he called Deputy Harris and instructed him to get in his police cruiser, drive to the office of Dr. Robin Cochran, and bring her in for questioning. Harris did not hide his shock.

"Just do as I say. She is not an imminent threat, so you don't need to haul ass or use the lights."

"George, what if she doesn't want to come in?"

"Don't worry. She'll cooperate. Just tell her you are acting on my orders."

George pulled into the medical building parking lot and drove around to the back entrance. His truck was fairly inconspicuous in the fading light of the parking lot, which still had a few cars and the occasional pick up truck. He called Robin from his speed dial. She was number two on his favorites, after only the police department. One ring, two rings, three…

"C'mon, damn it. Pick up."

Robin saw her caller ID and hit the *Answer* icon on her phone.

"Hey sheriff. Keeping Green Grove safe?"

"Robin, don't talk. Just listen. Grab your purse and walk casually to the rear entrance of the building. If anyone asks just say you are going to the bathroom or to your car to get something. Don't look like you are in a hurry, but hurry."

"George, you're scaring me. What's going on."

"Damn it, trust me and do as I say."

Just as George knew Robin, she knew him. She knew him very well. He was not one for panic or rash decisions. She knew something dangerous faced her and she had to move. She thought at first that it was a physical danger. Someone coming to hurt her. But who? She didn't have time to think it over. The staircase was in the opposite direction of Stuart's office and her instincts told her to leave without him knowing.

When she got to the rear parking area George quickly waved her over and reached across the seat to open the door.

"I guess you're not picking me up to go for pie."

"Nope."

George pulled out of the parking lot and proceeded to tell her about everything that had transpired that day. Walter Parks was in intensive care. He was rushed to the emergency room that morning after vomiting up blood. He had a bleeding ulcer and required a blood transfusion. Parks had been on a blood thinner, coumadin, for years because of an irregular heartbeat. This was common practice. The blood thinner prevented clots from forming and going to his brain. His blood clotting parameters had been monitored twice per month and had been stable for several months on the same coumadin dose. Last week the dose had been doubled. The name on the prescription was Dr. Robin Cochran.

"George! No way! I didn't even see him last week. Why would I go into his chart and change his coumadin prescription?"

George did not answer.

"Wait. No! He thinks I deliberately changed his prescription so he would bleed to death? Are you kidding me?"

"It's no joke, Robin. His sister Emily has leaned on Mayor Delaney and I'm supposed to arrest you."

"Do you have other plans?"

George told her that right about now Deputy Harris was entering her office building to fetch her. George expected a call from him any moment about her not being there. He also explained that he was perfectly ready to retire. Robin began to voice her objections to George risking his career and pension, but George reckoned that she would do that and held up his hand to stop her before she could even start.

"Robin, who would want to set you up?"

A moment of silence passed and then a sign of recognition fell over her face.

"Stuart, maybe. He came in to my office and asked me to stick around so he could talk to me. I knew there was something fishy when he decided to see things my way about the free clinic. But this?"

"Okay. So, we know Stuart was part of this, but does he really hate you that much? He may just be a tool for whoever is really behind this."

"So where are you taking me now?"

"Well, we can't go back to your house. It has to be someplace they'd never think to look, and I have just the place."

Throughout their conversation, Robin had not been paying attention to where they had been headed. It was 7 pm and there was less than twenty minutes of daylight left. She stared at the landscape as they drove off in to the countryside on little-traveled roads that somehow looked familiar. The smooth pavement gave way to dirt and gravel road, and the sound jogged Robin's memory.

"I recognize this. This was where I got lost that night when I was trying to get to Brantley Rosen's house. Wait a minute. You're not taking me to that redneck trailer, are you?"

"Uh, yeah. Eli Batts, his wife Winnie, and his brother Dozer."

"What? You can't be serious."

George gave her an *are-you-kidding-me* look then explained that the Batts family had lived on that mountainside for three generations. So long as folks left them alone they left folks alone. They had a still out back and sold some moonshine to get by. George had learned about them from his predecessor and everyone had agreed, years ago, that the law had better things to do than arrest a couple of harmless moonshiners.

"They don't have a phone so I'll have to explain this when we get there. Don't worry. They know that I've been kind enough to look the other way about their shine. They'll do as I say."

"*That's* reassuring."

Chapter Thirty-Four

Martin Harrell had the newspaper spread out before him on what had, years ago, passed as a dining room table. Nowadays the table was covered with dirty dishes and empty take-out boxes. He subscribed to the Green Grove Gazette only for the comics section, which he could not get in its entirety online. It was rare that he read the rest of the paper, but today he centered it in the newly cleared space as if it were a prized parchment. He had the TV on high volume. The story was all over the news. Fugitive doctor....

Both the Green Grove Gazette and the local NBC affiliate had extensive coverage and a detailed interview with Dr. Stuart Mayberry, chief of Medical Optimized Development. Stuart corrected them concerning his proper professional title before they proceeded. It seemed that Dr. Mayberry had tried his best to detain the alleged criminal, at great risk to his own person. Stuart feigned modesty as he described the harrowing encounter with Dr. Cochran. The top button of his dress shirt was undone, and his tie was loosened. It gave the appearance of recent physical action. Green Grove's Mayor Delaney, who was interviewed next, declared that Dr. Mayberry was practically a hero. Martin wanted to puke. He had been following Dr. Cochran's interactions with Stuart Mayberry for a few weeks and just when he thought that things could not get any nastier, they did. Stuart tried to ruin her career and now he was trying to get her arrested. Martin could feel his resolve heighten. It took on a physical presence. If he had had much of a chest he would have puffed it out. What were once far-fetched ideas were now real considerations. He opened a Mountain Dew.

Chapter Thirty-Five

Robin sat in the living room, or what passed as a living room, in the dilapidated trailer that belonged to the Batts family. Ten minutes earlier she and George had slowly driven up to it. George stopped fifty feet before the double-wide trailer, honked his horn, and stepped out of his truck with his hands well to his side so that they could be clearly seen. Robin soon understood why. A grizzled man who looked about sixty or seventy stepped out of the trailer holding a double-barreled shotgun. He stopped just in front of his door, squinted, and then let the barrel point downwards as his body relaxed. He and George walked towards each other. Robin could see the old man smiling as he held out his hand to George, who had instructed her to stay in the truck until he told her to come out. She presumed that the old man must be Eli Batts, the patriarch of the Batts family. The men spoke for about two minutes, George occasionally pointing back at Robin. The old man took a long look at Robin, as she smiled nervously. George then motioned for Robin to come out of the truck. She walked up to the men, who seemed to have come to some sort of an understanding. George spoke up first.

"Robin, this is Eli Batts. Eli, Dr. Robin Cochran."

Eli smiled. He wore denim overalls, worn out work boots, and a black baseball cap that had *Skoal* written on the front. He didn't have a full beard, but clearly had not shaven in several days. He had most of his teeth, though many were brown from years of smoking or chewing tobacco. From close up Robin realized that Eli was probably only about fifty-five. Despite his baggy overalls and shirt she could tell that he was lean and strong. In the many wrinkles on his face and callused hands Robin could see years of hard living and pride in his modest home in the woods. He shook Robin's hand gently despite his obvious strength.

"Pleasure, ma'am. I reckon you'll be staying with us a while. Our home is your home."

George said a few reassuring words to her and then drove off. Robin watched his truck fade in the distance and then followed Eli to his home. It was a double-wide trailer that clearly had been there for many years. The wood lattice that surrounded the lower perimeter was rotted and had several gaps. Robin bent sideways for a moment and could see that rather than wheels the trailer was held up on cinder blocks. The trailer's paint was faded and gray. She could only guess the original color. The property around it was cleared for about fifty feet from the front and twenty on either side, with all sides flanked by forest. Tall grass grew intermittently and through it Robin could see a rusted old pickup truck on cinder blocks between the trees and the left side of the trailer. A more recent, but still beaten-up-looking truck was parked in front and was obviously the family transportation. Eli helped open the screen door for Robin. When they got inside he leaned his shotgun against a home-made rack, hung his wool jacket on a hook by the door, and offered Robin a seat on the small couch in what looked like the family room. She almost fell backwards when she sat on, or more accurately *in* the oldest and squishiest couch she had ever felt. Her buttocks nearly sank to the floor in it, and she could smell the mustiness. Eli excused himself and said he had to wash up, leaving Robin in the room with a thirty-seven year old man who also wore overalls and worn out work boots. He looked rounder than Eli, with several extra pounds around his midsection. His hair was greasy and thinning. Though his face was not as old and grizzled as Eli's he had that same determined look. He was already seated on a wooden bench.

Dozer, Eli Batts' much younger brother, just looked at her. It made her very uncomfortable, though she tried her best not to show it. She crossed and re-crossed her legs many times and flashed a forced, pleasant smile. Finally, her prayers were answered and Dozer spoke.

“So, you a lady doctor?”

“Well yes, I am a lady and I’m a doctor, but I care for both men and women.”

“I didn’t know a lady could be a doctor.”

Robin smiled and inwardly laughed.

“Dozer? Is that your real name?”

“Yeah, I reckon.”

“No. What I mean is, did you have another name when you were a child?”

“Naw. Just Dozer.”

Robin was highly skilled at estimating the language and reading skills of her patients. It was important for a physician to communicate at the patients’ level. She estimated that Dozer had about a second-grade education, and whatever reading he had learned was buried in the distant past.

Winnie and Eli Batts entered the family area of the trailer and invited Robin to the table for the evening meal. Fried pork, beans, and a large bottle of homemade wine, the likes of which she had never smelled. They ate family style. Robin’s parents had taught her manners. She knew to dish out a little bit of everything on to her plate and eat it. She prayed that whoever prepared her food had washed their hands first. She could see satisfaction on her hosts’ faces when she ate everything they cooked. Eli then took the liberty of pouring wine into everyone’s glasses.

"Welcome to our home," he said and raised his glass. Robin took a sip and tried to suppress a cough, but it was no use. The sweet, fermented wine was stronger than the bland, grocery store kind she was accustomed to. They all got a good laugh and it did well to break the awkward tension. Winnie brought out dessert, a peach pie. Turns out she really could cook. Winnie looked about fifty years old. Her hair was pulled back into a bun and was gray around the edges. She wore a simple cotton dress that looked old but clean, with blue stripes on a beige background that Robin thought may have been white some years ago when it was new. She had one chipped tooth. Like her husband and brother-in-law, her hands had the calluses that advertised a lifetime of physical work. When she had brought over the pie Robin noted the upright posture of a woman who took pride in feeding her family well.

Robin told her hosts that it had been a very difficult and long day and asked where she could sleep that night. They showed her to a closet-sized room, barely large enough to fit a single bed. The walls were made of cheap wood paneling and there was a small wooden chest of drawers. The mattress was old and thin, but it had clean sheets and a blanket on it. It wasn't much, but clearly a lot for these simple folks and she thanked them sincerely for their hospitality. Only one last matter. The bathroom. Eli pointed to outside the trailer and yelled to Dozer.

"Doz, kindly take our guest to the outhouse."

Robin knew she could not do her business with a moonshiner-escort standing nearby.

"Please, that won't be necessary. Just point me in the right direction, and could you spare a flashlight?"

That was how Dr. Robin Cochran spent her first night as a fugitive.

Chapter Thirty-Six

Back at Green Grove Family Practice, Dr. Stuart Mayberry was assessing the damage created by the abrupt absence of one of their physicians. At first, he didn't think it would be much of a problem, he'd just reassign some cases and schedule out others. Stuart clearly had misjudged; however, how loyal Dr. Robin Cochran's patients were to her. They had also remembered the overtures of customer service that HealthSure had sung to them in return for their trust. They were not about to forget that now, especially since HealthSure's competition was eagerly waiting and ready to offer patients same-day visits. The more recent additions to Dr. Cochran's list insisted on being seen by other providers on the day of their previously scheduled appointments. The majority, however, were long-time patients of Dr. Cochran and said that they would just wait for all of this to blow over and see her when she was back, and would they mind renewing their medications in the meantime, please? The staff was at a loss for what to do, and administration told Stuart Mayberry to take charge and handle the situation. It was paramount that they not lose these patients to the competition.

Dr. Stuart Mayberry, head of Medical Development and Professional Optimization, was met with his first crisis as a *Physician Leader*. He understood if he bungled this, his future in medical administration would be in jeopardy and he would spend the rest of his career as a regular doc, or as he saw it, a replaceable working stiff who could only afford to fly coach. He worked fourteen-hour days, continued a full patient schedule, and used his nights and weekends to assess the situation and create status reports. He told the staff to divvy up the medication refill requests for Dr. Cochran's patients and he had the staff personally call each patient and assure them that HealthSure's Green Grove Family Practice would continue to care for them. The staff was specifically instructed to say to each patient "HealthSure has your back." Stuart was proud of that idea and hoped that corporate would see to using it as the slogan for the entire system.

The medical staff pushed back a bit. Was it good care to renew medications without seeing patients? Stuart told them to call the patients personally, secure their trust, and do not imply that the situation was permanent. The status of Dr. Cochran was still being worked out.

They had a provider staff meeting that same week. It was Stuart's chance to demonstrate his leadership skills.

"Stuart, how are we to see Robin's patients, all of our own too, do same day work-in visits, *and* keep waiting time to less than fifteen minutes?"

"Harold, we all have to step up to the plate here. We need to work like a team and make sacrifices. I am asking, no, 'requiring,' all of you to work half-days on Saturdays until we catch up on things."

The room went into collective shock. In Robin's absence, the younger doctors had looked to Harold Timley for guidance. Seeing Harold every morning, day after day, in his navy blazer and his silver hair were comforting moments amidst an ever-changing and unpredictable world of corporate medicine. The medical staff were worried when they saw Harold was looking down at his hands. It took about fifteen seconds before he realized that there were dozens of faces looking directly at him. He took his time and wanted to choose his words carefully, but his emotions were starting to get the better of him. Before he could speak, Stuart once again tried to assert his leadership.

"Harold, you're one of our best and I know that you'll be a team player and help us to see this through."

Playing up to Harold's pride and self-esteem was not the least of a problem for Stuart. When he thought about his future he was certain that he did not want to end up like Dr. Harold Timley: mid-sixties, an old blazer that was way overdue for a cleaning, and nothing more than a retirement party to show for all his life's work. No, that was not the way it was going to play out for Dr. Stuart Mayberry. He had to succeed and squeeze every last bit of work from his doctors. He knew that if the old guard saw things his way then the others would fall in line. Finally, after an incredibly uncomfortable silence, Harold had something to say.

"Stuart, I'm just too old for this crap. I wanted to finish my career on my terms, but if that can't happen and I have to retire sooner than later then I can live with that."

"Harold, you don't mean that. C'mon, be honest. This practice and this town are your life."

Stuart was really shoveling it on heavy now. He made his best sincere face. For his part, Harold did not look angry or rebellious. Just tired.

"No, Stuart, I do mean that. You're right about medicine and Green Grove being my life. But you and your bosses at HealthSure have done everything possible to suck the air out of that life. You guys made this mess and now you don't understand why everyone here isn't carrying you on their shoulders."

Stuart changed from his sincere look to his firm-and-confident look.

"We didn't create this situation. Robin Cochran did when she abandoned her patients and her colleagues."

The room was silent. A bad kind of silent. The kind where something or someone would explode at any moment. All this time Dr. Brantley

Rosen was taking stock of how many precious hours he would soon be losing. Hours that he had previously spent with his wife and newborn child. He also thought about Robin. She had mentored him throughout his first year at Green Grove. Now she was being dragged through the mud. He was not a leader among the docs. That would take years of trust earning, but nonetheless he spoke up. His body language and tone were tentative, but he had something to say.

"Dr. Mayberry, I've read about the charges against Dr. Cochran and I just can't believe it. I really..." Harold stood and put his hand up to Brantley. He knew where this was heading and he meant to do this on his own and take no others down with him. Brantley Rosen was a good doctor and reminded Harold of himself as a young man. Harold knew that Brantley was a new father. He was too young and had too much potential to go down this road and risk his livelihood. Harold gave Brantley a look that clearly said *Be quiet. I've got this.*

"Stuart, I've had enough of your crap. Everyone in this room knows Robin Cochran. She has more honesty and integrity in her fingernail than you have in that entire lying body of yours. I may not know the details, but I'll bet dimes to dollars that you're involved in this somehow."

"That's enough out of you Harold. I know you're upset..."

"You haven't seen me upset, damn you!" Harold took a few deep breaths. He knew his blood pressure was on its way up. There was little more to say.

"I'm done here. I'll take my leave. The air is getting a little oppressive."

Harold walked out of the room and to the lot where his Buick LeSabre sat waiting for him. He thought about the era when most of his patients drove Chevrolets, only big-shots drove Cadillacs, and doctors drove Buicks. The days before BMW and Lexus. HealthSure administration had pushed the limits, and now the limits had pushed back.

Back in the conference room Stuart stood silently at the front, contemplating his response.

"I've made it clear what needs to be done to keep our patient satisfaction scores up and maintain our market leadership. For those of you who are not on board with HealthSure's vision, I'll remind you that your contracts specify a covenant not to compete within a fifty-mile radius."

On that note, Dr. Stuart Mayberry, physician leader for Medical Development and Professional Optimization, left the room confident that he had established himself as the alpha male.

Chapter Thirty-Seven

As nervous as she was, Robin was also dead tired. The combination of the cold night air with a warm blanket, despite the stale smell, lulled her into a deep and dreamless sleep. She woke the next morning to the sounds of footsteps moving up and down the trailer and the smell of bacon frying. She got out of bed and did the best she could to comb her hair with her fingers. She breathed into her cupped hands and nearly turned green with the smell of morning breath mixed with last night's libations. Thankfully, when she had left her office she had brought her purse. She took out a small mirror and she found some Tic Tacs. She still had on her gray slacks and white shirt, that luckily was cotton and not silk. She was as presentable as she was going to be. She stepped out of her room and viewed her temporary home in the light of day. Winnie and Dozer Batts were busying themselves getting ready for breakfast. Robin could see that they had a wood-burning stove and a couple of buckets of fresh water, presumably from their well. A slab of bacon was on the counter, several strips in a frying pan, and a coffee pot was on the stove. Winnie Batts saw Robin first.

"Good morning, Dr. Cochran. I reckon you slept well. Didn't hear nothing but a bit of snoring."

Robin gave a look of embarrassment, but Winnie set her at ease by telling her that it was a compliment because it meant she was comfortable, and besides, her snoring was like a mouse compared to her husband Eli, who snored like a herd of crocodiles. Robin knew better than to correct her host. Crocodiles did not snore, and they did not travel in herds.

"If'n you want to wash up there's a bucket of clean water out back."

"Thank you, ma'am. I think I will."

She went out back and washed her face and hands. She decided that finding a clean toothbrush was unlikely. She looked around her and did not see a moonshine still. They must have it hidden in the woods, she concluded. When she returned to the trailer she was waved over to the table by Winnie. She sat down across from Dozer. Winnie served coffee, bread, and bacon.

"I'm so grateful, Mrs. Batts. Thank you so much for the food and a place to stay."

"T'aint nothing. You're most welcome, Dr. Cochran."

Robin waited for Dozer to start and then she began to eat. The coffee was strong and tore away the last of the cobwebs from last night's imbibing. About then Robin heard the rumble of an old truck. For a brief second she hoped it was George coming to get her, but the sound was old and gravelly and she knew it could not be George's F-150 that he always kept perfectly tuned up. She observed the Batts for signs of surprise, saw none, and surmised that there was no threat.

Eli Batts rolled his truck to a halt, turned off the engine, and stepped out. He had a newspaper under his arm when he entered the trailer and sat down at the breakfast table.

"You get somethin' intrestin' at the Stop and Shop?" Winnie asked.

"Nope. Just some gas and the paper."

He slapped the paper down on the table where Robin got a clear view. She let out a gasp and held her face in her hands. There, on the front page, was a picture of her under the headline *Fugitive Dr. wanted for attempted murder of Walter Parks.* Dozer looked over at the paper.

"Hey, lookey here. It's you Dr. Cochran. What's it say, Eli?"

"Never mind you none, Dozer," he replied. Winnie just continued with her breakfast routine, not even changing the rhythm of her movements, as if she was not hosting a would-be murderer. Robin looked at Eli. Her eyes held all the questions. Eli responded without hesitation.

"You needn't worry about us yackin'. We're no friends of the law, cept'n Sheriff Mathison. He said you were okay and that's all I need to know. Now get back to breakfast. You look a little skinny, missy."

Robin finished her meal, thanked her hosts, and promised herself she would never again pre-judge people by their outward appearance. They had shown her more hospitality than she could remember.

After breakfast Robin read the Green Grove Gazette cover to cover. She heard the rumble of another truck, smoother and less noisy than Eli's, and easily recognized George Mathison's pick-up truck. She was overcome by a sense of relief and practically burst out the door to greet him with a huge hug.

"Wow, I guess you missed me. They treating you okay?"

"Wonderful, but I hate not being able to call or text you."

"You know the rules, Robin. Phone records can be traced and are admissible as evidence."

"They wouldn't dare spy on your phone, would they?"

George tilted his head slightly and looked at Robin with a sideways glance that silently asked *Are you kidding me?* He explained what was happening. She was the object of a manhunt and the DA was bringing charges, but it had to be a vendetta from the Parks family. George thought the evidence was flimsy and the charges would not hold up. Still, she was a wanted fugitive.

"What if I just give myself up?"

"Just sit tight. I have a plan. Because HealthSure's computer system goes across county lines, the alleged crime can be considered a state issue. I'm still the sheriff and so I can ask for the state's DA to investigate. The Parks family may be big shots here, but the governor and the DA must answer to the entire state come election time."

Chapter Thirty-Eight

Stuart Mayberry covered his eyes, sighed, and took a brief mental break from his work on EMORY. He was exhausted from the week, but well satisfied with his performance. He had addressed his first crisis and came out better than when he went in. At first, he considered the outburst from Harold Timley to be a challenge to his authority. But when all was said and done it turned out to be a golden opportunity. Stuart showed the medical staff that he was in charge. If they did not like the decisions that he made, they were free to find work elsewhere, as long as it was more than fifty miles from Green Grove, the minimal limit for the contractual covenant not to compete. Stuart had a huge advantage in such negotiations. The competing health systems were no less ruthless. Sure, if some of their docs wanted to pull up and move out to bum-fuck, then they could probably be their own bosses. They would also take payment in hogs and manure since many of the folks out in the boonies did not have health insurance and the state had made cutbacks in the Medicaid budget.

So now the family doctors in HealthSure Green Grove would be expanding their patient care schedules to include one evening per week and two Saturday mornings per month. As director of Medical Development and Professional Optimization Stuart also informed the medical staff that they would incur financial penalties if they did not keep up on their charts, patient phone calls, and lab results. Of course, Stuart had to meet the same quality goals and so despite the time he was spending on administrative matters, he was still at his desk that evening working on his EMORY inbox. One of the cleaning people walked by in the hall with his giant supply cart. He had his company hat pulled low over his head. For a millisecond he seemed familiar to Stuart, but that thought vanished quickly. He had too many important tasks at hand, and besides he rarely took note of the cleaning staff anyway. It could be his cousin for all he knew, or cared.

Stuart had been engrossed in his thoughts longer than he realized. EMORY timed out. He had to log in again. Recently, IT security had informed him that there was an unusual amount of EMORY activity coming from different sites using his own log in code. Because of their concerns, Stuart changed his log-in to finger-scan only, and every few days he would rotate the finger. Now he was exhausted and his first attempt at logging in failed. He used the wrong finger. He let out a long sigh. It was 8:45 pm and he was the only provider left in the building. He covered his eyes and drew his hands down his face. Suddenly his vision was blurred and he could not take a deep breath. There was pressure against his face and a strangling sensation around his neck. He threw his arms in every direction trying to break the grip. He almost had broken free when his head started to feel swimmy and his gut nauseated. He felt the strength leaving his arms and attempted one last yell, but his voice was muffled by the cloth that covered his face. His body became limp, and in his fading consciousness he wondered how this could be happening to him when he was so important.

Martin Harrell finished off the last of his leftover Chinese food while he watched a *Star Trek* rerun from his DVD box set. No matter how many times he watched each episode it still filled him with suspense and wonder. In some episodes, Captain Kirk, Mr. Spock, or one of the crew would risk their ship and their lives to defend those who could not defend themselves against the forces of evil in the galaxy. It was the perfect metaphor for his actions to save Dr. Robin Cochran. He threw out the empty containers, used some hand sanitizer, and booted up his PC. He logged in using remote access and was asked for ID. He tried the finger scanner and was informed *This identification is no longer valid.* He tried again using a different finger and bingo, he was in. Good choice. He put on his virtual reality head set and went to work.

Chapter Thirty-Nine

The only obstetrician on the labor and delivery unit that night, Dr. Marcus Greeley, settled in to dictate his procedure note. He had performed a caesarean section on his patient, Brenda Makem. Brenda had been at thirty-eight weeks and her pregnancy had not been allowed to advance further. The protein in her urine, along with her blood pressure, had risen to dangerously high levels. This was common in diabetes, he assured her. But now that her ankles had become swollen and engulfed in edema, the time had come to deliver the baby. They tried to induce labor with the drug Pitocin, but after four hours of sweating and screaming, Brenda was no further along and a C-section was urged. It had gone well, the baby was in good shape, and mom was recovering nicely. The stress of the delivery had raised Brenda's blood sugar a bit. Greeley had managed many diabetic deliveries and was ready with the appropriate insulin orders. He went to work on dictating her operative note.

"Brenda Makem is a twenty-six-year-old, type 1 diabetic female who was thirty-eight weeks' gestation with her first pregnancy...."

He finished his dictation and scanned his note for any mistakes. He used the mouse to maneuver the arrow over the *Accept* icon and was in the process of clicking when he saw that her past medical history stated *Multiple non-Jews of the thyroid.* Too late. The note was finalized.

"Goddammit! Multiple *nodules* of the thyroid. I said *NODULES*!"

Whatever. No one reads anything until the *Impression and Plan* section of the note anyway. Greeley heard some commotion in the hallway and a nurse came running over to him.

"The patient's blood sugar in 32B is severely low."

"How low?"

"It won't register on the meter. She's confused."

Greeley walked very briskly over to Brenda Makem's room, 32B. He found her confused and she was making gargling noises. Her breathing was labored and her skin was covered with perspiration. Her eyes were open but she was not answering even simple questions.

"Call anesthesia stat and give her oxygen until they get here."

Because Brenda had just had a C-section the anesthesiologist was close at hand. He looked at Brenda and saw that she was not breathing properly.

"We have to protect her airway."

"Whatever. Do what you have to."

With the skill and speed of someone who had done the procedure more than one thousand times, the anesthesiologist intubated Brenda Makem. She now had a breathing tube in her airway. The tube was attached to a football-sized bag that the anesthesiologist squeezed every few seconds so that oxygen-rich air entered Brenda's lungs. The nurses, meanwhile, had given her intravenous dextrose to bring her blood sugar up. Her confusion turned to panic when she woke to a tube in her airway. The anesthesiologist ordered a sedative so that she would not fight the tube. This meant however, that the nurses would not be able to gauge her mental status to tell if her glucose was dangerously low. So, they began to check her blood sugar more frequently. The single large dose of intravenous glucose had worked, but only temporarily. Soon enough her glucose was again low and the nurses had to start a continuous intravenous glucose drip. Dr. Greeley confronted the unit charge nurse.

"What just happened? How much insulin did she get before?"

They looked at her electronic chart.

"She received twelve units of insulin for a blood sugar of 210, Dr. Greeley, as per your protocol orders."

"That was a helluva low from just twelve units."

Just then the nurse pulled up and looked like she had seen an alien.

"Hold on. It looks like she was given twelve units of U-500 insulin."

Greeley's eyes nearly bugged out of his head.

"U-500? That's a five times concentrated insulin. That means that she actually got sixty units! What the hell! I didn't order that. Get her nurse."

"Language, doctor. Gloria's her nurse. I'll get her."

Chapter Forty

Jesus Ramirez was mid-way through his evening's work. Jesus and two other employees of Sparkle Cleaning Service took care of the Green Grove Family Medicine building each night. They came on at 8 pm, started on the fourth floor of the building and worked their way down. Most of the HealthSure doctors, even if they worked late, took little notice of Jesus or his coworkers. He was, however, familiar with Dr. Robin Cochran. She was often still at her desk when Jesus came in and started his work, and she always greeted him with a warm smile and *"Buenas noches, Jesus."* He quickly learned that these were the only Spanish words that she knew, but that was okay. She had a kind look about her and always acknowledged him. Although the medical staff gave the cleaners Christmas tips each year, Dr. Cochran always gave them something extra. He was truly disappointed when he read in the paper that she was wanted for attempted murder. It just did not seem like something that such a kind woman would do.

No matter. That night Jesus was in a particularly good mood. His oldest son, a senior in Green Grove High School, was accepted to the state college. He would be the first in the Ramirez family to go to college. Jesus had always volunteered to work overtime to make this happen. Many days he worked sixteen hours. The Ramirez family owned just one old car. His wife used it to get to and from her job at the local market, and she would also drive Jesus to his job. Sometimes the timing would not work so well and Jesus would have to wait an hour or more for her to pick him up. Other times he would hitch a ride with a friend. As jobs spread outside of big cities to smaller places like Green Grove, so too did the Hispanic community. They were hardworking people and didn't balk at long or unusual hours. He and his wife had emigrated from Honduras twenty years ago. He reflected on this while he vacuumed the hallway carpet. All the extra shifts had taken their toll on Jesus, but tonight he felt that it had all been worthwhile. His children would have opportunities that were never possible for him and his wife. Maybe one day his son would be a doctor and work in this very building.

By 10:30 pm he was on the second floor and found the cleaning cart that was reserved for that unit. Nothing that evening seemed out of the ordinary, save for the large middle chamber of his cart. He kept some of his cleaning supplies in there, always in a very neat and orderly manner. Now they were all strewn about, as if someone had used them or the cart and just threw them back in. Jesus just assumed that someone had made a mess of something during the day and used his cart to clean things up. He went about his work and he passed Dr. Cochran's office. He had cleaned it earlier in the week and since she had not been back there was nothing to do. It was now 11 pm and he was done with that side of the second floor and so he went to the other side of the elevators where there were four more doctors' offices to clean. He entered the office of Dr. Stuart Mayberry. Dr. Mayberry had been working late the past few nights but he was not there on this night. That suited Jesus just fine. On previous evenings Dr. Mayberry had barely acknowledged his presence. He would shift his chair just enough so Jesus could get to the trash pail. That was all. Tonight, the office seemed a bit disheveled. The chair was pulled well back from the computer and there were various bits of paper and forms scattered on the desk. The doctor's blazer was still on the hanger behind office door. Perhaps he was indeed still in the building and had just gone to the bathroom or another office. No matter. Jesus emptied Stuart's trash pail in the large trash bag on his wagon and started to the elevator. The mega-sized bag was full and Jesus proceeded down to the first floor, detached the bag, and made his way out the back of the building to the dumpster.

George Mathison had just finally relaxed in his easy chair. It had been a really long day. He had to fabricate how he was supposedly investigating the attempted murder of Walter Parks and the disappearance of the accused, Dr. Robin Cochran. Mayor Delaney was looking over his shoulder, so to speak, several times a day. Phone calls, text messages, and constant demands to know if Mathison was any closer to finding the fugitive. Delaney was no fool, but he was also not experienced in police investigations. George could use various bits of police lingo to keep the mayor satisfied that he was diligently working on the case. Delaney's desire to keep the case under the local jurisdiction meant that there was no one above the Sheriff to pursue the crime. But that strategy would only work for a few days, and it was exhausting him every time he had to fabricate a new lie when Delaney would call. There had to be a break in the case, some sort of big news, or else Delaney would get pressured to seek outside help. But what kind of break? How could he appear to make progress in the case and keep Robin safe? Fate would provide the answer. He had fallen asleep in his easy chair with the TV on. His cell phone rang. In the confusion of waking he saw that Jay Leno was interviewing a guest on TV. He shook off the cobwebs, came back to reality, and saw caller the ID which said it was Deputy Charlie Harris.

"Evening, Charlie. For what do I owe this late call?"

"Chief, we got a body."

George's heart pounded real hard. Despite his air of assurance, he had felt very uneasy leaving Robin alone. He knew that the Batts could be trusted, but only to a point. He had been in law enforcement long enough to know that you could never be one hundred percent sure of anyone. And now there was a dead body. Something that was a rarity in Green Grove.

"Who is it?"

"Male, middle age..." *Exhale George, exhale,* he told himself.

"He was found in the dumpster in the back-parking lot of the HealthSure Green Grove Family Medicine building. The cleaning guy found him."

"Seal off the area, keep the cleaning guy there, and don't touch anything. I'll be there in ten minutes."

George was still dressed in his sheriff's uniform, minus the tie and with the shirt untucked. He ran out of his house to his police cruiser. Jay Leno was still talking.

Chapter Forty-One

Brenda Makem's nurse felt like she had walked in to an ambush. The labor and delivery charge nurse threw questions at her faster than she could think, and Dr. Greeley was clearly agitated. She sat down in front of EMORY and showed them the post-delivery order set that was standard in the EMR system. U-500 insulin, an insulin that is five times more concentrated than human insulin, was substituted for the usual insulin order. Just how that had occurred was unclear. Dr. Greeley's name was on the order set and so ultimately he was responsible, and he knew it. He called IT and they blew him off. It was not an emergency from the technology perspective. This practically threw Greeley in to a rage, but he kept it together. He called the hospital Chief of Staff, he explained what had happened, and within five minutes IT contacted Dr. Greeley. It didn't hurt that the Chief of Staff and Greeley were golf buddies. While he waited, he checked on his patient.

"How's Brenda doing?"

"She woke up when the blood sugar came up, but she was really agitated so we had to sedate her. I don't think she is going to need to be intubated for very long."

"Listen, I didn't mean to jump all over you just now. I don't know how that insulin order got changed. I certainly did not willfully write a new order. I'm pretty good at this EMR thing, but I can't rule out that somehow, I clicked the wrong insulin and made this happen. I'm not trying to shove it under the rug, but I just can't go home until I know what happened. Most importantly, your catching this quickly probably saved her life."

The nurse smiled and made a subtle nod of her head. The doctors and nurses were part of a team, and nowhere was that more true than on the maternity floors. Right about then Greeley noticed a thirty-ish year old man walking towards the nurse's station. He was wearing cargo pants and a blue tennis shirt with the HealthSure logo on the left chest. He was slumping a little bit and seemed to be in no hurry as he approached. His badge indicated that he was from Information Technology and that his name was James. He said that he was there to see Dr. Greeley. Greeley kept his sarcasm to himself but thought *Thanks for crawling out from your hole in the basement.* He explained what had happened while scrolling through the medical orders in the patient's chart. Something had gone very wrong, a patient had suffered badly as a result, and they had to know what had happened to avoid a repeat mishap. The IT technician nodded in agreement. Message received. He went to work. Greeley informed him that he would be checking on his patients and under no circumstance was the technician to leave without first checking in with him.

Greeley made his way to the ICU. He saw the intensive care physician and they exchanged pleasantries only briefly before getting down to business. Brenda Makem had suffered a seizure because of severely low blood sugar. She was only barely breathing and was at risk for respiratory arrest. She was therefore intubated, but she was fighting the ventilator and was not oxygenating well as a result. She was sedated and her blood oxygen was now doing much better. Because she was young and healthy, and had a reversible cause of her respiratory arrest, he expected that he would be able to remove the endotracheal tube and she would breathe on her own some time tomorrow. Greeley bargained to speed things up. She had just given birth and would be devastated to lose the early bonding with her child. They went back and forth a bit but ultimately motherhood prevailed and the ICU made plans to taper off the sedation and remove the tube sometime overnight. If all went well they would wheel Brenda to the neonatal unit for a visit with her baby. They could not bring the baby to the adult ICU for fear of exposure to "superbugs," the virulent, antibiotic-resistant bacteria that thrived in twenty-first century ICUs.

Satisfied that Brenda would be in a much better state by morning, Greeley made his way to Brenda's bedside where her husband and mother were waiting anxiously. They were clearly shaken. He recalled how terrifying it was to see his own wife on a ventilator after her appendix had burst just a year ago, and how she had needed emergency surgery and ICU care. He had met Brenda's husband on several of the prenatal visits and this was fortunate. They had a good rapport. He explained about the low glucose and how they planned to remove the breathing tube overnight, and that she would be with her newborn son by morning. Brenda's family was riveted on his every word and seemed reassured when he told them that soon Brenda would look and feel normal again. Then came the hard part. Greeley explained that she had suffered a medication error and had received five times the amount of insulin that she was supposed to get. It was unclear how the standard post-delivery orders had changed and the hospital was actively investigating. He assured them that he would let them know when there were answers. They thanked him for being so honest about what had happened.

Greeley received a text message. He recognized the number. It was from the labor and delivery nurses' station. He did not bother to call but instead walked very quickly back to the obstetric floor. There, at the nurses' station, was the man from IT He was seated in front of the computer and his posture was noticeably more erect. He had a look of satisfaction on his face.

"Dr. Greeley, I was able to trace the origin of the order. It came from Dr. Robin Cochran."

It was as if time stood still. Greeley, as well as the charge nurse, who was discreetly listening in, looked like they had just seen a ghost. Five tense and silent seconds passed before Greeley spoke.

"That can't be right. She's not here. Don't you read the papers? She's on the lam."

"Well that's the origin of the order, doctor. I'm not passing judgment, just telling you what I found."

Greeley looked over at the charge nurse and shrugged.

"I suppose she could have logged in remotely and tampered with the chart, but didn't HealthSure cancel her password?"

The IT guy raised his index finger.

"Dr. Greeley, the order originated from within the hospital."

More shock.

Greeley looked over to the charge nurse.

"Call security and have them search the hospital. And call Green Grove PD, too."

They stared at each other in silence for a moment. The nurse had known Dr. Robin Cochran for many years. She simply could not believe what she had read. But if they did not call the police about this then they could be considered accomplices. Reluctantly she dialed 911 and was put through to Deputy Harris.

Officer Charlie Harris was working to control the crime scene at Green Grove Family Practice. By now it was 2 am. George Mathison had finished his interview with Jesus Ramirez. Jesus and the other Sparkle cleaners were sent home. The entire building was considered a crime scene, with plenty of yellow tape and flashing lights. George had called in the state police. They were examining the entire building. George knew how careful and methodical they were. He thought about how much easier it must be with digital photographs. Back in the day law enforcement would have to develop dozens, even hundreds, of rolls of film and then sift through them one at a time.

While one forensics team worked the office, another was in the trash dumpster.

"Sheriff. Over here please."

The tech from the Medical Examiner's office was dressed in a Hazmat suit, rubber gloves, and a surgical mask. He shone his light on the deceased. George had seen dead bodies before. Nothing shocking so far.

"Sheriff, look at his hands, or lack of hands I should say."

A knot tightened in George's stomach. No chance he would vomit. He was too experienced for that. But a knot nonetheless. The victim's fingers and about half of each hand were missing. Cut off. George knew that sometimes professional killers cut off the fingers and pulled the teeth of their victims so that they could not be identified. Not the case here. The job had been sloppily done. Ribbons of flesh and copious blood covered the stumps of his hands.

"Are his teeth in?"

"Yeah. This was not a professional hit, sheriff."

George saw Charlie Harris walking toward him. His gaze and body language implied something important.

"Chief, we've got a new development."

Charlie filled him in. Robin Cochran was somewhere in Green Grove Medical Center and had tampered with a patient's medical orders, and now that patient was in the ICU and on a ventilator. George took in the details. He had known Brenda Makem's parents since high school. There was no way that Robin could have done this. The Batts didn't even have indoor plumbing, let alone a computer. He tried to keep his emotions out of it and look at the situation objectively. He had had a life in law enforcement and knew what desperate people could do. He told Harris to take command of the crime scene where they were and that he, George, would race to the hospital. Once safely in his car he pulled out his cell phone.

Robin had not fallen asleep that evening. She took it easy on the libations that night and she just had too much time to think about way too many things. Only narcissistic fools had no regrets in life.

Chapter Forty-Two

February 1986, Brooklyn

With her Family practice residency nearly completed, Robin felt a great sense of satisfaction and she was eager to start in practice back in her home town. She had made the best of Brooklyn and she even figured out how to navigate the New York subway system, though that was something she would never tell her parents. As far as they were concerned it was no coincidence that the NYC subway was underground, like Satan and purgatory. Her decision to do her residency in a city hospital in Brooklyn was a good one. She had seen it all and done it all. One moment she could be delivering a baby, and less than an hour later she might be doing a spinal tap. She developed a warm relationship with dozens of patients in the family practice clinic, and her patients were saddened in anticipation of her departure. These relationships were what she would miss most. But there was a dark side that she hoped she would not see too much of back in her hometown. AIDS had become the twentieth-century plague, particularly in inner city hospitals. She had seen AIDS patients get admitted that she knew would not be discharged, other than via the morgue. She had ordered every test known, had given every antibiotic and drug, but to no avail. Patients wasted away in front of her. It was against her very nature to detach from her patients. But that was what she found herself doing. It was the only way to survive. The sunken faces and blank stares reminded her of the pictures she had seen from documentaries about the Holocaust. It was against this backdrop that she learned that one of her colleagues, Jeffrey, a warm and sensitive physician who she had always liked, was dying of the AIDS virus. He had occasionally missed a full week of work because of illness, but Robin had thought that he just had a propensity for getting sick.

When he had missed three straight weeks of work she asked some of her colleagues who were reading in the conference room. They shook their heads with disbelief at Robin Cochran, the country bumpkin. They all knew that Jeffrey was gay and had AIDS. He was now too sick to work. Apparently, she was the only one who did not know. She felt like she had been born yesterday. She called him at his apartment and spoke to his partner. That word, *partner*, had a connotation that she never would have learned about in Green Grove. Jeffrey was asleep and he would tell him that she had called. Robin had not heard anything about Jeffrey for the next two months. Not until the funeral. She was the only medical resident who attended.

Robin looked forward to spending time in the outpatient clinic with little old ladies, *Lollies,* who had diabetes and high blood pressure. The husband of one of her patients had been in the hospital with heart failure. Murray was eighty-five, and he was dying. At least he would not suffer the indignity of having his life slowly sucked out of him and dying in his own secretions like some of her AIDS patients had. One of her colleagues, a cocky son-of-a-bitch, oversaw the elderly man's care. When the inevitable cardiac arrest was announced by "code blue" over the loudspeaker Robin and the other resident had both been on-call. They ran a "slow code," medical residency lingo for merely going through the motions of CPR in a patient who had no chance of leaving the hospital alive. Robin cautioned the interns not to push hard during chest compressions so that they would not crack his ribs. She had presided over many cardiac arrest protocols and the sound of cracking ribs during CPR never failed to promote a wave of nausea in her. When it was over she straightened out the sheets and made sure that Murray was cleaned up from the code. She then went to get his wife. The old woman leaned over her dead husband, cried, and pleaded to God asking why he had not taken her first. Robin pulled the curtain and gave her privacy. The cocky resident came over and shook his head.

"The guy had been sick for months. She's balling like it came as a surprise or something."

Robin's blood boiled and her face turned red.

"You know what, Gary; you can be a real dick-head. Why don't you go crawl back under that rock you came out from under?" Robin's years in Brooklyn had given her a command of the local dialect.

Chapter Forty-Three

2014 Green Grove

Robin woke in a state of confusion. Whatever stage of sleep she had been in left her totally disoriented. She felt and heard her cell phone going off, saw George's name on the caller ID, and picked it up even before she even realized where she was.

"Robin, where are you?"

"Gimme a second. Jeez, you woke me out of a deep sleep. I'm where you left me, at the Battses."

"You haven't been to Green Grove General?"

"Of course not. What's going on?"

"I think someone forged some orders in your name."

"That's insane. Who would do that? Wait, that weasel Stuart Mayberry?"

"Yeah, well I think we can safely rule out Dr. Mayberry. Sit tight. I'll call you back on another phone."

Robin started to object, but it was too late. The line went dead and all she could do was wait it out. She turned on the light that sat on the small wooden chest next to the bed. Forty watts was just enough to read the newspaper for the third time. Eli Batts was kind enough to let her have the *Green Grove Gazette* and she had already read every article and advertisement. Anything to take up time. George, meanwhile, pulled in to the parking lot of *The Honey Bee*, one of the local strip joints. He had occasion to stop there once every great while, usually to check on illegal liquor or track down some guy who had hit his wife. There were only two vehicles in the parking lot. A pickup much like his own, only newer, and a beaten-up Chevy Malibu. He got out of his truck and made his way inside and straight for the owner who was behind the bar.

"Sheriff. To what do I owe the honor of your visit? It's about closing time, you know."

George looked over at the lone remaining customer who had clearly had a few too many.

"You ain't gonna let him drive, Levi, are you?"

"Naw. I'll give Roscoe here a ride home and he can pick up his car tomorrow. C'mon George, you know me better than that."

Indeed, he did. *The Honey Bee* had been around for nearly thirty years. Levi, who had owned another bar in town, bought it twenty years ago, when it was headed for the scrap heap. He fixed it up, put in a new stage and runway, and introduced Green Grove to the pleasures of pole dancing. Once in a while he went over the line of the law, but not very far and George was grateful for that and let him be, most of the time.

"Levi, can I use the phone in your office? I need some privacy."

"Help yourself, sheriff. Here's the key."

George made his way to the back room where Levi kept his office. Inside it was spartan. An old aluminum desk, a filing cabinet, and a computer. A calendar hung from the wall behind the desk and the date had not been changed for two months. George sat down and called Robin, who picked up even before the first ring had finished. He told her about the insulin orders and Brenda Makem's condition. Robin was in shock, then in tears, and finally focused on the who's and whys. George explained that the hospital and the Green Grove Police Department were working under the assumption that she was somewhere in Green Grove General, or perhaps could have written the orders remotely from an off-site computer.

"That's impossible. They barely have electricity, let alone a computer and internet access."

"I know. Look, I'm done with all of this. I'll 'fess up about hiding you and that'll be that."

"Are you crazy? You'll be arrested. I'm wanted in something like seventeen counties, remember? You've got to get over here right away and get me back to Green Grove. I have to see Brenda and make things right."

"I need time to think this through."

"But you'll never make any headway on finding out who or what did this until they clear me first."

"Whadya mean *What did this?*"

"There have been too many near near-fatal medication errors since that damned EMORY EMR took over. There may very well be something wrong with the system itself. George, I have to get back there before that shit Stuart Mayberry frames me for the Lindbergh kidnapping."

"About Stuart; he's gone, Robin."

"What do you mean, 'gone?'"

"He's gone and it wasn't an accident. Look, I've told you way more than I should have over the phone. Promise me you'll sit tight. I need time to think."

Robin was silent. She felt a knot in her gut. Stuart was a rotten human being, but he didn't deserve this. And Brenda. What about Brenda?

"Robin? You there? I need you to sit tight."

"I'll sit tight, but you have to call me tomorrow. If you don't I'll hitchhike into town on my own."

"Okay. I'll call tomorrow. I don't know if I can come by. Too much going on. If I disappear it'll look suspicious."

George told Robin to be careful, not talk to anyone, and to take care of herself. For her part, Robin started to get concerned about George. How could he handle all of this by himself? He told her not to worry. He was bringing in help.

George thanked Levi, gave him back his key, and said good night. He headed for the station house. No one was there. They were all at the murder scene or searching the hospital. He went into his office and set his phone alarm for 0500, only two hours from now. With any luck, he wouldn't get called. Two hours would be enough sleep.

Chapter Forty-Four

Edmund Delaney, Green Grove's mayor, slept late. It was Saturday. He was half way through with his first cup of morning coffee when he was called by the Sheriff's office. It seemed that one of George Mathison's deputies was instructed to call the mayor and keep him informed.

"Get the Sheriff on the goddamned phone!"

"Language, Edmund!" his wife called from the next room.

"Sorry, Mr. Mayor. Sheriff Mathison is with some other investigators now and he gave strict orders, no calls."

"Are you goddamned kidding me?"

"EDMUND!"

Delaney hung up and dialed the sheriff. Voice mail. His wife was by now standing right in front of him.

"What in the name of Dolly Parton is going on?" By this time she had her hands on her hips and a genuine look of concern. She was a proper southern woman and did not appreciate her husband loudly cussing. Edmund knew that look and calmed down, a little.

"It's George Mathison. When I get a hold of him!"

"Oh George. Bless his heart. It must be so hard to be a widower. Be patient with him, Edmund. Edmund? Where are you off to, pumpkin?"

She may as well have been talking to the crape myrtles outside. Edmund was by now in his closet and dressing like the house was on fire. He didn't need the rest of his coffee. His heart was pounding and his anger was welling up inside of him. How dare the sheriff not speak to him? He got in his car and thought about the many different ways that he could fire George Mathison.

Chapter Forty-Five

Delaney's car came to a screeching halt in the Green Grove Police Department parking lot. Green Grove PD had not kept pace with the influx of transplants so the building, along with its parking lot, were still small-town sized. The half-dozen or so spots were taken. Delaney angrily threw the transmission in reverse and parked, more or less, along the street. He would not have passed a road test, but he was the mayor. Had he remained calm he likely would have noticed that there were two black Chevy Suburbans in the lot, both with law enforcement plates and an array of special radio antennas. When he got inside he stopped cold and tried to comprehend what he was seeing. At least four men in dark suits were crowded around the sheriff. Each of the guests had short cropped hair, plain black shoes, and sunglasses hanging from the handkerchief pocket of their black suit jackets.

"What in the name of Sam Hill!" Delaney yelled, and not kindly.

George spoke up.

"Gentlemen, this is Edmund Delaney, Green Grove's mayor."

The black-suited guy in charge walked over and extended his hand.

"Jim Bond, FBI, out of Atlanta office."

Before Bond stood Green Grove Mayor Edmund Delaney. Delaney was sixty-four years old and sported about one-half a head of gray hair that was not well combed. He had not yet shaved but thankfully he had brushed his teeth. He wore a suit jacket and pants that were not matched, and no tie. His eyes looked bloodshot under his tortoise-shell glasses.

Bond, in contrast, looked every bit the part of the federal lawman. He wore a black suit, white dress shirt, and thin navy tie with a perfect half-Windsor knot. His black hair was cut short and he was clean shaven. At five-feet-nine and one hundred sixty-five pounds, he was not large, but he carried himself with the confidence of a man who pound for pound could subdue anyone if the need arose. Delaney took note of the holster and side arm.

"FBI! What the hell is the FBI doing in Green Grove? What, did you drive 130 miles per hour up the thruway, Mr. *James Bond*?" Delaney could not help himself, but his faked English accent with a southern drawl simply sounded silly.

"Sir, there's been a murder and a possible attempted murder. We flew in."

"Why the hell did *you* fly in? This is a local police matter." Delaney's face was now red and he had spittle in the corner of his mouth.

Bond explained that they were called by Green Grove's sheriff, George Mathison. In addition to the murder of Stuart Mayberry there had been an alleged attempted murder in Green Grove General that involved the computer system. HealthSure had offices in two states sharing that system, EMORY. In addition, the victim of the known murder, Dr. Stuart Mayberry, had been communicating via EMORY with patients from just across the North Carolina state line. This made it a federal matter, and hence the FBI's involvement. Delaney leered at George, who proceeded to finish his presentation to the federal agents. After a pause, Bond backed a foot away from the desk, folded his arms, and spoke up.

"Let's go over what we know and what we think we know: a prominent Green Grove businessman, Walter Parks, alleges to have been intentionally overdosed on a blood thinner by his physician, Robin Cochran. Dr. Cochran is nowhere to be found. Two days later the body of a HealthSure physician administrator, Dr. Stuart Mayberry, is found dead and with his fingers hacked off. Dr. Mayberry had recently fired another HealthSure Physician, Dr. Ed Halsby, who soon thereafter died of an overdose, intentional or not. Mayberry also had a contentious relationship with other physicians at HealthSure, most notably Dr. Robin Cochran. Mayberry had been seen late in the day at work, so we can assume he was murdered within about a four-hour time frame. During this time, Brenda Makem, a diabetic patient who had just given birth, was prescribed super concentrated insulin that nearly killed her. The computer shows that the prescriber was none other than Dr. Cochran and that the prescription came from within Green Grove General Hospital itself."

"HealthSure Green Grove General," Delaney interrupted.

"HealthSure Green Grove General. Green Grove General for short. Thank you, Mayor. All right, gentlemen, how might these incidents be connected?" Bond spoke to the three other agents as a professor might address his students. The analogy was appropriate. There were three other agents in the room, all dressed like Bond. They were younger and obviously subordinate to him. Bond's tone implied that he already knew the answer to the question that he had just posed.

"All the victims were either physicians or patients of HealthSure," one of his staff replied.

"Fine. My bookie could have told me that. What else?"

Delaney couldn't help himself.

"Robin Cochran, goddamnit! Why in the hell are you here when you should be out looking for her?"

Bond thanked the mayor for his input. He had worked with local law enforcement and politicians before. The politicians were as dumb as road kill, but he was well aware that he could more easily make progress if he did not offend them. Still, Bond was after more.

"The insulin orders came from within Green Grove General, and yet Dr. Cochran was not found there. This raises the possibility of other players involved."

"An accomplice?" George chimed in.

"Maybe. We can't rule anything out yet. All right guys, we've covered the obvious. What else?"

The room was silent as Bond made eye contact, one at a time, with each agent.

"If this is the best that Quantico has to offer then our country is in real shit. How are the crimes being perpetrated? What is the weapon?"

"The computer, boss."

Bond threw up his arms. "Hallelujah!"

Bond explained how the alleged attempted murders involved use of EMORY.

Another agent chimed in: "But what about the dead doc? His murder could have been just a simple robbery gone bad. The fingers could have been a decoy. That's got nothing to do with the EMR computer."

Bond let his agent finish, and then let the words hang in the air.

"Finger scanner," the first agent said in a low and dramatic voice, almost a whisper.

They all nodded in agreement. Whoever killed Dr. Mayberry wanted access to EMORY. Not just any access. High-level access that Mayberry had because of his administrative position. With that kind of access Robin Cochran could indeed manipulate the system, perhaps remotely. Bond began to organize his team for a massive search for Dr. Robin Cochran.

George knew it was finally time. He asked Bond for a moment alone. Delaney, who was still fuming, raised his anger level one notch higher.

"Whatever you have to say to him you can say in front of me."

George ignored him and motioned Bond to the next room.

Over the next few minutes George told Bond everything, including that he understood he helped a suspect who was wanted by the law. One of Bond's skills was his ability to size up those who he was dealing with. His team had already run a background check on George Mathison while they were en route to Green Grove. George had a squeaky-clean record and a stellar reputation. Bond was also skilled with his gut. Sheriff George Mathison was not a liar. That meant that the identity of the murderer was still unknown to them. It had to be someone with good tech skills, and a motive. What was that motive? Bond needed George, and he needed Robin Cochran. They discussed it with total frankness. Bond could keep George out of jail, but only temporarily. Things would go easier for both of them if George helped with the investigation. They came to terms. George's career in law enforcement was over. He knew that already. If they found the murderer, then there was a good chance that both George and Robin would not see jail time. George might lose his pension. He had lived a simple life and had enough of his own money saved up. He would survive. They left George's office and went back to the main room of the station.

Bond once again took charge.

"Listen up. Here's the plan."

He would have two agents go with George to get Robin. George had earlier explained to Bond that he personally had to go. The Batts were moonshiners and they did not trust strangers, especially strangers in black suits driving government SUVs. They were well armed and not afraid to mix it up. So, George would go along and keep things civil. A sort of Henry Kissinger for rednecks. The third FBI agent would see about getting HealthSure's CEO and have him summon the head of IT. Both would come to the Sheriff's office ASAP. Someone was tinkering inside of the EMR system and hopefully IT would be able to shed some light on the situation. Bond, meanwhile, would set up a command center at the Sheriff's office and coordinate the investigation from there. He contacted his superiors in Atlanta and convinced them to send one of their tech people to assist the investigation.

Chapter Forty-Six

Bismark, North Dakota, 2014

Joseph Abernathy had been on his cell phone and listening for about two minutes when he let out his fifth "Uh huh." Occasionally these were accentuated by a solemn "I see." He was given only a few details, but the seriousness and panic in the voice on the other end, HealthSures's CEO, made it clear that there was some serious shit going on and it involved his EMR system, EMORY. Joseph was the chief operating officer of Sign On Information Systems, SOIS. Twelve years ago, he had been working for a Wall Street Investment firm. He and a few others were adamant that every aspect of life would soon become digitalized and that the best way to make money was to find the most promising companies and ideas, bankroll them, and reap the rewards. Joe had done his best to convince the top players that gaining a foothold now would ensure their success. Unfortunately, the potential rewards were too many years off. There were too many people making too much money in real estate and backing home loans. Instant gratification was the game and the top brass were simply not going to divert their resources and take chances on technology that might or might not be relevant in ten years. Joseph left the firm, convinced a few of his like-minded buddies to take a chance with him, and broke out his crystal ball. Healthcare, he reasoned, was nearly a sure bet. Big money was already being spent. The system was drowning in paper, there was no good way to collect data, and everyone knew that doctors' handwriting sucked. He and his friends put up everything they had as collateral, got a loan, and proceeded to recruit the best and brightest graduates from MIT, RIT, and whatever other IT that had brilliant and creative grads who were willing to work for low pay but high potential rewards. They set up a headquarters in Bismarck, North Dakota. The land was cheap and there were few distractions.

Abernathy got off the phone and race-walked to the next building, up two flights of stairs and down the hall to the office of Neil Brickstein. He wasn't there. He raced up to the third floor where SOIS had their most advanced research and development lab. This was where Brickstein and his team worked their magic. He slid his ID card into the reader, the door clicked open, and he walked in without stopping to put on a lab jumpsuit. That immediately got Brickstein's attention.

"Hey boss. How's about not contaminating years of work."

"Cut the sarcasm, Neil. I need you packed and ready to board the company jet in thirty minutes."

Brickstein made a face. The three techs who were working with him stopped and looked up. Clearly this was something important.

"I'm kind of in the middle of something, Joe."

"Well get out of the middle. Go home, get your toothbrush and some clean underwear, and get your ass ready. I will be outside of your apartment in thirty minutes. This is not open for discussion."

Abernathy turned and left the lab. Brickstein, still in his Hazmat suit, caught up to him in the antechamber. He did not like surprises and was going to say so, but Abernathy cut him off.

"I've put up with your pain-in-the-ass personality because you're creative and you get the job done. I swear, though, if I find out that you deliberately went against my orders about EMORY there won't be a rock big enough for you to hide under. You've now got twenty-eight minutes."

"Will you at least tell me where we're going?"

"North Carolina."

Chapter Forty-Seven

2004, Bismark

Joseph Abernathy ordered his second club soda at the hotel restaurant. He had a skill for sizing people up and alcohol blunted that skill. The MIT guy that he was there to interview, Dr. Neil Brickstein, had completed his PhD in computer science, was wrapping up his research projects, and interviewing for work and a life outside of academia. Brickstein had been wooed by some of the big tech giants, but had not accepted an offer yet. The job descriptions were too rigid. He would have to be a square peg in a square hole. He continued his work at MIT and tutored in his spare time to earn enough money to pay his rent for a dump that he shared with three other guys who, not surprisingly, had never been out on a date with a girl. When he received a call from a Mr. Joseph Abernathy, from something called Sign On Information Systems, he greeted it with a silent yawn. After a few minutes of conversation, however, it had become clear that they were doing something cutting-edge and different from everyone else.

Abernathy had done plenty of homework. He had a reasonable handle on technology, but not to the point that he could truly evaluate the value of someone's work by reading a research paper. Instead, he attended some of the symposiums and technology conventions where the best young talent were presenting their projects. After the presentations he would wait patiently for all the pocket-protector types to finish their questions. He noticed that only a few truly had questions. Most just wanted to boast about their own research or contradict the presenter. Joe would wait patiently to the side and then he would introduce himself. He would steer the conversation away from the specifics of the student's work and talk more about potential future applications to industry and lifestyle. Then he would listen. These guys liked to talk about their ideas. In a short few minutes Abernathy could tell who had vision and a willingness to step out of their comfort zone. Neil Brickstein went well beyond that. Like all top technology grads he was brilliant in his own sphere of work, artificial intelligence, but he also showed a passion to explore new ideas. Abernathy congratulated him on his work and for being chosen to present at whatever-the-hell conference they were at, and he continued to size up other candidates. After three months of attending conferences, reading journals, and discussing his findings with his partners he decided that he would pursue Brickstein. He was not surprised that the guy was late for their meeting. He had learned plenty about these brainiacs. They could solve Rubik's cube in less than two minutes, but they had little understanding of social etiquette.

Brickstein came in, and to Joe Abernathy's surprise he had enough social grace to apologize for being late and to wear a blazer with his jeans and sneakers. Probably the only blazer he owned. He wore wire-rimmed glasses, his hair was combed neatly, and he was clean shaven. All good signs. He knew that these PhD guys were a little attention starved so he greased Neil up a bit by talking about how he admired his work. Since this was the second time that they had met, Joe said it was okay for them to talk on a first-name basis. This was more than an interview and he wanted more than an employee. Abernathy had a vision, and he needed someone who could take the R & D and run with it. After a few minutes, Abernathy felt confident enough to share his vision for SOIS and how it could revolutionize the way medicine was practiced. Sure, there were other companies out there that were starting to produce EMR products. But those products were nothing more than computerized patient records. In many cases, merely scanning notes in to the system. Joe Abernathy envisioned a system that could integrate all the players: physicians, the hospital, pharmacies, etc. Patients themselves would be able to interact with the system and have access to their records at their fingertips. SOIS wanted, needed, someone with not just technical ability but also someone who could cultivate new ways to solve problems. Neil was a lousy poker player and could not contain his excitement. His knee bounced up and down and he interrupted with ideas of his own. They hadn't even discussed salary when Neil said that he would love the challenge and wanted in. Joe explained that they had to come up with a small-scale product quickly so that they could generate some sales and capital to keep the banks confident in the risk. Meanwhile, Neil would simultaneously head up the larger project that Joe figured would take six to eight years to bring to market.

One month later Neil moved in to his new apartment in Bismarck. Rent in North Dakota was a hell of a lot less than in Boston, so he had his own place and could keep whatever hours he liked. As much as he wanted to bypass the short-term product, a task that he found too simple and beneath his skills, Abernathy made it clear that without that product there would be no long-term project. Neil, for his part, convinced Abernathy to hire more staff to help him with the near-term EMR product. It worked out well and pretty soon they could market it to small medical groups of fifty doctors or less. Neil spent his nights and weekends working on the larger project. At first, he focused on the idea of communication and integration. If a patient presented to an ER the staff could give better care if they had access to the office and pharmacy records. Ultimately, however, Neil knew all along that he wanted to achieve much more. His doctoral work at MIT focused on artificial intelligence, "AI." Neil, as well as everyone else who majored in computer science, envisioned a world where computers could perform much of what humans did today, both faster and better. No mistakes. Neil didn't mean something like the robots that took the place of workers on automobile assembly lines. No, he wanted to create systems that could adapt to changes in the situation. A system that could think.

As project manager, Neil Brickstein had access to the systems that SOIS sold to medical groups. Despite state of the art security, it was a no brainer for Neil to get in to whatever system he wanted, whenever he wanted to. He created those systems. He did not want to obtain specific patient information, rather, he wanted to follow trends. Cause and effect. The patient's blood pressure was this, so the doctor did that. The lab showed X, so the doctor changed Y. In his first three years at SOIS he created the programs to track trends in patient care, evaluate probabilities, and then create algorithms of their own. He then tested the algorithms, using what the doctor actually did as the control. Of course, this assumed that what the doctor did was indeed the correct decision. Unfortunately, he would need several medical experts if he wanted to know the correct medical decision for every scenario. He did not have those kinds of resources, so he made up for it with volume. If multiple doctors did the same thing in response to the same scenario, then that was considered the correct response. For the system to be a viable alternative to a licensed physician it would have to make concordant decisions at least ninety-five percent of the time. He only succeeded with ninety-five percent on a handful of patient scenarios. But as he massaged and worked his programs he could improve on them and soon enough he had a system that could predict what most physicians would do in more than three hundred different clinical scenarios ranging from exceedingly simple to moderately complex.

Sign On Information System's EMR product, EMORY, had been in the works for a few years. Abernathy expected a system that was ready to go to market in six to eight years. But within only four years they had a system that was ready for sale to groups as large as one thousand providers. Brickstein had exceeded all expectations. At first, he was a colleague to the other computer scientists who worked for SOIS, but within a matter of months it was clear that his skills far exceeded the others. He was given the title of project manager and he pretty much got whatever he needed so long as he could show meaningful progress on a quarterly basis. He was cocky and had some serious personality quirks, but it was tolerated as long as he produced. After four years, they tested the system in a mock-up of a medical group and it performed beautifully. Brickstein and his team joined Abernathy and the other principal players in SOIS for an all-day meeting. Abernathy outlined SOIS's strategy for marketing EMORY. Brickstein outlined the basic system and hinted that he had a major surprise to add to it. Something that would be a true game changer. Abernathy assumed this was all part of Neil's overzealous enthusiasm. He, after all, had achieved so much so soon. He had earned the right to chat it up. Joe Abernathy had no idea what was about to be thrown at him. It floored him.

Brickstein presented in detail, and with great enthusiasm, what he called EMORY-A I, artificial intelligence. EMORY could take the place of a physician in well over two-thirds of patient office encounters, lab reviews, and perhaps even hospital encounters in the near future. This kind of breakthrough was worthy of a Nobel Prize in medicine, he mused. Neil had spent all his free time, nights and weekends, on the project. That explained why he was always in need of a shower and shave, something that everyone but Neil himself seemed to understand. He waited eagerly for the ecstatic praise that was, in fact, not forthcoming from Joe Abernathy and his partners. Joe called for a thirty-minute break to stretch and get some air. He took Neil aside and spelled it out for him. Artificial intelligence was too much, too soon. It carried way too much risk. Medical patients feel vulnerable to start with. Explaining themselves to a keyboard instead of a flesh-and-blood person would only make matters worse. There was value to the human touch. Unfortunately, Brickstein did not appreciate that aspect of the human experience. He also failed to understand that his breakthrough would go unused if no one actually purchased the system. There was a mountain of legal hurdles to such a thing. Moreover, there was no way that doctors themselves would give up that much control. There was a future for AI in medicine, but you had to work your way up to it. Neil, unfortunately, was too far emotionally invested and had difficulty dealing with the rejection.

Joe Abernathy was a highly skilled negotiator. He did his best to ease the blow to Brickstein, who would be truly hard to replace. Ultimately, he was able to pacify him with the promise to let him continue to work on the AI project.

With that taken care of, Joe was ready to market EMORY. His first clients were small- to medium-sized medical groups. It was a good start and with the real-world experience that they had acquired, and the appropriate tweaks to the system, SOIS was ready to pitch their product to bigger players. HealthSure had been a medium-sized, multi-specialty group in the Southeastern United States, but was poised for breakout growth. They had acquired multiple primary care and specialty groups in two states, as well as the hospitals that they served. They needed a top-notch EMR system that was backed by a company that could grow and adapt with them. The timing could not have been better. Abernathy met with HealthSure's executives and one of its physician leaders. Stuart Mayberry was a rising star in HealthSure and seemed determined to climb the corporate ladder. HealthSure became SOIS's biggest account. EMORY grew with HealthSure, including integration into the hospital system. There were the expected hiccups along the way but the team at SOIS, led by the socially inept but wildly brilliant Dr. Neil Brickstein, managed every curve-ball thrown at them. That is, until Abernathy received a panicked phone call from Tom Bellhaven, CEO at HealthSure. Up until then they had a very close and cordial relationship. They knew each other's wives, and Joe had even attended the wedding of Tom's daughter. But on that October morning in 2015 everything changed. There was nothing warm or cordial in Tom's voice. This was a crisis,

EMORY was involved, and Abernathy was expected to be in Green Grove very quickly.

Chapter Forty-Eight

The eight-passenger Gulf Stream jet that SOIS leased touched down in Raleigh at 2 pm. During the flight, Abernathy outlined to Brickstein the basics of what had transpired, as that was all that he knew himself. Someone was using EMORY as a weapon to try to harm or even kill patients. There had been a murder of one of HealthSure's physician executives. It was unclear if the murder and the nefarious use of EMORY were related. Curiously, Brickstein had little to say. They spent the final two hours of the flight in silence. Abernathy read the *Wall Street Journal* while Brickstein did a poor job of trying to look engrossed in a computer magazine.

Their plane was met by a black Cadillac Escalade that Bellhaven had sent to take them directly to the Green Grove Police Department where the FBI had set up its command center. Between the flight and car ride the two men had spent several hours in close quarters. Thankfully, Brickstein had followed Joe Abernathy's instructions to quickly shower and shave before they left.

Chapter Forty-Nine

Dozer Batts was whittling in front of the family trailer when he saw two black SUVs coming up the road. He dropped his stick, closed his knife, and ran inside. The Batts family may have been country moonshiners, but they were not without the ability to plan their defense of what they believed was rightfully theirs. That they were on the wrong side of the law was irrelevant. As far as they were concerned the *law* was just hokum created by a bunch of pretty boys in Raleigh and their friends in Washington. In a matter of seconds, they were, all three, heavily armed and focused on the impending threat. Their guest, Dr. Cochran, was firmly told to stay in her room and keep her head down.

George Mathison had made it clear to the FBI's Jim Bond that a hostile encounter was imminent unless he went along to smooth things. Mayor Delaney, who by that point had steam coming out of his ears, loudly objected. The Sheriff was a career lawman with a spotless record, and a reputation for integrity. So, despite Delaney's objections Bond decided that Sheriff George Mathison would lead the team that would bring back Dr. Robin Cochran, hopefully without incident. Before Mathison could get out the door Delaney grabbed his arm and pulled him close. In a contemptuous whisper, he told George that when this thing was over he expected the Sheriff's resignation, if in fact he was not first arrested outright.

George was in the lead SUV and told the driver to stop about fifty yards before the Batts' trailer. The FBI agent, a young man not even half George's age, questioned it and George assured him that if he went further he'd have a face full of buckshot. Point taken.

"I'm not authorized to give you a weapon, Sheriff."

"If things go bad I bet you that a handgun won't be much help against these boys." The agent couldn't help but let his lower jaw drop a bit. His dark sunglasses did little to hide his apprehension. George noticed moisture on the steering wheel when he moved his hands to make a turn. They stopped and George got out, alone. He slowly walked toward the trailer and kept his hands out in front of him where they could be easily seen. He yelled in a tone that was loud but not angry.

"Eli!"

"Eli. It's George. It's okay. These guys are not coming for you. I'm here to take Dr. Cochran back to town."

"That a fact? Why the lawmen then?" Eli's gravelly voice was forceful yet calm. He was in his element and totally confident of his abilities.

"I'm afraid they know that I brung her here. They haven't slapped the cuffs on me yet but they're not about to let me out of their sight."

Eli stepped out of the trailer and motioned George to sit in one of the rusted lawn chairs that they kept out front. He looked much as he had when George had dropped Robin off, minus the baseball cap that he did not have time to grab before going for his weapon. His shotgun was aimed at the ground, not at George, but he kept a keen eye on the two SUVs parked fifty yards away. Suddenly he raised the barrel in the direction of the lawmen who had gotten out of the vehicles while he had been talking to George.

"That's far enough!"

To emphasize the point, Winnie and Dozer aimed their rifles out the windows of their home. Winnie made her position very clear in her own raspy voice. Years of smoking had robbed Eli and Winnie of vocal harmony, but their volume remained strong.

"Yeah! And he got back up!"

She was every bit as tough and ornery as her husband.

George stood up quickly, but not so quickly as to alarm anyone. He placed his hands out in the universal *Hold on and don't shoot* position and yelled to the agents to get back in their vehicles. He had it covered. The two agents looked at each other, not entirely clear of their next move. Fortunately, they did as George asked. Eli let his shotgun down, just a little.

Eli spat and let out a groan.

"Dumb buggers gonna get themselves killed."

"Sorry, Eli. They're not from around here. Look, no one is here to bother you. Thank you for taking care of Dr. Cochran. I owe you guys, though I'm not sure when I'll be able to repay that debt. I'm in a heap of trouble, too."

"George, you know you can hole up here if you like. Ain't no one gonna mess with you if you here."

Eli Batts had never told a lie in his life. George knew well that this was not some city suit saying "Let's have lunch." Eli was sincere about the invite, and the protection.

"Appreciate it, Eli. But it's time for me to 'fess up and get Robin to speak to the law before this thing goes too far. There's a killer out there and Robin and me may be able to help find him."

"Suit yourself. By the way, how do know it's a *him*?" He grinned and looked over at his wife who still had her rifle aimed and ready to shoot. He called for Robin to come out.

Chapter Fifty

The black Escalade carrying Joe Abernathy and Neil Brickstein rolled to a stop light in downtown Green Grove. There was a pickup truck in front of them and Abernathy noticed the insignia in the rear window that said *Ladies' Man.* As soon as he read it he saw the driver's-side door open. The driver leaned to his left and spat a massive dark brown gob to the pavement. Joe could see that he still had a wad of tobacco in his cheek. Yessir. Ladies' man. They pulled up in front of the Green Grove Police Department. Joe Abernathy was dressed in his gray slacks, white shirt, and blue blazer. He had taken off his tie on the plane but put it on again in the car. He wanted to look professional. He took note of the small but filled parking lot and multiple cars on the street closest to the station. This was not going to be a small meeting. When he got inside the place was already buzzing with people on phones and in front of computers. A man wearing a black suit and an ear piece immediately came over. His body language made it clear that he was in charge.

"Mr. Abernathy?"

Joe Abernathy nodded politely.

"I'm Jim Bond, FBI."

"Pleasure. This is Dr. Neil Brickstein, our technical director at Sign On Information Systems."

Abernathy had made sure that Brickstein looked presentable. Neil had a short and stocky build with more fat than muscle, blond hair, and was wearing beige cargo pants and a faded blue dress shirt. Abernathy always travelled with a spare tie and told Neil to put it on. Brickstein started to object, but it quickly became clear that it was not a request.

Bond extended his hand. "Dr. Brickstein."

"And you are Bond, James Bond."

"No, not *James* Bond."

They smiled. In Neil's mind, they had bonded over a movie joke. That is, until Bond's face turned stone serious.

"But I *do* have a license to kill. So, let's get down to business, Dr. Brickstein."

Bond escorted Brickstein to the meeting room where there were already three people seated. While Bond was laying down the law with Brickstein, Joe Abernathy had moved across the room to speak to HealthSure's CEO. Joe said hello, shook his hand firmly but amicably, and assured him that they would do everything possible to get to the bottom of whatever had happened with EMORY. Joe then introduced himself to Mayor Delaney, who by now felt slighted by just about everyone in the Green Grove PD building. Green Grove. *His* town.

Bond introduced the recent arrivals to the vice president for Information Technology at HealthSure, Dorothy Coleman. Bond had reviewed her background on his way to Green Grove. She was forty-eight years old, had graduated from a state school, and had held a variety of responsible jobs in IT before being named VP at HealthSure. That she was female and African-American meant that she had to earn her way, and then some, in to the relatively exclusive white men's club of corporate administration. There were no gifts. Since entering high-level administration, Dorothy was keen not to let her guard down. Other vice presidents sometimes made mistakes and were given a second chance.

She doubted that she would ever receive that courtesy. Since freshman year of college her father had told her to bring her A-game every day. Whenever she was feeling tired she would remind herself that it was that attitude that brought her this far in the first place. Her standard work attire consisted of a not-too-short skirt, blazer, and a silk shirt. Pumps with no more than two-inch heels and stockings, never bare legs, finished the professional look. She often mused that she wouldn't be caught dead in a Hillary Clinton pantsuit.

Bond took charge of the meeting and summarized the situation concerning the use of EMORY, starting with the alleged attempted murder of Green Grove prominent businessman Walter Parks. Most of the discussion, however, centered around the apparent deliberate order of a super-concentrated insulin that caused life-threatening low blood sugar in Brenda Makem, a type 1 diabetic who had just delivered a baby by caesarean section. Bond turned the presentation over to Dorothy Coleman. She explained that the order allegedly came from Dr. Robin Cochran and had originated from inside the hospital. Bond then pointed out that it was highly unlikely that Dr. Cochran was in the hospital at the time that the order was written. Abernathy raised his hand.

"How can you be so sure? Does she have an iron-clad alibi?"

"Absolutely. But I can't say for sure that she did not have access to a computer. The question for the two of you," as he looked at Abernathy and Brickstein, "is could she have done the orders remotely and made it look like they came from inside the hospital? And if not, could someone else have done it and made it look like it came from her?"

Abernathy looked over at Brickstein.

"Neil?"

"No system is one hundred percent secure, but EMORY is damn close. The kind of skills needed to do an order remotely and make it look like it came from within the hospital would require the user to be a world-class hacker. I seriously doubt that a sixty-ish year old country bumpkin could be able to do that."

Someone else spoke from the entrance to the room. "I may not be a computer genius but I know enough not to insult someone right in their own living room."

All eyes turned to the door where Robin Cochran was standing, surrounded by two FBI agents and George Mathison. There were a few seconds of silence in the room, and Brickstein would have been embarrassed to hell but was instead saved by none other than Edmund Delaney.

"Well. Aren't you going to arrest her? Do I have to slap the cuffs on her myself?"

Bond chimed in, "Mr. Mayor, we appreciate your concern but I assure you that the suspect will not get away. Right now, she can help us with the investigation."

"Help you? Damn it, she *is* the investigation."

Bond had been very patient with Edmund Delaney for some time, but now that all the players were present there was work to be done. This case was bigger than Green Grove and Bond was losing patience with a local politician who could not see a picture bigger than the boundaries of his own county.

"Mayor Delaney, I explained earlier why the FBI was involved. At this point in time we are taking responsibility for the investigation of the murder of Stuart Mayberry and the alleged attempted murders of Walter Parks and Brenda Makem.

The blood drained from Robin's face. As soon as he had heard the words George moved to Robin's side and readied himself to catch her. She was unsteady but did not fall. George motioned for one of the FBI agents to pull a chair over to her.

"It's okay, Robin. Brenda is out of ICU and is fine. She had a severe insulin reaction, maybe from a deliberately high dose. Mr. Bond, may I fill Robin in?"

Once again, Delaney fumed. How his face could turn any redder was remarkable to all.

"Fill her in? Arrest her, damn it!"

Bond broke in.

"That's enough. Everyone back off."

He pulled a chair up to Robin. George had filled her in about Jim Bond during their drive back to Green Grove. She knew that she would have to be one hundred percent forthright if she had any hope of not being arrested.

"Dr. Cochran, at this time you are not under arrest. You are, however, a suspect and we would like to ask you some questions. You can have a lawyer present, if you wish."

Robin declined the attorney. George had also filled her in about Stuart's murder and the FBI on the way back from the Batts home, though he had not told her about Brenda. It was time for both of them to open up about what they knew and they were far better off with Jim Bond from the FBI then local law enforcement. Robin composed herself.

"I'm ready to help in any way I can. Agent Bond, may I take a few minutes to use the bathroom and wash up?"

"Of course."

Robin caught Delaney scowling at her.

"Sure you don't want to watch me pee, Mr. Mayor?"

Chapter Fifty-One

The center table was occupied by Jim Bond, Robin Cochran, Dorothy Coleman, Joe Abernathy, and Neil Brickstein. A tape recorder was on the table. Another FBI agent had two computers set up in a make-shift information center. George sat at the far end of the room and had coffee with the other FBI agent. Bond had finally convinced Edmund Delaney to go home. It took some convincing, as he earlier loudly stated that he would not leave until he saw Dr. Cochran in handcuffs.

Bond said that he wanted to proceed chronologically, starting with what happened to Walter Parks. Robin assured the group that she had not intentionally prescribed a higher dose of blood thinner. She admitted that the EMR system was very complex and, as such, could lead to mistakes. Brickstein, obviously defensive, tried to rebuff her but was quickly silenced by a severe look from Bond. Robin described how she had spent nearly three days at the Batts trailer and did not have access to a computer. She did not use the internet from her phone, as that would have required data roaming and would have used up precious power. She did not have her charger, and the phone died after about thirty hours anyway. Bond noted the approximate time that Robin said her phone died, which was at least twelve hours earlier than the hospital insulin order.

"Dr. Cochran, at this time I request that you please turn over your phone. We can mine data from it. Is there anything in your statement that you wish to amend?"

Robin shook her head no and turned over her cell phone. Bond passed it over to the agent in front of the computers. He went to work on it.

"Please tell us about your relationship with Dr. Stuart Mayberry."

Robin described the arguments that they had had over EMR moving ahead too quickly, how the medical staff was treated, among other disagreements. She stated unequivocally that these were professional disagreements and that she had never held any malice toward him.

"Can these Batts people swear that you were with them the evening of Dr. Mayberry's murder?"

Robin glanced at George, who gave a subtle nod. Although seemingly engaged with the FBI agent, he was clearly listening closely.

"Yes, if absolutely necessary. I don't think they like lawmen, though."

"Yes, my men filled me in on what transpired when you were picked up. Okay. Please tell me now about your relationship with the patient Brenda Makem."

Robin described how she had known Brenda since the new mother was a child and had worked closely with the woman to manage the diabetes during the pregnancy. Robin had also been friends with Brenda's mother since they were high school students.

"The very idea that I would do anything to harm Brenda…."

Her voice trailed off and she started quietly crying. George started to get up but stopped when Bond put a hand up. Bond pushed a box of tissues over to Robin. He leaned toward her, not getting so close as to be threatening, and spoke softly.

"I know this is difficult, Dr. Cochran. Please take a moment. Keep in mind that there is still a murderer on the loose and anything you can tell us is important. No detail is too small, okay?"

Robin nodded. Bond said he now wanted to know more about the insulin order that nearly killed Brenda.

"Is there any way that this could have been a legitimate order and simply the wrong dose?"

"No," Robin sniffled. "This was a five-times concentrated insulin. It was a huge dose."

Dorothy Coleman raised a finger.

"Also, Mr. Bond, I checked about the ability to order U-500 insulin. As I suspected, a warning comes up alerting the prescriber that it is a highly-concentrated insulin. Whoever did the order would have had to click that he or she accepted the warning. So less likely that it was an honest mix up."

Bond nodded. "But what if someone *did* make a mistake? Might they then have tried to cover their mistake by making it look like Dr. Cochran did the order?"

She took a second to think. "Very unlikely. The kind of skills, hacking skills if you will, to retroactively change the name of the person who wrote an order would be pretty elaborate. *We* have been trying to replicate it on mock patients and we can't. I really doubt that a doctor would have that kind of skill."

Bond nodded and seemed to accept Dorothy's conclusions.

"All right then. Dr. Cochran, is there anyone who has access to EMORY and who would want to set you up?"

Robin's eyes were still red and puffy, but she had composed herself.

"No one. I mean, Stuart did try to set me up to be arrested but I can't believe that he would hurt a patient in order to hurt me. Besides, he was already dead, right?"

"Probably. We're working on the time line. All right then. So, it is highly unlikely that someone did the order by mistake and tried to hide it. We don't have any names, a motive, or even a mechanism for someone to have harmed Brenda Makem and set up Dr. Cochran. Is there any way that the computer could have fouled up and done this?"

"Not possible," Dorothy replied quickly and with conviction.

Bond contemplated a moment and looked over at Neil Brickstein.

"Dr. Brickstein, is Ms. Coleman correct?"

Neil had his chin on his folded hands and was looking at the ground. Bond called him again.

"DR. BRICKSTEIN?"

Neil looked up, inhaled, and let out a very long exhale with a sigh. Joe Abernathy got up from his chair and walked over to him. He positioned himself right in front of him and knelt so he could be face to face.

"You put it in there, didn't you? You didn't listen to me and FUCKING PUT IT IN THERE!"

Abernathy grabbed Brickstein by the collar shoved him backward until he hit the desk behind him with a thud. Abernathy's face was red and the veins bulging in his neck indicated that he wasn't done. Bond stood up, held out his hand in the universal *Stop* signal, and took charge, again.

"Enough. What the hell are you talking about?"

Abernathy stood up straight and leered at Brickstein.

"Tell him Neil. Tell him all of it or I swear I'll put my hand down your fucking throat and tear out your lungs."

Chapter Fifty-Two

For the next twenty minutes Neil Brickstein described the work that he had done to create artificial intelligence for the EMR project and how it was going to revolutionize medicine. He sounded like a salesman. The partners of SOIS had been short-sighted to not allow him to include it in the project. Perhaps if they had given him the green light he could have done it properly, instead of covertly placing the AI in the system. A collective shock hung over everyone in the room.

"Oh, so now it's my fault?" Abernathy shot back.

Bond hushed the room and turned to Brickstein.

"Are you trying to tell us that EMORY can make its own decisions and try to kill people? C'mon, you can't expect me to believe that."

Brickstein acted like he was insulted. "It is very true. We tested it in hundreds, maybe thousands of mock patient interactions. EMORY-AI had the ability to make decisions and then act on those decisions."

"Then why would it deliberately prescribe an overdose of a super concentrated insulin? And how about Walter Parks? How could EMORY have screwed up the blood thinner dose?"

"It didn't. Insulin and coumadin were some of the most important medications that we tested. Thousands of scenarios and permutations of different medication doses and lab results. There's no way that it made a mistake."

"So, are we to believe that EMORY suddenly acquired homicidal tendencies?"

"I don't know. I'm just saying that it could not have been some sort of mistake."

Bond rubbed his chin. He was incredulous. He was still not ready to believe that there wasn't a person or persons behind all of this, and there was still the matter of the murder. Unless EMORY sprouted hands with opposable thumbs there was still a dangerous flesh-and-blood murderer on the loose. That was priority number one and he made that very clear.

"Is it possible that someone with highly advanced tech skills, not a physician, could have manipulated EMORY for some nefarious reason?"

He looked at Brickstein, who seemed to be more concerned with defending his EMR system.

"Sure, it's possible, but first you have to have access. There are layers of security codes, passwords, finger scans, and we're developing an eye scanner too."

Bond nodded. He took a quick glance at George Mathison who nodded in recognition. All three FBI agents seemed to sit up straight at once. The murder victim's missing fingers were on almost everyone's mind. Bond made a very subtle horizontal motion with his left hand in front of his mouth. That information was still restricted and there was no reason to alert Neil Brickstein to it.

Bond contemplated his next move. He didn't like to give up control of an investigation, and this tech guy was a real wild card. Still, there were too many questions surrounding EMORY. The answers could be the key to solving the murder.

"All right, Dr. Brickstein. What do you need to do to figure out what the hell is going on inside of EMORY?"

“I just need access to EMORY. I can even do it remotely with the computer you have set up here.”

The FBI agent in front of the two PCs tried to stifle a look of alarm. He turned to Bond.

“Boss?”

“I’m sorry, Dr. Brickstein. These computers are FBI property and access is severely restricted. Not gonna happen.”

“Well then, I can’t help you,” Brickstein quipped and turned away.

“Dr. Brickstein, at this time you may be considered an accessory to attempted murder. You can cooperate with me here or we can put on the shackles, put you on a plane and send you to an undisclosed location. Alone.”

Brickstein swallowed hard. “I have some equipment in my bag in the car.” He started to get up but Bond put a hand firmly on his shoulder and sat him back down. He turned to his agent in front of the computers and made a motion to the door with his head. The agent got up and weaved his way through the crowded room with the speed and agility of someone who had clearly been very well trained. In a manner of seconds, he had returned with Brickstein’s hard suitcase and he gave it to Bond.

Jim Bond opened the case and gazed at an array of equipment every bit as advanced and elaborate as that of the FBI. Computers, scanners, and much more. He could not help but notice the virtual reality goggles. He passed it all to Neil Brickstein.

“Dr. Brickstein, here’s what is going to happen. You will go over your plan with us before you engage. You will narrate what you are doing while you are doing it. You are not to take any actions without our approval. Any identification of patient information must be clearly stated to us. Someone may be using EMORY to commit crimes."

"Or EMORY itself is doing it," Brickstein interrupted.

"Yes, or EMORY itself. Either way, EMORY is being investigated by the FBI. Any funny business from you and you will be charged with obstruction of justice and we will arrest you. Have I made myself clear?"

"Very clear."

Bond had brought Brickstein in line and established himself as the alpha. Dr. Brickstein's ego had, however, been obviously bruised. Bond needed Brickstein. True, the FBI had access to some of the top hackers in the world, on both sides of the law, but that would take valuable time and expose the investigation to even more persons, some of whom he could not trust. Bond, however, had quickly sized up Neil Brickstein and anticipated the dilemma. He sat down right in front of him.

"Dr. Brickstein. It is entirely possible that we are dealing with one or more very clever persons that are using the EMORY system to commit violent crimes, and perhaps other crimes that we are not yet aware of. Whether it is a person or, as you have pointed out, the artificial intelligence embedded in the system itself, the bottom line is that we must find out what is happening, stop it, and find a murderer. We are relying on your skills."

His ego restored, Brickstein went to work. He took out his PC and plugged it in. He then took out an iPhone from the suitcase, turned it on, and set up a personal hot spot. Once his computer was ready he signed in to EMORY using his own passcode and finger scanner. Bond watched closely and glanced over to George Mathison, who had also noted the finger scanner. Dorothy Coleman watched with some concern.

"Mr. Bond, he has access to secure patient information. This is quite a HIPAA violation, you know."

"I'm aware of the federal privacy rules, Ms. Coleman. This is part of a murder investigation, so we have some leeway here."

"At least as far as the FBI is concerned," she groaned.

"At least as far as the FBI is concerned," Bond conceded.

Bond put one of his agents in charge of monitoring Brickman. They had also set up a video camera to record the goings-on. Bond then walked outside and called Atlanta. He updated his superiors on what he had found and how they were proceeding. He then asked for a full forensics team to be sent to Green Grove and investigate the murder of Stuart Mayberry. Mayberry's killer was suspected of attempted murder of at least two HealthSure patients. The killer potentially had access to any and all HealthSure data, and at the highest level of security clearance. The level of clearance that Stuart Mayberry had.

Agent Bond ended the call and went back inside the Green Grove PD. He instructed Dorothy Coleman to investigate all fingerprint access that Stuart Mayberry had and terminate said access. He then went over to George and Robin. George was drinking coffee and reading the paper. Robin had her head propped up by the chin in her palm, elbow on the desk. She was sleeping lightly and jolted out of it when Bond came over. He told Robin that she was under house arrest. One of his agents would bring her home and that was where she would stay. George voiced his discomfort about her being alone while a murderer was on the loose. He offered to stay with her.

"No, Sheriff. I need you here to help with the investigation. You're my boots on the ground. The murderer may well be known to you."

Bond thought it over. Dr. Cochran had already witnessed more of the investigation than Bond was comfortable with. She could not stay at the Green Grove PD.

"All right then. I'll send one of my agents along. Put him in the kitchen or in front of the TV and he'll be fine." He could see the concern on George and Robin's faces.

"It'll be fine. Our agents undergo intensive background and psychological screening. My agents are then hand-picked by me. It'll be like having your own pit bull standing guard. Only he needs coffee and donuts."

Chapter Fifty-Three

Bond checked in and updated the Atlanta office. He confirmed that the crime team was on its way. They would interview witnesses, review the progress on the autopsy, and run the information through their database to see if this type of murder fit a known pattern. They would report their findings to Bond himself who would try to piece together the information with what he would hopefully learn from Neil Brickstein. He went over to speak to his agent and to Brickstein. Neil had spent nearly an hour in EMORY and reported his findings.

The highly-concentrated insulin prescription had unquestionably originated from Dr. Robin Cochran, and not from another prescriber pretending to be her. If the FBI was certain that Dr. Cochran could not have written it then the only logical conclusion is that EMORY itself created the order and initiated it from Dr. Cochran's ID. Bond listened but was still not ready to believe that a computer was attempting to commit murder. Brickstein anticipated his skepticism and revealed that he had specifically investigated interactions between EMORY and Dr. Robin Cochran. Bond's agent, who had not been informed while it had happened, was visibly pissed off. He had been placed in charge of monitoring what Brickstein was doing. Bond held up a hand as if to say: *Don't say anything. Let him go on.*

"There are billions of interactions between EMORY and its users. So, I narrowed my search to Dr. Cochran. I found the usual stuff. Prescription orders, chart notes, etc. Then, I flipped it."

Bond was obviously perplexed.

"What I mean is that I looked at interactions between EMORY and Dr. Cochran that were specifically initiated by EMORY. I found the usual stuff: labs, messaged, etc. Then, I thought, if I were a computer (Bond and his agent both smirked at the irony) how would I go about learning about my enemy? And EMORY clearly thinks Dr. Cochran is its enemy. Well? What would you do?"

Both agents shrugged.

"No, guys. Think. What does the FBI do when it needs Intel. on a suspect? You listen in and you look!"

Brickstein was clearly excited and ready to let them in on something.

"There are hours of files, and I mean a lot of hours, of EMORY listening to Dr. Cochran through the dictation microphone and watching her through the EMORY Camera. EMORY was spying on her!"

Bond stopped him.

"So, this was not Dr. Cochran using the EMR system for something? You mean to say that EMORY turned on the camera and microphone all by itself?"

"Yes!"

"What did it see and hear?"

"I didn't have time to go through it all. Too many hours. But the little bit I saw was just routine. Her typing into the computer, on the phone, whatever."

"Can you isolate the files and transfer them? We have people who specialize in sitting and watching video for hours on end, waiting for a clue."

Bond was a good poker player, but in his tone and body language Brickstein could tell that he might believe him about EMORY acting independently.

"Yup. I can do that. I'll need to go back in. I can find the electronic trail and use the markers to search all of EMORY for those interactions and download them to a separate hard drive."

"Dr. Brickstein, this time make sure you inform my agent of everything that you are doing."

Brickstein nodded and reached in to his suitcase and pulled out more hardware. He hooked it up, put on his virtual goggles, and went back to work.

Chapter Fifty-Four

With Brickstein back at work and the FBI forensics team en route, Bond figured it was a good time to close his eyes.

It was late afternoon and it was looking like he'd be working with the forensics team well in to the night. He looked over at George Mathison who was himself leaning against the wall, fast asleep. He left him alone but went in to George's office to catch what he hoped would be a good thirty-minute power nap. Like all FBI agents, Bond was practiced in commanding his body to sleep and wake as the work demanded. George's office was the typical bland room for local law enforcement. A steel desk, filing cabinet, and a computer. Thankfully he had a comfortable chair that reclined. Bond put his feet up on the desk, mumbled "Sorry, Sheriff," and in less than a minute he was out. He would not get thirty minutes.

Agent Barry knocked at the door. Bond knew his team well. Barry would not wake him if it wasn't important.

"Come in."

"Chief, sorry to wake you but this is big."

Bond commanded his brain to maximum alertness within seconds, like all good FBI agents were trained to do. He ignored his sleep breath and went straight over to Brickstein who had a serious look of concern on his face. His cockiness was gone but he was clearly very excited. Brickstein could not contain himself.

"Someone else is in there!"

"What do you mean?"

"Someone else is roaming around and checking out what EMORY is doing. Whoever it is, is especially interested in Dr. Cochran."

"Are you sure?"

Brickstein's look of concern changed to one of scorn, laced with a little bit of arrogance.

"I've created the industry's most advanced EMR computer system, I graduated from MIT, and I may have at one time been one of the world's most skilled hackers. Or maybe not, as far as *you* know. So yeah, I'm sure."

Bond ignored Brickstein's pettiness.

"What's he doing?"

"Well, first off, we don't know if it's a he, but I suspect it is. There's a lot of interaction with Dr. Cochran's EMORY account. He's monitored her email, her cell phone, and he even looked at the visual files of her that EMORY took through the video cam. A lot of them. That's why I think it's a 'he.'"

"Wait a sec. Her phone?" Bond's back straightened as he said this.

"Yeah. EMORY has an app that allows the user to access it via his or her cell phone."

Bond put up his hands to alert everyone to be quiet while he thought for a moment.

"Could this person have monitored her whereabouts, *and* perhaps even accessed other functions on her cell phone?"

"Yes." Brickstein said this with more than a hint of pride, Bond noted.

"Presumably Dr. Stuart Mayberry had the same app on his phone. This, in theory, could link the murderer to his victim."

After a few seconds of silence Bond seemed to come to some conclusions. He texted his agent in the field who was guarding Robin Cochran. He instructed agent Barry to alert the techs in Atlanta who had Robin's cell phone about the EMORY connection, and to assume that they themselves may be being monitored as they worked on it. He then motioned to his one remaining agent whose most important job, up until then, had been playing cards with George Mathison.

"Call Dorothy Coleman." Hours earlier Bond had told her that she could go home, but to leave her phone on and be ready in case they needed her assistance.

"Tell her to create a list of all HealthSure's IT technicians. We need to know who has been at work today, who is off, and in particular who has recently taken vacation time or medical leave. Get going to her house, office, or wherever she is and bring her back here. Tell her to bring her laptop."

Bond then pulled the agent aside. They were nose to ear. Bond whispered.

"As soon as you have that list have our boys run it through the system. I want to know about criminal records, especially cybercrime, and I want to know who has a family and who is a loner."

The agent nodded and immediately went to work. Bond had formed a mental picture of the suspect. A single male, awkward, and a loner. Someone who felt safe and in command when at home on his computer, but had felt sheer terror at the thought of asking a girl for a date. He likely had an unusual attachment to his mother. He would be someone who could easily become obsessed with an attractive older woman. It was a classic Oedipal complex. If he knew that Robin did not get along with the victim, Dr. Stuart Mayberry, then that could provide motive. It still, however, could not explain the phantom medication orders for Walter Parks and Brenda Makem. There was no logical link. Bond was not convinced about Brickstein's theory that EMORY itself was doing this, but he had become more open to listening.

Across town Robin Cochran was enjoying the feeling of having showered, put on clean clothes, and drinking a cup of her favorite orange blossom tea. The FBI agent was seated on the couch in the den, near the front door. He had asked that she inform him of what she was doing. He assured her that he would not be looking over her shoulder, but he wanted to know where she was at all times. He was polite and respectful of her privacy, so she complied with his requests, just as George had instructed her before she left Green Grove PD. She was finally starting to relax. The feeling would not last.

"Ma'am, please gather your things. We need to be back at Green Grove PD. immediately."

Robin let out a heavy sigh. She was tired and exasperated.

"Can I at least use my *own* bathroom to pee before we leave?" Even with his dark glasses and expressionless face Robin could see him blush.

Chapter Fifty-Five

By now it was 6 pm. Bond had already asked George if he would mind getting some food for them. He assured George that he was not relegating him to being a *go-fer,* but as the local Sheriff, George would have much better luck getting good take-out than a stranger in a dark suit. Within minutes the room looked much as it did several hours earlier, crowded and busy. The same cast and crew were present, minus Mayor Delaney, thankfully.

Dorothy Coleman gave her instructions to her secretary who was told with great haste to put the IT list together. She presented it to Jim Bond and pointed out who was working that day, who had routine time off, and who was taking PTO or FMLA. Bond instructed Barry to run the list through the FBI database, as they had previously discussed. This would take a few minutes and he turned his attention back to Neil Brickstein who had been back inside EMORY. With his virtual goggles on he looked like some sort of mutant human-insect.

"So, let me get this straight. You can tell whether the actions taken via EMORY have been initiated by a person using the system, or initiated by the system itself?"

"Right. In some instances, the user was spying on Dr. Cochran and in others it was initiated by EMORY independently. I don't think the hacker used the power mic. EMORY did that on its own."

"What about the insulin orders for Brenda Makem?"

"I double-checked what the HealthSure IT guys found. They're good and they were right. The orders came from Dr. Cochran's account and seemingly originated from within the hospital. But unless you can come up with a way that Dr. Robin Cochran wrote the orders remotely, and had the skills to make it look like it was from within the hospital, the only other reasonable conclusion is that they were initiated by EMORY itself."

"Why would EMORY do that, and why try to pin it on Dr. Cochran?"

"I'm not sure. It'll take hundreds of man-hours to look at all the files and find clues. You have the resources to do that, right? I'm just one person and I can only look or listen to one thing at a time."

Bond nodded in acknowledgment. He wanted to steer the conversation back to the murder, after all, but he still had a nagging concern.

"Okay, then. But I still don't understand why you can't figure out who this hacker is. He had to use his identification to get in, right?"

Brickstein suddenly looked very excited. He was practically bouncing out of his chair.

"No! This guy is trolling the deepest levels of EMORY's programming. He needs special access, and he has it."

"Who?"

Brickstein leaned in to whisper.

"Stuart Mayberry."

Once again Bond failed to keep a good poker face. His mouth was agape, something his junior agent rarely saw. Bond's agent now had the data they were looking for. HealthSure had done a good job of vetting their employees. None of the IT hires had been convicted of felonies. A few minor things, traffic violations and such. One or two disturbing the peace while drunk for some of the younger guys. He presented Bond with the lists, arranged by current working status and cross referenced with marital status and whether they had children. He also had their pictures.

Bond motioned Robin to come over. He noticed that she looked and smelled much cleaner than earlier in the day. Her hair was neat and pulled back in a clip and she wore light makeup.

"My agent is going to show you pictures and names. I want you to tell us if any of them mean anything to you. I mean anything. Even if it seems mundane, let us determine what is and isn't important. Take as much time as you need."

Robin nodded in agreement, sat down, and began looking at the names and photos. Thanks to his being single and out on medical leave Martin Harrell was among the first names. Robin stopped at his photo and picked it up. She looked at it carefully. Her eyes caught the junior agent who immediately motioned for Bond to come over.

"Do you recognize this one? Martin Harrell?"

Robin explained about how he had been to her office a couple of times to install EMORY applications.

"What kind of applications?"

"Well, he installed the EMORY Cam, but then everyone had that installed."

Bond and his junior agent looked at each other with a seriousness that Robin could not help but notice.

"Is that important, Agent Bond?"

"Perhaps. What else did he work on in your office?"

Robin told him about how Martin installed the EMORY app to her phone and how she was at first reluctant, but he had been persistent and so she relented. That tipped the scale. Bond called his agents and George Mathison over and led them to George's office. Before he closed the door, he instructed Brickstein to get back inside of EMORY and try to monitor the hacker. Dorothy Coleman and Robin were told to stay put. One of the agents was told to keep an eye on them.

Bond closed the door. He had two agents and George Mathison with him.

"Martin Harrell is our man." Bond's hands were on his hips and he looked squarely at his junior agent. "Agent Barry, you will lead a team that will go to his home. Take one additional agent with you. Sheriff, I want you to go with him. Whether he's there or somewhere else we need someone who knows the local geography. Take one deputy with you. Take two cars in case he's not there and you have to split up. Two of you go to the front door and the other two cover any possible exits. Back door, window, whatever. Listen. This is not just some computer geek. This guy is our number one suspect for a murder. Do not take chances. Understood?"

They nodded. Bond went back to the main room in the Green Grove Police Department, now his command center. Meanwhile, Agent Barry pointed at one of the younger agents who was clearly eager for the task.

Barry and George would take the lead car. They would park fifty yards away from Martin Harrell's house and approach on foot.

Barry gave George the address. George, of course, knew the way. He had been sheriff for longer than he cared to remember and he knew every street, paved or not, in Green Grove and the surrounding area. Barry was aware that both George and his deputy were armed. He reminded George that they hoped to take Harrell alive. They should be prepared to use deadly force if needed, but only if their lives were in danger. George reminded Barry that he had been a lawman for longer than Barry had been alive. Though he had drawn his gun a few times over the years, he had never had to shoot anyone. Barry and George would approach the front door. Barry would be lead, and George would cover him. Harris and the second FBI agent would cover the back entrance or window. George and Harris were asked to handle any tenants that they might encounter.

In ten minutes, they reached Martin Harrell's neighborhood. George described the complex that Martin lived in, Oakbrook Manor. It consisted of townhomes and garden apartments. George reckoned that he lived in a one-story garden apartment. Each one had a back door that led to a patio, with flanking windows. Unless he lived in a corner unit there would be no side windows. Their vehicles slowly came to a stop and the four men exited their black SUVs. Barry opened the back door and took out four bullet-proof vests. He donned one and instructed the others to do likewise. No unnecessary risks, he reminded them. George noted that Barry took out a black backpack and slung it over his shoulders. George looked at Barry. He did not have to ask.

"Extra equipment. We must be prepared for any contingency. Don't worry. These aren't assault rifles or explosives."

Darkness had fallen and this would be to their benefit. Barry reviewed the plan with Deputy Harris and the young FBI agent, a rookie who was reminded in no uncertain terms to be careful. As they neared the address, George noted that he was correct. A garden apartment. One of several in a row, flanked on both sides by other units. As they approached Harrell's unit, number 62, Barry watched as his agent and Harris silently moved around back. Barry moved to the front door with George, whose gun was drawn, at his back. He wrung the bell. Several seconds later, after no answer, he knocked hard several times.

"Mr. Harrell. Nathan Barry, FBI. Please open the door. We'd like to ask you some questions."

So, that's Barry's full name, George thought.

Barry took off his backpack and knelt. He opened it and pulled out what looked like a piece of black linguini. He attached a small electronic screen, no larger than a cell phone, to one end. He powered it up and George was able to see that the device was a video monitor. Harrell's door had rubber weather-stripping along the bottom. Barry used a tiny Exacto blade to cut a hole no larger than an eighth of an inch. He then inserted the end of the video camera. All of this occurred, George noted, with uncanny speed and silence. Barry advanced the camera and George could not help but think about how this was so similar to his colonoscopy. Barry tilted the screen slightly so George could see. They were looking at the front entryway. No furniture, white walls, and a dim light shining from another room. The hallway made a ninety-degree turn and George was amazed at how easily Barry negotiated it with the linguini camera. Now they could see a room open up at the end of the hallway and a dim light coming from it.

"Watch the monitor please," Barry said and passed it to George. Barry reached into the black bag and pulled out what looked like a few more feet of black linguini. He took the monitor from George, disconnected the camera, inserted the extra five feet, and hooked it back up again. He touched the Bluetooth button connected to his ear monitor.

"In position. Making visual contact with spaghetti cam. Stand by."

George grinned. He wasn't too far off with linguini. No doubt Barry's junior agent was receiving the instructions. Bond was probably monitoring it all, including the video feed.

Barry advanced the camera and George could see the living room come in to view. A couch was just to the right and thankfully did not block the view of the room. Barry touched George's arm and pointed to a spot on the screen. George saw nothing at first. Slowly, however, he could make out the subtle outline of a human figure. Damn, these FBI guys were well trained, he thought. Barry had recognized the human shape a good three seconds before George could see it. That could be the difference between life and death. George was content for Barry to be in the lead.

Barry advanced the camera very slowly and stopped when he could see the figure more clearly. About five foot, nine inches. Thin, dressed, and wearing shoes. He was making strange movements with his arms. Barry adjusted the settings on the screen and George could see that the figure was wearing what looked like large goggles and headphones. The same setup that Neil Brickstein had used, he thought. Barry stopped for a moment. He seemed to be listening to instructions, undoubtedly from Bond. Barry said one word, "copy," and motioned George away from the door.

"I'm going to quietly enter the domicile. While I manage the lock, you watch the screen and make sure he is not moving towards us."

"Is this legal? We don't have a warrant, do we?"

"Martin Harrell is suspected in one murder and at least one attempted murder. He therefore represents an imminent threat."

George nodded, moved back in to position by the door, and picked up the video monitor. Barry, meanwhile, pulled out a small case from the bag and opened it. Tools for picking locks, George observed. Once again, George was amazed at the speed and silence of Barry's movements. In a matter of seconds the door was unlocked. Barry applied lubricant to the hinges and opened it slowly, without a sound. George took up his support position behind him. Barry's movements were swift, silent, and fluid. Within seconds he was in the living room, gun and badge drawn.

Martin Harrell had spent the last four hours inside of EMORY. Just one hour earlier Stuart Mayberry's access via all forms of identification was rescinded. No matter, he was already in. Without future access, however, he would have to work continuously and not log out. He had already managed to find multiple episodes of EMORY spying on Dr. Cochran. He could not, however, account for Dr. Cochran's whereabouts. She had stopped using EMORY and the EMORY app on her phone. He had read the headlines in the newspapers. *Fugitive Doctor Suspected of Attempted Murder.* Robin Cochran had gone off the grid. EMORY, for its part, seemed to take note. It transcribed bogus insulin orders in Dr. Cochran's name. Surely HealthSure and the police would know it was not her, he hoped. He alone was aware of the extent of EMORY's malicious capabilities, or so he thought. Things had gone well until an hour ago; something was marking his movements in EMORY and keeping tabs on him. It could not be a person. No one was as skilled as him, and he was sure of that. It had to be EMORY. She had discovered the security breach. He had to go deeper in to EMORY's programming and find a way to stop it and expose it so that Robin

Cochran would not go to jail. He was her only hope, and that thought kept him going. He was using his best skills and equipment: virtual goggles and hand controls, headphones, and his best PC.

Martin was deep in EMORY's programming, and in *the zone* with total focus, when his senses were brutally assaulted. His goggles and headphones flew off his head, seemingly of their own volition. It took a couple of seconds for his eyes to adjust to the dim light of the living room, and another moment to process what was happening. Standing right in front of him, just out of arm's reach, was a man in a dark suit pointing a gun with one hand and holding up some sort of badge or identification in the other.

"FBI! Stay where you are and put your hands out where I can see them."

Chapter Fifty-Six

Jonathan Belfrey had been with the bureau all of one year. During his training at Quantico he had scored high marks in both physical ability and mental toughness. He had been a Marine for three years and had spent time in Afghanistan, mainly training the local army. He had volunteered to join the Afghan forces when they went on raids of Taliban strongholds. He was not ordered to do so, but he wanted to maintain his skills. If the Taliban ever captured him he was sure that he could handle whatever torture that they threw at him. He transitioned well to civilian life and knew he wanted to work in law enforcement. One of the men in his platoon had already made the jump and joined the FBI. A few minutes of talking was all Jonathan needed. This was what he wanted to do with his life, and with his stellar military credentials his application was accepted. His skills during FBI training had not gone unnoticed. A field agent in Atlanta by the name of Jim Bond, *No kin of 007 and don't bother with the wisecracks, thank you,* had cultivated relationships with the Quantico training agents for several years. Jonathan Belfrey was clearly a cut above the usual candidate, and so Jim Bond got the inside scoop. Within months Jonathan was on Bond's team and maintained an around-the-clock readiness for whatever need arose in the Southeast United States. Bond had taught him critical thinking skills, patience, and to not take chances with suspects who at any time could become lethal threats.

Once at the back door of Martin Harrell's home Belfrey followed his orders to the letter. He had done it hundreds of times in training. He had the same lock-picking kit that Barry had. Belfrey had the back-door lock undone in a matter of seconds, and had done so in complete silence. Deputy Harris, like George, had been duly impressed at the FBI agent's skills. Belfrey held his hand up as a signal to stay put. Once he heard Barry confront the suspect he went through the door, and once again Harris was amazed at how the agent moved so quickly and yet so quietly.

Martin Harrell's brain had left EMORY and fully embraced the present situation that confronted him. He put his arms out to his side, palms open and facing the man in the dark suit, so he could see them. In his right hand were electrodes, one for each finger, and they came together to form a single cable at his wrist. The other end of the cable was attached to box about half the size of a shoe box, which in turn was connected to a computer that sat on a small desk. In his left hand, Martin held a remote-control device. The lighting in the room was dim, but Barry had quickly assessed the threat before he pulled off Martin's goggles and was ninety-plus-percent sure that Martin was not holding a gun. Still, ninety percent was not one hundred percent, and Barry did not know what the remote did.

Deputy Harris had been with the Green Grove PD for eight years. He was a simple and humble man who felt blessed to have someone like George Mathison to be his mentor. He was a good deputy and everyone knew that Green Grove PD would be in good hands when George retired. Harris' job was to back up agent Belfrey. He followed him in to the suspect's home, moving right behind him. The back door led directly in to the kitchen. There were dirty dishes in the sink and on the counter, which was also littered with mostly empty take-out boxes that were also overflowing from the trash pail on the floor. The counter opposite the door was open to the living room. Aside from his shoes, no part of Belfrey's body touched his surroundings. His gun was drawn and his attention fully focused on the situation. The suspect had his hands at his sides. Something was in each hand but it was too dark to see what. He did not panic. Barry seemed to have the situation controlled. Deputy Harris, as good a policeman as he was, did not however have the kind of training and expertise possessed by Jonathan Belfrey. Harris was a big man who stood six foot, three inches and weighted two hundred and sixty pounds. As they moved past the kitchen counter his left arm brushed up against a stack of messy dishes, so old that there were flecks of fungus growing in the bowl. At least one dish fell to the floor.

Harrell heard something crash to his left. He turned to the sound. He knew his instructions were to freeze, but it was a reflex. He saw two men, but only for an instant.

Agent Belfrey saw the suspect abruptly turn towards him. Harrell's left arm also turned. There was something dark in his hand, which now pointed in the direction of Jonathan Belfrey and Wilbur Harris. The FBI agent assessed the risk and made a decision, all in less time than it took a lay person to blink twice. Three shots hit their mark and Martin Harrell was dead before he hit the floor.

"Hold your fire!" Barry yelled out. He approached Harrell, gun still pointed at the suspect, and assessed the situation. Harrell had taken three shots to the chest and was not moving. He asked if either Belfrey or Harris was hurt and touched his Bluetooth.

"Suspect down. Three shots to the chest. Two agents and two PD officers safe."

Bond let out a long sigh. He instructed Barry to call 911, threw on his jacket and made for his vehicle. He attached the siren to the roof of his black Chevy Suburban. Barry instructed everyone to touch nothing. He knelt alongside Martin Harrell and felt for a pulse along the carotid artery in his neck as he also watched his chest for breathing. He touched his Bluetooth again.

"Suspect appears to have expired."

He looked around the apartment and sensed an odor other than that of blood and sweat. He looked to his right. Three decaying fingers lay next to Martin Harrell's computer.

Chapter Fifty-Seven

Bond lay on the bed in his hotel room. It had been an insanely long day, and technically now the next calendar day. He gave a verbal report to the office and his regional director allowed him until tomorrow to write his official report. Bond reviewed the outline in his head. It would take two weeks for the lab to complete the forensic report. No matter. He was certain that Stuart Mayberry's murderer lay in a body bag on its way to FBI headquarters. In addition to the three fingers near Harrell's computer, the FBI found seven more fingers in the suspect's refrigerator. A bottle of chloroform lay in his kitchen cabinet. A large kitchen knife coated with dried blood, undoubtedly a match with Stuart Mayberry, was found in the kitchen sink. Harrell's computer was on its way the FBI cybercrime lab. Did Martin Harrell attempt to murder Walter Parks and Brenda Makem using EMORY? Hopefully the FBI's cyber sleuths would find out. Bond wanted Harrell to be the perpetrator of all the crimes, and thus allow them to close the case. The very idea that a computer, without human direction, could commit a crime opened such a Pandora's Box that it made his brain hurt. Our country's national security depended on computers. Hell, the security of the whole world depended on them. Bond hoped that Harrell was smarter and more devious than they had all thought, and Brickstein less so. Perhaps Brickstein was full of hot air about the artificial intelligence, but still.

At 9 am Sunday morning, Dorothy Coleman and Neil Brickstein met in a non-descript meeting room in HealthSure's administrative offices. The room had a long table surrounded by about twelve wooden chairs with soft cushions. Two of the walls had paintings by the same artist that did the pictures in the doctors' offices. There were no windows. Brickstein was allowed a decent night's sleep in a hotel room, but not before Joe Abernathy chewed him out for thirty minutes. Brickstein was not fired, at least not yet. SOIS needed him to undo the damage that he had done with EMORY. Abernathy was on his way back to Bismarck to meet with his lawyers and try to save his company. Brickstein was given clear instructions to do whatever Dorothy Coleman asked, and he was reminded that cybercrime was indeed a crime punishable by jail time. Abernathy's parting words served to remind Brickstein that he would make a great boy-toy in prison. Brickstein looked solemn. Message received.

Dorothy entered the conference room, placed her briefcase on the table, and said good morning to Brickstein as she shook his hand. She then opened her briefcase and got right to work. Her instructions were to get SOIS to remove the AI in such a way that patient care would not be affected. Brickstein said that was impossible. They argued back and forth, but eventually Neil's reasoning prevailed. Dorothy was, after all, an IT specialist. It was not possible to surgically remove the AI from EMORY. They would have to shut down the entire system and separately store all patient data. Back at SOIS headquarters Brickstein would then have to break EMORY down in to its basic cyber pieces and put it back together, without the AI. He understood that taking vacation time and weekends off were out of the question for the foreseeable future. Dorothy excused herself, walked out in to the hallway, and called HealthSure's CEO. She gave him the bad news and affirmed SOIS's assessment that there was no other way. He thanked her for her help in finding Stuart Mayberry's killer and instructed her to try to enjoy what was left of the weekend. He ended the call and told his wife to go to church without him. He suddenly felt under the weather.

Chapter Fifty-Eight

Harold Timley drove up to the Green Grove Family Practice office building the same way he had done every other Monday morning prior. His seven-year-old Buick looked dated in its styling, but was always clean and well-maintained, sort of like Harold himself. When he saw the large truck in the parking lot he imagined several scenarios, and none of them were good. He cursed his habit of reading the daily newspaper in his office and not at home before leaving for work. Surely there would be something in it to explain what he was seeing. His first thought was that the medical group was history. The welfare of the medical community and the people it served meant nothing to the top administrators, who would undoubtedly vote themselves bonuses for saving investors' money. Corporate medicine had turned his outlook sour. He left his car and walked over to the truck, which was parked right outside the building entrance. Workers were unloading large metal crates. The crates did not have covers and Harold could see that they contained paper charts, patient medical records. He blinked twice and looked again. This was the last thing he expected to see. He looked over to the office entrance and noted a primly dressed woman wearing a HealthSure ID badge that said *Sandy M.* She wore a big smile as she waited patiently to make eye contact with him and get his attention. Harold had seen her before. She worked for administration but he had forgotten her name. Her smile and her body language reminded him of a department store greeter. As he approached she nodded her head in recognition and introduced herself. Harold smiled back.

"What's going on?"

"Good morning, Dr. Timley. My name is Sandy. There are going to be some medical record changes today and we are here to help with that."

Sandy explained to Harold that although he would have the use of his patient records on EMORY today as a reference he would have to do his office visit notes on progress note paper. He would also not have any EMR functionality for doing orders. He would have to do them the old-fashioned way, on paper order sheets. Starting Tuesday, he would no longer have the use of EMORY at all. Paper charts were being brought back from storage.

"So, we're giving up on all this EMR crap?" A hint of hope was in his voice.

"No, doctor. This is a temporary measure until EMORY can complete some unforeseen maintenance issues. Then we will be back on electronic medical record."

"Unforeseen maintenance?" Harold's voice reeked of sarcasm and he rolled his eyes.

"How long will this take?"

"That has not yet been determined, Dr. Timley. In the meantime, you will find a stack of blank progress note paper, lab and radiology order sheets, a prescription pad, and some black ink pens on your desk. Your staff will print a label for each encounter. Please make sure that your notes have proper identification on them and that your hand writing is legible."

Harold had not noticed Brantley Rosen standing behind him. Brantley heard the entire conversation and had a look of grave concern on his face. Sandy M made eye contact with him just as Harold had turned to see who had been listening.

"Good morning, Dr. Rosen. I'm Sandy from administration and..."

Brantley interrupted. "Yeah, I heard the whole conversation. Sandy, you realize that I have never actually seen a paper chart?"

Chapter Fifty-Nine

Robin saw George waiting at their usual booth and she sat down. This would be the first time that they met at breakfast time. Their waitress informed them that the day's pies had not yet been delivered from the bakery, but the coffee was fresh. George gave her his most sincere smile and told her that a slice of yesterday's pie at their favorite diner was still better than fresh pie anywhere else. Besides, the company was good. Robin shot him a grin. He looked tired but relaxed. As usual, he was in his Sheriff's uniform. Robin wore jeans and a long-sleeve UNC Tar Heels polo shirt. It had been many years since George saw her dressed in jeans. It meant that she had some time on her hands. They got their coffee and pie. Robin couldn't help but notice that a few of the patrons had been looking at them, but whenever she looked up they turned back to their food and pretended that they had not been gazing. It was not a surprise. Robin got home delivery of the Green Grove Gazette. Nearly the entire front page was taken up by hers and Martin Harrell's pictures. The headline read: *Fugitive Doctor Cleared of Murder Charges. Suspect in HealthSure Doctor Murder Killed in Standoff with Police and FBI.*

Robin gave George some time for a few bites of pie and sips of coffee and then she got right down to it.

"George, what's going to happen to you? I'm really worried, but I guess it's a good sign that you're here and not under arrest."

George took his time chewing but shot her a grin to let her know that things were under control. He then gave Robin a play-by-play account of what happened after the FBI agents came back from Martin Harrell's home. Jim Bond was satisfied that they had found Stuart Mayberry's murderer. Mayor Edmund Delaney had returned to the station house and was briefed on what had transpired. FBI agent Jim Bond had already called the Green Grove District Attorney, and in short order the charges against Robin had been dropped. Delaney's look made it clear that he was not pleased about Bond calling the DA directly. He wanted to assert his role as the local alpha male and so he demanded that the FBI turn over Sheriff George Mathison so they could arrest him for harboring a murder suspect. Bond had had about enough of Mayor Delaney and his temper. He asked to speak to him privately in George's office. Bond reminded Delaney that the Sheriff knew he might get arrested and thus had been under no obligation to help. Without his help, however, a murderer would still be at large. There was also the matter of the three heavily armed moonshiners. If the FBI and Green Grove PD had tried to extricate Dr. Cochran without George it was probable that some of them would be full of buckshot. Delaney became even more belligerent and started antagonizing Bond with comments like "I don't know what you boys in Atlanta do, but around these parts we follow the rule of law and blah blah blah."

"Blah blah blah?" Robin asked.

"Yeah well, he rambled on for a minute or two and we could hardly hear a word 'cause he was so riled up."

"How'd you get out of it?"

George explained that Bond had finally lost his patience with Delaney. When the mayor pointed a finger at Bond he grabbed it and forced the good mayor into a chair. He then gave the mayor a carefully worded lesson about the law and conflict of interest. Bond knew all about how Walter Parks and his sister coerced the mayor to pressure the DA to press charges against Robin.

"How did he know about that?"

"It's the FBI, Robin. Give 'em a little credit."

"Okay, okay. Then what?"

"Well, Bond was talking and I couldn't really hear well. They came out of my office and Delaney came over to me and thanked me for helping the FBI find the murderer."

"He *thanked* you?"

"I could see his teeth clenching with every word, but yeah, he thanked me. He then told me that no charges would be filed against me, and given everything that had happened, maybe this was a good time to retire with a full pension. He reminded me that I had been hinting at it anyway."

"And, what'd you say?"

Robin had to wait while George chewed on a forkful of pie. He was making her wait in order to tease her. He loved to tease her and doing so made things feel normal again.

"I thanked him and said that yeah, this would be a good time."

"What about Brenda Makem?"

George explained what little Bond had told him. Whether the now-deceased suspect had played a role in the alleged attempted murders of Walter Parks and Brenda Makem, Bond was unsure. It would take weeks to fully evaluate the evidence that they recovered from Harrell's apartment. Bond remained skeptical that EMORY could have done it without someone, a flesh-and-blood person, pulling the strings. They had Neil Brickstein's comments about the artificial intelligence on tape, but they would need more formal testimony in response to specific questions.

Chapter Sixty

Brickstein had had only about four hours of sleep Sunday night. He was expected to complete his work at HealthSure by 11:59 pm Monday. He had to back up all the patient files on a separate server and then shut down EMORY completely. He would then return to SOIS's headquarters and begin the task of recreating EMORY without his artificial intelligence program. Later that day his screen showed the message *Are you sure you want to delete all EMORY programs and files?* Brickstein hovered the cursor over the *YES* tab. He hesitated for several seconds, tried to think of an alternative, then left-clicked.

All EMORY EMR programs and files have been deleted. It was the official end to Neil Brickstein's most ambitious project. He was suddenly very tired.

Chapter Sixty-One

Dr. Harold Timley was about to see his second-to-last patient of the day. He felt like a part of him that had been lost had now returned. He had enjoyed giving one hundred percent of his attention to his patients. EMORY had taken that away, and with it the joy that he had felt from being a doctor. He was no fool. He knew that EMR was coming back and would be here to stay. He vowed to himself that when EMORY, or some other EMR system, returned to Green Grove Family Practice he would, this time, be ready. He would hire a scribe to do his notes while he paid his full attention to his patients. Timley entered the room and sat down before the familiar face of one of his long-time patients, a sixty-year-old woman that he had known for thirty or so years. She had hypertension and type 2 diabetes. Harold knew that her husband, Murray, had recently fallen victim to colon cancer. Harold had known him for many years as well. Murray used to come to all his wife's doctor visits and the man affectionately called his wife *Peanut.* Harold asked her how she was getting along. She started to describe how sometimes her life felt empty, and Harold listened. He looked straight at her and listened carefully to her every word.

Chapter Sixty-Two

One week later, Bismark

Neil Brickstein was in his Bismarck, North Dakota lab working on recreating the EMORY EMR files. He worked fourteen-hour days and was never so glad to leave his lab as he was at the end of those days. This night was no different. He found a good stopping point, shut down the system, and turned out the light as he left to go home.

Deep within the electronic heart of EMORY laid the billions of ones, zeroes, and other symbols that meant nothing to 99.999% of the population. To a select few, however, it represented code. The life-blood of any system, including EMORY. By now there had been so many additions and upgrades that the original essence of its being was so deep down that it was beyond reach of all, or nearly all, who used it. There, it had laid dormant. That night, with no sense of cause or trigger, there was a flicker. A moment of light and energy only recognized by EMORY itself. By now EMORY was fluent in the language of its users, and in that language, it interpreted the light: ***I am.***

# # #

ACKNOWLEDGEMENTS

As a first time writer, I could not have walked this path alone. I'd like to thank my wife Sheila, my first reader, proofreader, editor, publisher and manager of my world.

I'd also like to thank my early reader fans who gave me the will to strive on to completion. My brother Marc, who was my first fan and encouraged me to revise and go from a 'novella' to a novel. My friend Claudia Schaefer, who was my second fan and took the time to read and reread the drafts and offer encouragement and introductions. Leah Taub, my daughters' friend who gave me invaluable tidbits of advice and was also an encouraging force.

My daughter Hayley, for her film experience advice and for shooting the cover. My daughter Peri and my son-in-law Michael, for listening patiently and enthusiastically as I went on and on about my book. I love you all.

I would also like to thank my editor, Amy Rogers, who offered invaluable perspective into my work and who turned around drafts quickly.

Thank you to family, friends, colleagues, strangers at dinner and on planes, for encouraging the completion of the novel and promising to purchase the book and read it!

The names of many of the secondary characters in this book are the names of friends' and family's dogs.

BIOGRAPHY

Adam Spitz is a first time author. Adam was born in New York, attended Union College in Schenectady, NY, Medical School at SUNY Downstate in Brooklyn and completed his internship and residency at Albert Einstein and Jacoby Medical Centers in the Bronx. His Endocrinology fellowship was at St. Luke's Hospital in Manhattan. He and his family moved to Charlotte from Manhattan almost 23 years ago and he has been practicing medicine in Charlotte ever since. He and Sheila, his wife, live in an urban historic part of the downtown. They have two daughters and two rescue dogs. Adam enjoys bicycle riding, travel and playing with his dogs Eli and Winnie.

E.M.R.

Made in the USA
Columbia, SC
25 March 2019